# KING

# TUT'S

# PRIVATE

# EYE

# KING

# TUT'S

# PRIVATE

# EYE

# LEE LEVIN

ST. MARTIN'S PRESS ❧ NEW YORK

A THOMAS DUNNE BOOK.
An imprint of St. Martin's Press.

*Design by Songhee Kim*

Library of Congress Cataloging-in-Publication Data

Levin, Lee.
    King Tut's private eye / Lee Levin. —1st ed.
        p.    cm.
    "A Thomas Dunne book."
    ISBN 0-312-14274-9
    1. Egypt—History—Eighteenth dynasty, ca. 1570–1320
B.C.— Fiction. 2. Tutankhamen, King of Egypt—Fiction.
3. Private investigators—Egypt—Fiction. I. Title.
PS3562.E88964K56 1996
813'.54—dc20                                         95-53311
                                                        CIP

First edition: June 1996
10   9   8   7   6   5   4   3   2   1

For

my lovely wife,

Sunie, who has

been insisting

for years that I

sit down

and write

# ACKNOWLEDGMENT

I wish to extend my deepest appreciation to my fine agent, Rhoda Weyr, who took the time to meet with, and work with, a new author when her time was certainly more than filled with representing the established writers with whom she already dealt.

In the same manner, I wish to extend my thanks to Ruth Cavin, senior editor at St. Martin's Press, for the encouragement she gave when the original manuscript was first submitted, and for her cogent and thoughtful insights that made the revised book "work" so much better. She very willingly took time to meet personally with the author of a first novel despite a workload involving the publication, for St. Martin's, of better than one new book per week.

## Acknowledgment

Elisabeth Story, associate editor, Melissa Jacobs, editorial assistant, and David Goldberg, publicist, all have shown great patience in dealing with my queries and have invariably been prompt and efficient in getting back to me with accurate and detailed answers.

I suppose, too, I should thank all the archaeologists and Egyptologists whose meticulous researches and findings have made it possible to reconstruct so much of the vibrant life of ancient Egypt.

v

# INTRODUCTION

**Y**ou are about to read the first detective story in the history of the world. How this came to pass is a curious tale. I shall try to be brief, although, being a college professor, brevity does not come naturally to me. For virtually my entire career I have been Professor of Egyptology at Crown College, Yardley University, which is to say I have never actually worked for a living.

The events I relate took place in February 1996. I was on my last archaeological visit to the Valley of the Kings, this being my final trip before retirement. Naturally I scheduled it for mid-winter. No fool, I. Who would stay in England in February if they could arrange otherwise, particularly at public expense? Still, February or not, the Valley of the Kings is a beastly place. Flies, gnats, and winged creatures of unknown species and proclivities make the Valley of the Kings an uncomfortable destination, albeit a warm one and, for me, a free one.

I had managed to wangle one last grant from the university and was spending it as parsimoniously as possible save, of course, for my own creature comforts. The amount they'd given me was pinchfist by former standards—the times and all that, you know—but even so it bought the services of about a thousand fellahin for nearly three full months. Now, I'm a flaming liberal, but this was *my* grant I was spending. Ordinarily, I'd be most eloquently indignant at the exploitation of these pathetic Egyptian laborers, working in the cruel sun for the few pennies a day I paid them, but I cheerfully rationalized that it was for the good of humanity and that I needed all those brawny backs to have any chance at all at a significant find. Besides, if I paid a decent wage to some, I could pay no wage at all to others, and where's the justice in that? In point of fact, despite my sympathies, I'm rather fortunate that the concept of trade unions hasn't taken hold in these parts.

I could easily have dodged this last trip. After all, I'll be retiring soon, which is precisely why I can be so candid. Besides, after having my snout buried so deep in the public trough all these years, a last-minute sense of shame made me feel I ought, at least, to give the taxpayers a shot at getting something for all the money they've put in my pocket these past forty-odd years.

I had another motive, too. This time, maybe, just maybe, I'd actually find something worthwhile. It would be nice, after four decades, to make a real splash in the tiny academic pond I wallowed in.

My previous digs had been awful scams and this one probably would be too. I'd find a shard or two, or maybe turn up a wall with a few hieroglyphic inscriptions, and make another book out of it. With a maximum of speculation and minimum of facts I'd puff up my finds as the most fabulous discovery since that Italian fellow sailed into that unmissable land mass on his way to China. With this technique I've been able to publish the minimum unread and unreadable books to keep the administration happy. I save my most stultifying writing for these tomes—only my colleagues read them, and it serves 'em right.

So here I was on this last boondoggle, with my workers mucking about, pretending to work while I pretended to pay them, as the workers in the Soviet Union used to say when there still was a Soviet Union. You can imagine my surprise when one of my workers—I don't even know his name—happened to be half-heartedly poking his shovel into the ground at a mastaba-tomb of the Eighteenth Dynasty I was lethargically looking into, and his shovel made a *thud*. It happens all the time and I wasn't too excited, except this time he unearthed a gorgeous inlaid box about four feet long and two feet wide. I won't bore you with a description of the amazing workmanship, save to assure you that the box alone, if I could find a way to smuggle it past the Egyptian authorities, would buy me enough U.K. bonds so that just the interest would give me a lifetime supply of London call girls, including meals and taxis. I've managed to stay single, and now that female creatures seem unwilling to cook or clean or sew for us, why any man would want to marry one of them is an increasing mystery to me. They rent themselves out so much more cheaply.

In any event, the box was so cleverly made and tightly fitted that you could scarcely detect it wasn't all made of a single piece. The wax seal had hardened into concrete, but I could immediately recognize it as belonging to Eye, grand vizier of the pharaoh Tutankhamen. I'm not a complete fraud—I do know my hieroglyphics.

The workers know they're required to report any finds to the Egyptian authorities supervising the site, but with a little judicious bribery I was able to get my man to part with it. The sum wasn't trifling, either—these beggars know what this stuff is worth on the European market. This wasn't the first time I'd managed to slip a find into my kit, little somethings that I'd wind up peddling to some of the tonier antique shops in Grosvenor Square. Tut me no tuts. The pension from Yardley is miserly, and besides, dear moralist, tell me how scrupulous *you* are when you send your income tax form to the Inland Revenue.

I'll leave it to your imagination to conjure my excitement as, with literally shaking hands, I took the find into my tent and broke the seal. I didn't let myself speculate on what might be inside, though I confess the thought flashed unbidden that maybe, just maybe, something might rest there that could make the end of my totally mediocre career a true spectacular. For a few minutes I'd be as famous as an American rock star. Well, in my circles at least. And so it proved.

I pried open the lid and saw inside bulky objects wrapped in linen. I extracted the objects, most carefully, I assure you, and found them to be scrolls. Very large ones, and in nearly perfect condition, particularly considering that they had been lying around for the better part of thirty-four hundred years. It took but a moment for me to realize that what I had before me was the private journal of Eye himself, written in his own hand.

As I proceeded with the work of translation I began developing a kinship with this Eye. I knew all about him. Eye (or Ay, or Aya) was the father of Tutankhamen's principal wife and the grandfather of Tutankhamen himself, making him a most powerful man of his time, and I alone held his private history in my possession. What a find! My God, my career had meaning after all! The man was cynical, jaded, and certainly no hypocrite—he was totally candid, and made no effort to gloss over with sophistry his cupidity and self-interest and unorthodox sexual practices. He wrote in a breezy, conversational style, at least for an Egyptian of his day, and I've made every effort to preserve this flavor in the translation that follows. In fact, to a certain extent, since I felt such kinship of spirit with the man as I worked on his scroll, I fear his voice has become my voice. But of course, Eye was still a man of his times, and couldn't completely rid himself of the conventions. For example, every time he uses a dignitary's name he gives all his ranks and titles, no matter how often the name appears. If I were writing for my colleagues, I'd translate precisely in that fashion, but you deserve better. Eye wrote in an insouciant, idiomatic style—after all, this is his private journal—and I've done my best to do the same, though I assure you I never skew the facts. As I read these amazing papyrus scrolls I very quickly came to realize that what unfolded was the first detective story in the history of the world. Well, of course, there's that messy business with Adam and Eve's boys, but no mystery in that, is there? And, on top of everything else, the most amazing coincidence was that Tutankhamen's grand vizier was actually named Eye. Thus, the title of the book which follows was almost inevitable: KING TUT'S PRIVATE EYE.

Crown College
Yardley University
May 1996

# THE PRIVATE SCROLL OF THE GRAND VIZIER EYE

# 1

## DAY ONE
## —
## THE BEGINNING

I write this in my own hand. I cannot entrust this work to my personal scribe, nor to any other man, for the intrigues in the palace of the pharaoh are numberless and no man may be trusted. I write this scroll in haste, for I know not the time left to me. I have offended my pharaoh greatly, for reasons not yet clear to me, and if it is his will I may face the sentence of the two hundred blows of the cudgel plus mutilation of ears and nose.

My heart is pounding so heavily I can feel it beating like hammer blows against the inside of my ribs. Perhaps it would be best if it were simply to explode right now. At least I would be granted an honorable end, and a swift one.

When mightily displeased, the pharaoh has been known to sentence men to have their privy parts separated from their bodies. Though I am fifty-seven years of age, I am still quite fond of mine. I might even be facing death, if that is pharaoh's will. A quick death does not frighten me, but the slow, lingering sort much favored by pharaoh is another matter altogether. For a man, whether death or the mutilation of his most precious organs would be the worse fate, each must decide for himself.

I cannot believe it has come to this, not after all these years of faithful service to my Egypt. Not after all I've done for my country. And certainly not over something so peculiar, so bizarre, as a murder that almost certainly never even took place.

My name is Eye, Grand Vizier of the Two Kingdoms, Royal Inscriber, General of Chariots, Divine Father, Royal Fan-Bearer. [*Translator's note: et cetera, et cetera, et cetera.*] I have held these posts under the reign of the god-pharaoh Tutankhamen and under the reign of his father, the pharaoh Akhenaten, may the gods curse his memory, may his monuments and inscriptions be eradicated, and may Osiris, Lord of the Underworld and Judge of the Dead, cast him into utter darkness. I spit upon the memory of Akhenaten, who even from his grave may after all these years be sentencing me to mine.

Akhenaten, that wicked man, led my beloved Egypt into many woes from which even I, with all my efforts, have yet been unable to extricate her completely. I thought I was through with him. Now, eight years after his death, he returns to bedevil me. The bile rises in my throat; the sweat pours from my body as I paint these hieroglyphs on this scroll. I have little hope of surviving these next days. It is my devout hope that if I do not, this testament survives so that generations not yet born shall know the truth concerning my fate.

I swear by the gods Re, and Hathor, and Osiris, and Toth, and Amun, and all the gods of Egypt great and small, that the events I relate in this scroll are true, and may Osiris bar me from the delights of the Netherworld to which I am otherwise entitled if I speak false in the most trivial particular.

I paint these words upon this scroll in my own hand for my own safety's sake. Besides, the curse of my life is nepotism. All of my servants and staff are relatives, and I cannot fire them. My scribe is the worst of the lot, but he is my nephew. I would dismiss him with the clap of a hand, if I could. I have told him a hundred times that it is 𓎛 before 𓄿 except after 𓊖 but he simply cannot seem to grasp it. And as for grammar, he has no concept whatsoever. It's appalling how the quality of the teaching in the schools has deteriorated since I was a boy. The pluperfect completely eludes him, and as for past participles . . . My tomb will make me the laughingstock of Egypt for a million years to come. I shudder every time I see the inscriptions carved there by that incompetent nephew of mine. I only hope I live until I retire, when perhaps I can arrange to have the work redone without antagonizing the entire family. Right now, this seems a forlorn hope.

I console myself with the thought that it is common for tombs and inscriptions to be desecrated by future generations, and for names to be chiseled out and recarved with new ones. Perhaps this scroll will survive even though my name carved in granite perishes; may survive even though the very location of my house of eternity forever disappears from the knowledge of man.

I have done well and risen to great power in Egypt. I am not a boastful man by nature but this is the plain truth. It is therefore most galling to face such terrible fear at this stage of my career, having risen so high and overcome so many difficulties. I was not born of the royal family but nonetheless have achieved fame and power by my own efforts. Being the father of Nefertiti, principal wife of the accursed Akhenaten, has of course been of benefit. Still, I have managed to stay alive during these tumultuous years, when many of higher birth and station have met ignominious fates. I freely admit it is a source of pleasure to me that not only have I succeeded so well but also that so many of my friends have failed. Is this not human nature?

The day started harmlessly enough, the day that caused the terrible events I now relate to commence unfolding. It was a day scheduled for yet another dreary audience at the royal palace. I used to revel in them, but over time they've grown most wearisome. Perhaps it's because I'm old. At age fifty-seven, spending an entire audience on one's knees, with the forehead on the ground and backside in the air, is not only humiliating but physically exhausting. The strain on the neck and eyeballs is almost unendurable. And that wretched boy-king Tut is impossible, even if he is my grandson. When Tut's father, that imbecile Akhenaten, died, I became regent of Egypt—or co-regent, to be exact, along with General Horemheb. After all, Tut was only ten years old. We thought we'd be able to rule for years without interference, but that little snake outfoxed us. By the time he'd reached fifteen, he'd managed to gather a considerable amount of power into his own hands, asserting himself a little at a time as he grew older. It's clear where all this is heading. Now that he's eighteen, he's become impossible. There's going to be a showdown. It's only a question of when.

Let me tell you, there's nothing more exasperating than dealing with a teenager, especially when he's a god. I'd hoped, by virtue of my services to his father and by being the ingrate's grandfather, I wouldn't have to prostrate myself before him. My bones really can't take it anymore. But no, over a year ago, the little weasel began insisting that everyone kneel. I, Horemheb, his wife, everyone. It wasn't a good sign.

Actually, I have to admit, the custom serves a useful purpose. Anyone who fails scrupulously to observe the ritual in the god-king's presence is subject to execution at the pharaoh's whim. All royal courts are corrupt, and many an administrator, unwilling to give up the stream of gold earned from bribes and the peddling of influence, has stayed on longer than his knees and joints could handle, and has been swiftly parted from his head and his wealth. The more prudent courtiers resign when their coffers are full enough.

I've often thought that this is why Egypt has endured when so many other kingdoms have vanished. The peril in Egypt of being unable to make proper obeisance is so extreme that administrators tend to resign at fairly young ages, thus ensuring fresh blood and ideas in the running of the country.

It is a peril which I myself consider most carefully each day I know I'm to be in audience at court. It's a delicate decision—another day of power, weighed against the danger of being unable to rise unaided and nevermore to be burdened by these worries again.

I am General of Chariots, which is to say commander of all the king's cavalry. I take this post seriously, and it is not a mere ceremonial honorific. Many is the battle I have fought in Egypt's service, and many a scar on my body I bear this day to prove it. My chariot is of my own devising. The one I ride in today on my way to my audience with Tutankhamen is one of which I am especially proud. I have contributed a great deal to the advancement and improvement of these war vehicles. By using heat-bent wood and connecting rods, plus delicate-looking but sturdy six-spoked wheels, combined with an open rear end, my design achieves great lightness yet great strength. And by setting the wheels farther apart I also achieve greater stability, so that these war machines cannot be easily overturned by rough ground or enemy action. I tell you this so that you will know I am no fool. And though what little hair I have left on my head is all gray, and though I am not as slender as when a youth, my mind remains keen and supple, which is why I survive thus far.

In any case, I would have greatly preferred a more ornate chariot—my rank certainly entitles me to one—but I have gauged our boy-pharaoh most carefully and noted the increasing touchiness he is showing toward matters of status. I am, I freely admit, as vain as the next man, and having risen to my station rather late in life, these outward shows and displays are still important to me.

You see, I am no hypocrite, and tell things as they are. Oh, at court I am every bit the sycophant and groveler. What courtier is not? But in this my private writing I make no effort to spare any man, and most particularly myself. Others may find fault with me, and as this scroll unrolls, they will. But I assure you, of all the faults they find, I find even more. By the same token, I am not a man given to false modesty. Though my faults are grievous, I do have virtues too. I have a keen mind and a keen eye. Few details escape me. I have a genuine reverence for our ancient gods, and put my trust in them. I have courage, and in my younger days proved it on many a battlefield against many of my country's foes. And I am no fool.

The pharaoh has become more and more petulant about anyone else's ostentation at court save his own, and for this reason I resign myself to using my simple field chariot instead of the elaborate ceremonial model I keep at my own palace. I have lived this long and gotten this far by keeping my eyes open at all times and probing as deeply as I can into the character of all who are in a position to do me ill. It is this which keeps me here today when, as I have already noted, so many of more noble birth and higher station have preceded me to the Netherworld.

I arrived at the god-pharaoh's palace at sundown. I had been able to persuade Tut to schedule his audiences in the evening, when it was cooler. That much at least I still could accomplish.

"Ho, General!" the captain of the guard greeted me, saluting smartly. I like Houy—he is a good man. He is splendidly muscular and clearly has that indescribable presence that stamps him as a natural leader. He will go far in the service—I have my eye on him; he is a comer and has already served me well. I have no doubt whatsoever of his personal loyalty to me. Of course, I further ensure the loyalty of my guard regiments by supplementing their pay from my own private purse, but nonetheless in Houy's case I feel I have earned his loyalty, not bought it.

"Greetings, Houy," I responded, returning his salute. "All is well?"

"I can't complain, General," he replied with a grin. "There are worse billets in the cavalry than palace guard duty!"

He pulled his splendid chariot aside while guardsmen dismounted to open the palace gate. Now these guard-chariots, *they* were really something! There were a dozen of them at each gate, all of eighteen-karat gold. [*Translator's note: of electrum, actually, an alloy consisting of roughly 75 percent gold, 22 percent silver, and 3 percent copper.*] They are so heavy that the normal two-horse team could never pull them, and I had had to have the design modified so that four horses could be yoked abreast, and even then they had to strain mightily to get up to walking speed. It was useless in the field, of course, but marvelous for show.

Forgive me if I digress at this point. It is essential for your understanding. General Horemheb and I had been colleagues through all the insanities fomented by Tut's demented father Akhenaten. His tampering with the ancient gods of Egypt brought nothing but woe and civil unrest to the land. And, while I felt the man was a disaster, Akhenaten was my god-pharaoh and I was bound by my oath to him, and I honored it. In those days I fought in the field at the head of my horse, staving off foreign invaders and crushing local uprisings. Horemheb and I were like brothers.

Still, Horemheb is an ambitious man, as am I. When the ten-year-old Tut became god-pharaoh, we ruled Egypt jointly in his name. It was an uneasy alliance at best. Horemheb commanded the infantry, I, the cavalry. Infantry's better. There are so many more of them. I lived in constant fear of a coup.

Therefore, one day, when Horemheb was in the field training his infantry and I at the palace, I brought before Tut one of these splendid ceremonial chariots for his inspection, one of these electrum-covered monsters, all ornately carved and glowing golden from every inch of surface, with specially modified wheels capable of holding the enormous weight. In addition, I unveiled to Tut charioteers and mounted guardsmen in splendid cloth-of-gold uniforms, with golden swords and golden spears, and elaborately carved and crested helmets all matching and coordinated. In short, breathtaking splendor to delight the insatiable vanity of this child-king. I had a purpose, needless to say.

Tut was ecstatic at the sight of these toy soldiers, as I knew he would be, once I made it clear that they were for his palace, not mine. "Grandfather!" he exclaimed, and there was a rare note of genuine affection in his voice, "Grandfather, they're splendid! They're magnificent! These are really for me, for my palace?"

"Of course, my Pharaoh (Life! Health! Strength!). You are pharaoh—they're yours to command."

"Then I shall commence drilling them personally. This very day. And I'll mount them on perfectly matched horses, to make them even more splendid."

That was a touch I hadn't thought of. There was nothing slow or dull-witted about Tut, although inevitably he was totally and completely spoiled. Becoming a god so young—he was, you remember, ten—cannot help but alter one's personality, and not for the better.

As you can see, it took no effort whatsoever to persuade him that regiments of these horse soldiers were far more impressive as royal guards than the infantry, which now looked so dowdy in comparison. The cost, to be ground from the peasants through even more taxation, was of course no consideration.

Thus, when Horemheb returned from the field, his infantry guards had been supplanted by my horse guards—four regiments of them. Horemheb was furious, of course, but could do absolutely nothing about it. The balance had now tipped in my favor. When it comes to palace coups, whoever commands the guards commands the country. And now four regiments fiercely loyal to me—for, as I've said, I see to it that my guard regiments are superbly paid—hold command of the king's palace compound. Rather neat, I thought.

I paid a price, of course. Horemheb, my former colleague, was now my implacable enemy. And Horemheb is no man to trifle with. He is built like a bull, and brave as a bull, too. Horemheb is, quite simply, a natural warrior, but that to some extent is where I have the advantage of him. Palace intrigue is not his style. He is too direct for that. Still, I never imagine the man to be a fool. I now control the palace guard, but he controls the infantry, and how long either of us can maintain control of Tut is truly an open question. Horemheb and I may have the military forces at our command, but a god has resources too.

I nodded to my driver to proceed, and with a flick of the reins he urged the horses through the opened palace gate. Although these royal audiences bore me nearly to sleep, the palace itself never ceases to delight me. The outer walls are of plain unbaked brick, but the interior is truly lavish. I pride myself on my discerning taste—I'm something of a dilettante—but I must confess that had I chosen the decor myself I could not have much improved on what I see. In truth, I *did* select or approve some of it myself, though I do not even attempt to take credit for the bulk of it. Shall I describe it in detail? I think not. It would be impossible to create in your mind a true picture of the wonders in gold and silver, in statuary and wall paintings, in fluted columns and graceful fountains, in ornate floors and decorated ceilings that delight the eye no matter where one turns. I find it hard to imagine that the very gods themselves, in their homes in the Netherworld, can be surrounded by more beauty than one finds in the palace of the pharaoh.

I reached the interior audience hall, through whose gate my chariot could not pass, so I dismounted and strode purposefully through to meet my king. The ceiling of the audience hall was enormously high—at least ten times the height of a normal man, designed to impress and overawe all who entered. This purpose it accomplished, but at a cost. The god-pharaoh, no matter who he is, is also but the height of a man, and the immense room dwarfs him too.

A portion of the corridor down which I approached the audience chamber was mirrored, and I took the opportunity to glance at myself. There was nothing I could do about my nearly bald head save wear a wig, and this is an affectation I refuse even to contemplate. However, in compensation, I display a most gorgeous beard, all most carefully coiffed and curlicued and shaped by my barber's irons, so that the perfectly symmetrical curls, trimmed spade-shaped, create a delightfully impressive picture and, to some extent, I hope, soften the prominence of my beaklike nose, regarding which I have never been overly pleased.

My tailors have outdone themselves in designing my robes, taking particular heed to make them loose and flowing to conceal, to the extent possible, my very generous girth. So I eat well. I'm the grand vizier. Why shouldn't I? In fact, it is most fitting that I be, shall we say, of ample size. A man of my position, my stature, should have a certain *gravitas,* a certain solidity, to emphasize the dignity of his station. I have always been able to indulge my appetite for rich and exotic foods, although of late from time to time I find my digestion troubled by them. My sleep too. And my dreams.

I gave myself one more swift look into the mirrors. Satisfied with my appearance, after pushing a few stray strands of beard into place, I moved forward, and as my eyes adjusted from the bright sunlight outside, I stiffened. There is an inlaid border of dark granite marking the boundary point at which I must kneel and put my forehead to the floor, then crawl and scoot forward in that ridiculous posture until I reach the foot of the king's throne. But for a certain distance I could walk, and see, and what I saw sent a shiver from my toes right through my scalp.

My dismounted horse guards were nowhere to be seen. In their place stood a phalanx of troops I had never laid eyes on before, gorgeously uniformed in scarlet and silver, with great plumes of horsehair bristling stiffly from their huge, lavishly carved and burnished silver helmets, and carrying brilliantly polished silver swords and spears. In an instant I knew exactly what had happened, but with a supreme effort of will let no trace of dismay or no pause in my gait indicate to anyone that I had taken notice. I was in serious trouble.

# DAY ONE

—

# LATE AFTERNOON

I was the last to arrive. The king was on his fabulous throne, in full regalia, wearing the ornate double crown of Upper and Lower Egypt, and posed in the ritual position with his scepters of authority crossed over his chest, the flail and the shepherd's crook. Tufts of curly, jet-black hair emerged from underneath the neckpiece of the crown. His hands were long and delicate—girl-like, really, and the fingers appeared to be overweighted with massive bejeweled rings. Queen Ankhesenamun sat next to him. How breathtakingly beautiful she was in her full-length, jeweled court gown, and I would describe her beauty as outstanding even if I weren't her grandfather. Of all my granddaughters, Ankhesenamun has always been my favorite, perhaps because she was the firstborn. This of course makes her many years older than her brother the pharaoh to whom she is wed, and of all my grandchildren, including for certain Tut himself, Ankhesenamun is the one with whom I have always had an instinctual rapport.

Standing immediately next to Tut was Aanen, High Priest of the Temple of Amun at Karnak. Other than the queen, Aanen is the only personage not required to perform the ceremonial grovel at the king's feet. His presence at these audiences is obligatory, to place the seal of Amun's approval upon the court's proceedings. Upon my entering the palace the priest's great choir commenced a sonorous hymn in my honor. When, all those years ago, I had heard it for the first time I was deeply moved, and I confess it still has the power to move me. All those mellifluous voices singing a hymn of praise and thanksgiving to me, to Eye, to one who has risen so high from such minor origins. It's heady stuff. Well, the hymn wasn't precisely to me, of course, it was the sacred hymn of the grand vizier, which amounts to the same thing. Aanen himself is a sour-looking, disagreeable, middle-aged man—purse-lipped, with an expression on his face as if he'd just eaten something vile but was too polite to spit it out. Most clerics have that look. I've never known exactly why.

General Horemheb, too, stood beside the throne. Obviously, Tut had given him permission to rise, but permitting him to stand next to the throne was an unusual honor, and the whole scene made the hair on the back of my neck stand up. Not the hair on my head, however, since, as you know, alas I have virtually none.

Tut's mother, my daughter Nefertiti, also stands next the throne, fully garbed in the regalia of the queen mother. She is still a stunning woman. Great tits. I know this full well from the days of the scoundrel-pharaoh Akhenaten, who had made the women of his court, including Nefertiti, dress in diaphanous gowns that were for all practical purposes transparent. This was one of the few radical innovations wrought by Akhenaten with which I had no quarrel.

Nefertiti is a woman of powerful appetites and immense ambition, and when she tried to seduce me, I almost succumbed. A woman that magnetic and good-looking is well-nigh irresistible, even when she is one's own daughter, but I knew her interest in me was to further her own intrigues. Believe me, I was well enough advised in the ways of the court to avoid that particular snare since, without doubt, whatever her game was, the profit in it would be hers and not mine. [*Translator's note: Incest in the royal court of Egypt was the norm, although typically of the brother-sister variety. More about this later.*]

Yuti, the king's physician, was in attendance too. But he wasn't standing. I could recognize him solely from that enormous butt wriggling in the air. His forehead, pressed firmly against the floor, made his features impossible to see.

I reached the granite line and, in the instant before making my absurd obeisance, glanced at Horemheb. He looked down at me with scowling eyes and a shit-eating grin on his face. [*Translator's note: I have searched my vocabulary in vain to find a more apt rendering of Eye's phraseology. Alas, I have failed.*]

I scrunched forward until I reached the king's feet, upon which I planted the ceremonial kiss. After a brief interval he signaled me to stand. That, at least, was a good sign. If I had been forced to remain kneeling while Horemheb stood, I would have known I was doomed. I hauled myself up with the heavy cudgel I had devised as my own symbol of office. I confess a certain smug satisfaction in having thought of it. As grand vizier I do have certain prerogatives, and this sturdy, ornately carved and gilded wooden staff extended my viziership by a good ten years. With it I could haul myself up from my kneeling position with little fear of making some stumble that could outrage the king's dignity and give him grounds for my dismissal or execution, depending on his frame of mind. Many a man in Egypt rests in his house of eternity for no better reason than that the king was suffering mild indigestion on the day the man happened to make his misstep.

"Ah, Eye, we are pleased to greet you once more," Tut intoned in ritual greeting. His voice always had an oily sneer to it, even when he was genuinely trying to be pleasant. I imagine you have already been able to tell that I really didn't like this little brat. I say little advisedly—he truly was small for his age, no more than three and a half cubits in height, and slightly built. [*Translator's note: A cubit is about eighteen inches, which would make Tut about five feet three inches tall.*] He had a nice-enough-looking face, with a rather solid chin and a straight, well-formed nose. I envied him that nose the most. Mine is more of a beak, like an eagle's, and there is more of it on my face than I would prefer. I have been told it gives me a look of power and presence, but those that say this have reason to flatter me.

It is Tut's eyes that trouble me. They have a glazed, remote quality about them that always makes it seem that he is never really *there*, that he is a distant spectator somewhere outside his own body, that he never truly makes contact with any human being, but only observes people at a distance. And there is something else about those eyes. His father Akhenaten had the same look about him. It is difficult to describe. Sneaky. Implacable. Conniving. Eerie, in a way. Whatever it is, it certainly has always made me uneasy, particularly now when he is showing every sign of wanting to shake off the regency and take all power directly into his own hands. Although there of course is no other way to keep the god-blood line pure except for brother and sister to marry, I sometimes wonder if centuries of inbreeding might not be producing occasional odd specimens.

As I rose to my feet, Tut waved his arm delightedly, pointing at the new troops. "My new guard, Eye. Aren't they magnificent? They're a surprise from Horemheb, on the occasion of my eighth year as pharaoh. He designed the uniforms himself. I couldn't be more delighted!"

"Truly delightful, O Mighty God-King (Life! Health! Strength!)," I replied as evenly as I could, gritting my teeth and glancing once more at Horemheb. A mistake, since it gave him the chance to give me one more of those triumphant smiles. "And just how many of these marvelous new guardsmen has Horemheb furnished you, O Mighty One (Life! Health! Strength!)," I continued, although I felt certain I already knew the answer.

"Four regiments," Tut responded proudly. "And you should see how perfectly trained they are! They march as a single man, and their height is perfectly matched too. They're the pick of the entire army. Their drill is far more precise than your cavalry guards, Eye. Far more precise."

So, I'd underestimated Horemheb, and underestimating my adversaries is something I rarely do. Maybe it's time for me to retire from all this. My principal wife, Tey, has been urging this upon me for years. "What more do we need?" she keeps asking. "What more do you want? How much better can we live?" You know how it is with wives. Maybe she's right. Who needs all this?

Horemheb had checked me, and was taking full advantage of the opportunity to gloat. But the fact that my horse guards still manned the outer perimeter of the palace meant that all he'd been able to accomplish was parity. Parity *inside* the palace, that is. With his infantry so heavily outnumbering my cavalry, the balance, viewed in total, had tilted once more in his favor.

I put the best face on it possible. Dignity, pride, and all that, you know. I had had years of practice, and there was no way I was going to give Horemheb the satisfaction of seeing me the least bit crestfallen.

Imperturbably, I opened the scroll that contained the agenda for the royal audience. There was nothing new in it. Criminals to be executed. Lax administrators to be flogged. Estates to be confiscated. New taxes to be extorted from the peasants. Strict new decrees to be promulgated, with heavier penalties for disobedience. The usual stuff.

I began reading, but Tut waved it all aside with a gesture of his hand. "Not tonight, Eye. It can wait. I have something more important for you, and I expect you to devote all of your time to it. You'll need every minute."

I sighed. What now?

Without further preamble Tut let me know. "Eye," he said, without the trace of a smile on his face, and a peculiar look in those strange, otherworldly eyes of his, "I want you to find the murderer of my father."

If Tut had asked me to conjure up a flying pig, I couldn't have been more surprised. "Your father's murderer?" I repeated stupidly, too astonished to think of anything else.

"Yes, fatso, my father's murderer," Tut repeated, mocking my tone of voice. The fatso crack was out of line. True, I was somewhat paunchy. But fatso? I took this as a sign that I was no longer entirely in his favor.

I pretended a coughing fit to give myself time to gather my wits. "Magnificent One (Life! Health! Strength!)," I said at last, "your father has been dead for eight years." I looked up and saw the expression on his face. "But no matter," I continued hastily, "rest assured I shall find the man for you." After gathering my thoughts, I relaxed a little. It was no big deal. I'd simply have a few slaves tortured, extract a name from them, torture whoever it was they denounced, extract a confession, and make this capricious boy-king happy.

Tut continued to look at me sternly, without any hint of a smile. "Don't think, Eye," he went on, "that you can simply have a few slaves tortured, extract a name from them, torture whoever they denounce, extract a confession, and make me happy. I know that game. *There will be no torture!*"

I looked back at him, stunned, probably with mouth agape.

"Anybody can get a confession that way. I want the real murderer. That means absolutely no torture. No torture of anyone. Is that understood?"

"But, Holy Pharaoh, (Life! Health! Strength!)," I protested, "how can I solve this great crime without using torture? That is our way. We *always* torture. We've *always* tortured. It's the basis of our legal system! Why on earth would any man ever confess if he knew he wouldn't be tortured?" I was truly indignant, but of course could not reveal this with even the slightest facial expression. My conviction rate had always been one hundred percent, and I was intensely proud of it. What was all this about?

"I want the real man who killed my father," Tut pursued, as though I hadn't spoken. "The true criminal."

*You're a god. Find him yourself,* I thought irritably. But what I said was, "Without torture, solving a crime that is now eight years old is grievously difficult. And, Mighty Sovereign (Life! Health! Strength!), are we quite certain your father, the god-pharaoh Akhenaten, was indeed murdered? As I recall—and do correct me if I'm wrong—the god-pharaoh Akhenaten simply became ill and died. I do not remember any mention of murder." Also, I thought peevishly, why do you even care at this late date? Even if he was murdered—which seems absurd to me—whoever did it did you a great favor, you little idiot. He made you pharaoh. I don't recall your ever liking your father that much anyway. Or anybody else for that matter. If someone killed him, I'd think you'd give him a palace. A banquet at the very least.

"My father was perfectly well," Tut snapped. "He was never sick a day in his life. And then, all of a sudden, in less than two days' time, he was dead. It was poison. Or magic. Regardless, I want the man responsible."

Everything has to start sometime, I reflected. People die. In two days. Of something. If I had to track down the supposed murderer of every man in Egypt who sickened and died in two days' time, I'd wear out an army of torturers—assuming I'd be allowed to use them. One thing was certain. There was more to this than I could sort out here on the spot. "O Transcendental God (Life! Health! Strength!)," I continued as evenly as I could, "I shall of course do your bidding. Without torture, however, I fear it shall take a great deal of time."

"You have seven days."

Seven days. I was aghast. "With all due respect, Most Powerful Lord, I surely shall require much more time than that."

"Seven days," he stated implacably.

"Most Puissant Master," I begged, "couldn't you give me at least a week?" [*Translator's note: Eye was not being sarcastic. The Egyptian week consisted of ten days. Each month had thirty days, and at the end of the year there were five extra days celebrating the birthdays of the gods of the Osiris cycle. It's a far more logical calendar than the one we use today.*]

"Seven days," Tut repeated implacably. "And if you use torture, I'll know it."

I was stunned. A mere seven days to accomplish a miracle. To my knowledge, no crime in the history of Egypt had ever been solved without torture. And I doubted very much if this was even a crime. Akhenaten had simply died, that's all, and Egypt was much the better for it. My mind was already racing. What was this really about? Certainly it was not filial piety. I knew this little monster better than that. What was he up to? What did it all mean?

In any event, he was absolutely right about one thing. If I tried to use torture, he'd know about it. This audience would be the talk of all Thebes before I even left the audience chamber. There are many who would love to see me fall, and any torture would be reported to the king straightaway, no matter how cleverly I tried to conceal it. No, regrettably I would have to play this one strictly by the scroll.

"Very well, my Pharaoh (Life! Health! Strength!)," I said gamely, "I shall have your murderer for you. In seven days, as you command. Perhaps less. And without torture. That I swear. And I invite all the nobles here assembled to a great feast at my palace, seven days from this very date, at which all shall be made known to you."

Now this was pure, reckless bravado on my part, but not nearly as foolish as it might seem. I had nothing to lose. If I could achieve this miracle, my stature would soar, and I would give pause to Tut's scheming, whatever his scheme might be, long enough to have a chance to counter it. I am a wily man myself. And if no miracle occurred, I might as well put on a bravura performance and wait for Tut's next move, knowing full well that whatever it was, it wouldn't be pleasant.

I made my exit as insouciantly as I could, scooting and groveling backward as I went, until I reached the granite line, at which point I pulled myself up with the help of my stout cudgel. I wanted to stay—I was most loath to leave Horemheb with Tut without my being there, particularly since he'd been given the signal honor of being allowed to stand next to the throne. But Tut had dismissed me, acknowledging my banquet invitation with the merest inclination of his head, while pointedly reminding me that I'd need every second of the time he'd allotted.

It had been a weird audience, very brief, and this time anything but boring. Nothing on my agenda had even been touched upon. It didn't take a pyramid scientist to figure out that I was in deep trouble. But why?

My mind raced. One of the drawbacks of a life spent in palace intrigue is that nothing ever seems certain. I could only speculate, and hope that my inferences pointed me in the right direction. What was Tut's insane demand all about? How could I be expected to find a nonexistent murderer eight years after the fact, the nonexistent murderer of a pharaoh who royally deserved to die? And then another thought came. Perhaps Tut really believed his father had been murdered, and believed that I had done it. That would explain just about everything. My obvious fall from favor. His refusal to permit me to use torture, since without torture I wouldn't be able to get confessions. And then there was Horemheb's apparent rise. Could it be—could it be that the creation of the new guards was actually Tut's idea, not Horemheb's? Perhaps it was Tut I was underestimating. But what could I do about it?

And then came another dismal thought. I'd have to return to my palace and tell my principal wife, Tey, that I'd committed us to putting on a full state banquet with just seven days' notice.

# Day One —

## Evening

I've been in better moods. As I made my way back to my own palace I tried to get my thoughts in order, but I was having a hard time of it. With the audience so brief, there was still a twilight afterglow as my chariot clattered down the sandstone-brick road. We had to swerve to avoid a massive obelisk lying at rest on rollers, with about two thousand peasants lying strewn in exhaustion by the roadside, their day's work done. In two weeks the huge granite monolithic pillar, carved out of a single block and weighing countless tons, had been hauled perhaps a mile.

I once more reflected upon how fortunate we are here in Egypt. The annual flooding of the Nile is truly a gift from the gods. Every year the Nile floods, so every year Egypt has these tens of thousands of idle hands, who have nothing to do until the river once more recedes. Idle hands, of course, make mischief, so what better than to enroll them on behalf of the state? The state could thus build all these wonders—temples, palaces, tombs, pyramids, and meanwhile the peasants in turn received—what? Well, no matter. It's not for me to question the way the gods order things. I certainly can't complain. I'm the one in the chariot; they're the ones sleeping on bare ground. I'm the one with the palace. And if the life of a peasant is hard, in compensation, it's short.

My palace is conveniently close to the king's, so the return trip didn't take long. Would you like me to tell you about it? My palace, that is. I thought not. It is quite impressive, if I do say so myself, but if I went into detail you'd think I was exaggerating. Besides, tonight I don't feel like giving a guided tour.

My servants greeted me with feigned delight and I feigned a smile in return. Tonight I wanted to be with Tey. I was in no mood for secondary wives or concubines. It really wasn't fair, I suppose, to go to her mostly when I had major problems, but I'd come to rely upon her solid good judgment and she was the one person I could absolutely count on to hold my confidences true. Tey loved me, and in my own way I loved her—whatever that means. In the end, forty years of marriage counts for something.

I entered her bedchamber, and she looked up at me. "Bad day at the palace, dear?" She could always tell.

I didn't pretend otherwise. There was no use, anyway. And I wanted to talk to her about it, wanted to get her insight. So I did. I told her all about the audience, about my fears, my concerns, my suspicions, and she listened carefully without interrupting.

When I finished she looked at me incredulously. "Fatso?" she exclaimed. "Tuttikins actually called you *fatso?*"

I hated it when she called him that. But I guess that's the way grandmothers are.

I shook my head wordlessly. I truly couldn't believe it. Here I'd told her that I might be on the verge of being deposed as coregent, might in fact have my head on the block, and all she could think about was that her grandson had called me fatso.

"I'm sure he really didn't mean it, dear," she said soothingly. "I can't imagine what got into the boy. It really isn't like him to be so—so—"

"Don't worry about it, Tey," I sighed. "It's no big thing." I looked at her affectionately. Tey, like me, had put on weight over the years. Not as much as I have—women tend to care for themselves better for the most part—but she certainly was no longer the slender sixteen-year-old I'd married. Her dark hair was streaked with gray, which she covered with some sort of wash, but of course I knew it was there. Her deep-brown eyes were a little worn- and tired-looking, but still honest, and she didn't have a corrupt bone in her body. Tey was a good woman. I don't know if a woman would regard that as a compliment, but when thinking or speaking of her, that's the first phrase that comes to mind. Remarkably for a woman of her age, her face is almost unlined. And she has an agile mind, a clear-seeing one with keen insight into human nature. If she herself is uncorrupt, she has no illusion about the generality of mankind.

"Let's think this thing through," she said at last, frowning and rubbing her stubby fingers along the side of her face. "Let's take it a piece at a time. I really can't believe he'd turn on you after all you've done for him, but I guess I'll have to believe it, won't I? Anyway, we know he either truly believes his father was murdered, or he doesn't. Let's start with the assumption that he doesn't believe it and see where that takes us."

"Well, if he doesn't believe it, obviously it's just a ruse."

"To what end?"

"To get rid of me."

"He could do that anytime. With Horemheb's support, all he has to do is fire you."

"True. But apparently he's learned a lot, spending his entire life in the royal palace. A tyrant can do as he pleases, but after a while, if he's seen to be too capricious, everyone around him starts worrying for their own heads and one day the tyrant wakes up with a dagger in his gizzard. A wise ruler, on the other hand, always appears reasonable. He finds acceptable reasons for doing what he wants done, no matter how unjust. He never wants his actions to appear arbitrary. That way, the rest of the court doesn't feel threatened. In this particular situation, if I fail to find a murderer that doesn't even exist, he can make a great show of his affection for his dead dad and claim that he's dismissing me, not to break my power as co-regent, but for incompetence. I knew that one day he'd make his move, I just didn't expect it quite this soon."

"So what can you do if this is what he has in mind?"

"That's what I'm asking you. So far, all I can come up with is bribery."

She looked at me disapprovingly. "Why not?" I went on defensively. "This is a special case. If he won't let me use torture, what else is there?"

She shook her head emphatically. "No good."

I thought she was objecting on moral grounds. She wasn't. "No good," she repeated. "Ordinarily it would work, but I don't think so this time. I wouldn't approve, but like you say, this is a very special case. Yes, you could certainly bribe somebody to implicate someone else. But even though you can't use torture, under the circumstances I doubt if Tuttikins will feel all that constricted himself. I still can't believe he's doing this to us, and I'll try to have a personal little talk with him. But anyway, if he has this mind-set, and knows his father wasn't murdered, he'll know the evidence you bring him is false."

Clearly Tey was absolutely right.

"So," she went on, her eyes reflecting her pride in having seen to the heart of the matter so swiftly, "a little torture in the dungeons of the royal palace and it won't be five minutes before he hears that you're the one that did the bribing."

I considered this carefully. "So what else is there to do?"

At length she sighed and uttered a single word. "Resign."

"No good either." This time it was I who immediately saw to the core of things.

"Why not? I've been begging you to give it all up for years. We have more than we'll ever need—much more. More than we can spend in the rest of our lives. How much more food can we eat?

How many more chariots can you drive? How many more servants do we need? What's the point anymore?" Believe me, I'd heard this dissertation many nights before this one.

"The point, Tey," I said patiently, "is something I've never tried to explain to you before. I didn't want to cause you anxiety, and I know how you feel about our grandson. I work with him all the time, and believe me, my feelings are nowhere near the same as yours. If I resign as grand vizier, whatever grounds I use, Tut will insist I resign as General of Chariots also. And if I do that, I'm at the mercy of my enemies. And I've made enemies. Nobody rises this high without leaving enemies behind. Sometimes enemies one doesn't even know he has. And clearly Tut now has me on his list as well."

"I can't believe that!" she protested, and from the grim look on her face I was rapidly beginning to regret ever starting this conversation with her. After all, I could just as easily be in bed right now with Tia or Gilupkhipa or any one of the dozens of concubines I keep about the place, just in case.

"I can't believe that," Tey repeated. "We're all family! And why should Tut wish you ill? After all you've done for him? It was you who made him pharaoh!"

"Well, yes, me. And Horemheb. And while I don't mind taking credit, since he's Akhenaten's only son, I don't see how there was any other nominee. Without civil war, that is, and Akhenaten had given us enough of that."

"But we're family!" she protested once more.

"Of course we are. *Everyone* in the royal palace is family. Or damn nearly so. Quite a few of the pharaohs lying in their tombs and pyramids were killed by family. And lots more family are in their tombs all over Egypt, killed by pharaohs. Family doesn't help a lot, Tey. Not when it becomes a question of power. And this is all about power.

"Tut's been chafing after it for a long time now, and at eighteen it's hard to stop him. I can't blame him, really. After all, at sixteen he became a man. But he's smart enough to know how the system works. He resents me, and knows he has to get rid of me to ever become pharaoh in his own right. He's the type that never forgets a slight or a wrong, and I'm certain every time I've thwarted him he's filed it in his memory. Under Ḫ for revenge.

"Some pharaohs are content to be figureheads. They're the smart ones. They live to splendid old ages. One of them ruled for ninety-one years. I doubt if anyone will ever break that record. But Tut's the kind that wants real power, and there isn't a head in the royal palace that sits easy on its neck when a pharaoh's on the throne with real power in his hands. Tut's still too young to realize that that includes his own neck too."

"But what about Horemheb?"

"Horemheb's time will come. After mine. Unless he strikes first. Creating those new regiments of foot guards was brilliant. Whether that was Horemheb's idea or Tut's, a palace coup in my favor is out of the question now. Even if I had that in mind, which up till now I haven't. And now it doesn't matter anyway—Horemheb has counterbalanced me."

"So what's to be done?"

"I'm thinking."

"Well, let's consider what can be done if Tut's right and his father was murdered."

"Not bloody likely."

"Think about it, Eye." She looked directly at me. Tey is a "now" person. She's always "into" whatever is going on at the very moment. Her mind is never disengaged from the matter at hand. "Poor Tut," she went on, "was only ten years old when it all happened. But ten-year-olds see a lot. That's an age when they absorb everything and miss nothing. Maybe he saw something. Maybe he sensed something. After all, he's right about one thing. Akhenaten was perfectly fine, and not two full days later he was dead. Whatever killed him killed him awfully fast."

"I've seen a man fall over and die in less than a minute."

"True. But usually physicians know what causes those things. The pharaoh's own physician was baffled. He never did figure it out."

"It's a shame there was no autopsy at the time. Maybe then Tut would know his father died of natural causes. But being a pharaoh, Akhenaten's body went straight to the royal embalmers. Yuti never had a chance at him once Akhenaten was dead."

"Well, nevertheless, Yuti is the best physician there is in all of Egypt, and if he couldn't tell for certain what happened to the pharaoh, I can understand why Tut could still be wondering. Anyway, Eye, based on what you've told me, if Akhenaten wasn't murdered, there's nothing you can do except wait to see what happens. So you might as well go forward on the basis that he was. I suppose the first thing is to make up a list of everyone that might have wanted Akhenaten dead."

"That's easy. Every man in Egypt."

"Be serious."

"I am serious. The man was a nightmare. A disaster. I never talked to you about it much in those days. After all, he married our daughter Nefertiti and lifted us out of the minor nobility into a place right next to his side. Believe me, I knew from which spigot my beer was poured. But he was a madman. Marrying Nefertiti when he was supposed to take one of his sisters as his principal wife was a great stroke of fortune for us, but a terrible shock to the country."

"You were magnificent dealing with him," Tey said, looking up at me proudly. "Most men would have been thrilled to have their daughter as the king's concubine, but you held out for principal wife."

I knew she'd picked up on the fact that I was a little annoyed with her and she was trying to mollify me with flattery. It worked. But she was right—of all the deals I've made in my lifetime, that one was the best. Akhenaten was besotted with my Nefertiti, and I knew he'd pay any price to have her. The strange part was that it was so easy. He didn't seem to have any concern about the scandal it would cause, marrying outside the godline. Maybe he knew that what he had in mind about the Aten would make his marriage to Nefertiti fade to insignificance, like the daytime moon being overwhelmed by the sun. If that is so, he was certainly right.

What the man was thinking I'll never truly know, taking the Aten, which after all was nothing more than a minor aspect of the sun-god Re-Horakhty, and raising it to the place of the *only* god. It was sheer, literal insanity. It was unbelievable heresy. It was sacrilege. I remonstrated with him in private, over and over again, but it was no good. He was determined to have his way.

I had no choice but to support him, considering that my lot and that of my family were completely tied to him. His extravagances in building new temples to the Aten nearly bankrupted the country. Then came the resistance from the priests of the temples of the old gods, and the shock to the peasantry at having their ancient deities suddenly stripped from them. It's a wonder the country survived, and if someone killed him, all Egypt's in his debt.

I also knew that Tey was right. I had no choice but to act on the assumption that indeed somebody had killed Akhenaten. But who?

Tey was reading my mind. That wasn't at all unusual—she seemed to have an uncanny knack of being able to do that with just about everybody. It had driven the children crazy when they were young. "So," she continued, "what choice is there? If nobody killed Akhenaten, and if you can't resign, and if you can't control Tut anymore, all you can do is wait to see what happens. So you might as well use the time trying to find a murderer. What's to lose? Maybe he exists."

"And maybe I can prove it," I replied sarcastically. "And maybe the Nile will start flowing backward. And maybe the sun will start rising in the west. And maybe, without torture, I can get somebody to say, 'Sure, I killed the king. It was me. Kill me in the vilest way you know how.' " I only said this to annoy her, but it was the literal truth. How was I to go about this? To the best of my knowledge, nobody had ever tried to catch a murderer this way before.

Tey knew I was only venting my frustration. As I said, most times she could read my mind. "You have no choice, Eye," she said wearily, shaking her head. "You have to try, because you have no other choice."

I waited, and she continued. "Let's think it through." She paused, her forehead wrinkled in thought, and she scratched the side of her nose as she always did when she was deep in concentration. "So everybody in Egypt wanted the king dead. Fine. That doesn't help much. But how many of them were in a position to actually kill him?"

She was right, of course. This limited the number of possibilities considerably. Naturally, I'd already thought of that before she said it. I was just being nice to her, letting her say it first.

"You're absolutely right!" I exclaimed, and she smiled in delight. "How many people actually had access to the king?"

It was a rhetorical question. I knew the answer, of course. After all, I *was* Akhenaten's grand vizier.

"Let me think," I went on, ruminating out loud. "It's hard to remember everything so far back. Interrupt me if you think of anything. But you're right—a lot of people had access to him, but only a few could have poisoned him. I'm assuming he was poisoned now. That's all it could have been. If it was magic, there are thousands of priests that could have cast the spell, so that's hopeless. I have to go on the assumption that he was poisoned. And if that's true, it has to be someone in the palace. Someone Akhenaten trusted completely."

"Couldn't a slave have poisoned him, at someone's orders?"

"Highly unlikely. As time went by, Akhenaten became more and more fearful for his life. With good reason, too, I might add. There were plenty of days I wanted to strangle him myself. The more fearful he became, the more precautions he took. He never went anywhere without at least a squad of guards. And believe me, I mean *everywhere*. Even when taking care of bodily functions. Even in the royal bedchamber. And he ate nothing without having it tasted first. He was very, very particular about that. No, there were but a handful of people he trusted."

"Who?"

"It's a small list. Nefertiti, of course."

"Forget our daughter," Tey said firmly. I rolled my eyes heavenward but decided not to dispute the point. I knew how Tey was about family.

"All right. There's Yuti, his physician. He had no choice but to trust Yuti. And Aanen, the high priest."

"Aanen, the High Priest of *Amun?*"

"Yes. He was one of Akhenaten's first converts to the godhead of Aten. And one of the first to convert back when Akhenaten died. Aanen's principles might be a little flexible, but he knew who his pharaoh was. And Akhenaten doted on him. Yes, Aanen could be alone with Akhenaten whenever he wished."

"Is that all?"

"I think so." I thought some more. "Horemheb, maybe."

"Akhenaten trusted *Horemheb?*"

"Not totally. But as General of the Infantry, Horemheb had access to him. He'd spend hours with Akhenaten, going over battle plans, and plans to put down peasant revolts. Usually there'd be guards present, but Akhenaten could have gotten a little careless. It's a possibility."

"Any others?"

I paused. "Well, there's always Tut himself."

Tey looked at me in sheer disbelief. "Tuttikins? Tuttikins! He was only ten years old at the time! And Akhenaten was his father! How can you even think such a thing?"

"You don't know Tut like I do," I stated sourly. "There's always been something peculiar about the boy. He may have only been ten years old, and ordinarily I'd agree with you that no ten-year-old boy could carry out a plot to murder a pharaoh, but in Tut's case I'm not so sure."

"That's absurd and you know it! Even granting the ridiculous notion that a ten-year-old boy could do such a thing, if he actually did it himself, what possible reason could he have for asking you to find the murderer if he knew that he himself had done it?"

It was a good question, and for the moment I had no answer. Perhaps one existed, but right now it didn't come to mind.

"Anyone else?" she pursued.

I paused for thought. There was always me, of course. I'd had complete access to Akhenaten. No point in mentioning it to Tey, though. If Tut seriously thought someone had murdered his father, there was no doubt from the start that I must be his principal suspect. After all, but for the unpredictability of fate, I might have been able to be regent in my own right, without sharing power with Horemheb, which for all practical purposes meant that upon Akhenaten's death I would have held the pharaoh's power in my own hands. Motive enough for murder. But no use even mentioning this to Tey. Instead, I merely sighed and said, "No, at the moment, no one else comes to mind."

"So we've narrowed it down to three," Tey stated triumphantly. She had a self-satisfied look on her face. "That's cutting it down pretty substantially from 'every man in Egypt.' "

I hated it when she looked so smug. And when she was right. But I had my own satisfaction too. The real total was six. I couldn't scratch Nefertiti off the list. I knew my daughter. I knew her appetites and her ambitions. No use arguing with Tey about it, though. It was *my* list, after all. And there was another name I had to add to it. Ankhesenamun. My granddaughter. Tut's wife. She was the king's favorite. She would have been seventeen—more than old enough to do the poisoning. Would she have? I very much doubted it. But yes, if anyone would have had a chance, she would have. She was on my list. I truly wished Tey was right and the real number were only three, but facts are facts. The number was six. Not counting myself.

I looked at Tey, and realized I hadn't yet told her that she was going to have to put together a state banquet in seven days. I decided to wait until tomorrow to tell her—I really needed to try to get some sleep tonight. And as I gave it further thought, I realized that the actual number of days left was six. Tut was counting this as the first day.

# 4

## DAY TWO —

## MORNING

I scarcely slept at all that night. A thousand thoughts whirled through my mind, every one of them useless. By dawn I was no farther along in my thinking than I had been when first my head rested on my bed. Oh, I'd had lots of ideas, but as I thought them through they all led absolutely nowhere.

Well, perhaps there was one thought I'd come up with that had merit. Maybe. It was a pretty obvious one in any case. I'd spent hours pondering the question of who might have had access to Akhenaten and, given the precautions he'd been at such pains to take, how they might have been able to accomplish their task. It now occurred to me that if I could get some inkling, anything, of *why* they wanted him dead, perhaps this might narrow the field of inquiry even further. Originally I'd simply assumed everyone wanted him dead—he was truly about the worst pharaoh Egypt ever had—but after a while I realized that wasn't enough. Wishing him dead was one thing. Having enough motivation to risk actually doing the deed was another thing altogether. If he was murdered—and what a big "if" that was!—the perpetrator would have to have more than a generalized dislike of the man. Killing a pharaoh is a dangerous enterprise. Our history records more executed plotters than murdered kings. Whoever would attempt such a crime must have had exceptionally powerful reasons indeed.

Now, you well may be thinking to yourself, Is this man really as clever as he claims to be? Please bear in mind that to my knowledge no man before me has ever been faced with the problem I've been given, not to mention the very short time allotted to solve it, so what may seem so self-evident to you was something I had to work out afresh by myself.

Having arrived at this preliminary conclusion, it was clear to me that my first step should be an interview with Nefertiti. After all, she had been the king's wife, and if anyone could add to my fund of knowledge, it would be Nefertiti. Also, of course, she was my daughter, and perhaps some vestigial filial piety might induce her to be more helpful than she otherwise would choose to be. Nefertiti, for all her beauty and charm, was cold at the core. Whether she would actually give me anything useful, or indeed could, was another question altogether.

I rose considerably earlier than usual, there being no point in staying in bed, and summoned my morning servants. They could scarce conceal their annoyance at being brought to my bedchamber at such an early hour. Well, too bad. That's what I'd bought them for.

You might think that under the circumstances I would prepare myself quite hastily, but you would be wrong. I know how long it takes for me to prepare myself for the day, and I know that Nefertiti, being a woman, takes much, much longer. Hence there was no need to rush. In fact, considering how early I had risen, I could prepare in an even more leisurely way than usual.

Since I would be calling upon Nefertiti at the royal palace, it was incumbent upon me to appear draped in full regalia befitting my post as grand vizier. I summoned Oudah to me—a pretty little thing, and lively too—and stepped into my basin so that she could give me my daily bath. She lifted a large and rather heavy spouted jug as high as her graceful arms could reach and poured hot waters over me, all nicely scented. The water contained a mixture of natron and a special sand that produced a pleasant foaming and bubbling when rubbed vigorously into the body, and had the property of easily bearing away all grime and perspiration.

After these preliminary ablutions, Oudah prepared a stiff paste of *souabou,* a concoction made from fuller's earth that also lathered nicely and was marvelous for deep cleansing of the pores.

To ensure my personal freshness, giggling, she rubbed powdered, sweet-smelling incense into my armpits and groin. I don't know if she enjoyed it, but I certainly did. In fact, to make the daily ritual even more enjoyable, I had her perform this service for me naked. Oudah naked, of course. I obviously already was. Don't frown. If you had the powers of a grand vizier, you would do the same.

If you could see Oudah's perky face you'd know why I was never in a hurry to leave my bath. But it couldn't last forever and, after having her assist me with my loincloth and linen undergarments, I dismissed her with a sigh of regret and, with a clap of the hands, summoned the rest of my morning staff. As yet I had not exercised my rights of ownership with Oudah—I was saving that, the more to savor it later, and besides, the early morning really isn't the best time for that sort of thing.

In came my barber, my chiropodist, my manicurist, and my cosmetologist. They gathered about me like pups at their mother's teat, chattering away incessantly as they shaped, tweezed, snipped, curled, shaved, and otherwise used all their arts to convert this paunchy, beak-nosed object into a thing of real beauty. Alas, it was a hopeless task, but they did their very best and for certain I looked much the better for their efforts.

The cosmetologist had the last go at me. She most carefully rubbed a concoction into my face, a paste derived from dried pods of the fenugreek plant, ground husks, and oils, which had the remarkable property of temporarily removing wrinkles almost entirely. The stuff was fiendishly expensive and the formula for its manufacture was held a closely guarded secret, but the important thing was that it worked.

Next, she enhanced my eyes, using green and black powders [*Translator's note: made from malachite and galena, ores of copper and lead, respectively,*] creating the almond shape so much in fashion these days.

Thus, save for donning my robes and jewelry, I was done. I picked up my shiny bronze mirror and gazed at my reflection. As always, they had done their work superbly well. With a sigh of satisfaction I lingered before the mirror. Eye, I thought to myself shamelessly, you're magnificent.

I took another paste of natron mixed with some other type of incense and rubbed it into my teeth and gums, then rinsed my mouth with rose water to purify my breath and keep it sweet. I was now ready for the royal palace.

It was nearly the time when the sun stands directly overhead when I reached Nefertiti's chambers. I would not want you to think I'd spent the whole morning dressing. However, as I mentioned, I knew that Nefertiti would, and that it would be useless to call upon her any earlier, so I managed to get a few odds and ends of work accomplished before setting out to see her.

Her servant ushered me in, and I could see immediately that I had been absolutely right. Clearly she'd spent her entire morning bathing and dressing. It was worth it. Although she was the mother of several children and approaching forty years of age, she remained a smashingly handsome woman. The gown she had chosen was most diaphanous—transparent, nearly—and I could see, most appreciatively, that the years and the childbearing had done little to diminish her charms.

She not only has, quite nearly, the body of a young woman, but the face as well. Her cheekbones are high, the skin over them tightly drawn, without blemish or wrinkle. Doubtless her morning servants used the same, or some similar, concoction on her face as did mine, but in her case I'm certain that not many wrinkles existed that required smoothing. Her posture is elegant—regal, queenly. This has been her bearing all her life, well before she'd been wed to Akhenaten. Her dark eyes retained their flash, but I well knew the ruthless intelligence behind them.

Nefertiti is a most impressive woman. She has presence. There is a self-assurance about her that is wholly natural. She assumes that whatever she wants will instantly be done. She's been like that all her life, even as a child. I still remember when she was but perhaps three years old, and our family relatively common, her ordering our few servants about with a peremptory wave of her little fist. More than once I heard a servant grumble, "That's sure one bossy little girl." It's not as though Nefertiti has no faults, however. For one thing, she is of the school that believes if a little perfume is good, a lot must be better. For another, she is cold as a desert midnight.

She motioned her servants to leave the room with a sharp clap of her hands, like royalty. Which she is.

"It's kind of you to see me on such short notice," I commenced.

"I was certain you'd be here," she replied calmly. "Please sit down, Eye," she continued, indicating a cushion-covered couch. I complied readily. Note that she calls me "Eye," not "Father," or even "Vizier." She's very much aware of her status as queen mother.

I settled myself comfortably. "So how were you so certain I'd be here?" I told you she was smart.

"I don't envy you the fool's errand you've been sent on," she continued, as though I hadn't spoken. "I'm sure you've been up half the night—all the night, more likely, trying to figure out what to do. And the only thing you could think of was to come to me. To Nefertiti."

She was right, of course. She always is.

"You need me. And here you are," she went on. "It took no particular genius to figure that out. If there's anyone at court that could possibly help you, it would be me. Although I truly doubt if anyone in this world can help you now, Eye. Perhaps the gods. Certainly no mortal."

"I'll appreciate all the help I can get, nevertheless." I found myself talking to this daughter of mine as though no common blood flowed in our veins. It's galling, but there it is. "It's clear Tut wants to be rid of me," I pursued. "I can even guess why. It's certainly no surprise, other than the timing. But, Daughter, is there anything else you might know that would be useful? Is Tut up to something special, is there some special significance to his making this move now, right now?" Note my shameless use of the word "Daughter," for which I had little expectation of any positive result, and certainly not the result that occurred.

Nefertiti looked deeply into my eyes, insinuated herself onto my couch, and smiled that languorous smile of hers. She took one of my hands into hers, and rested the other on my knee. The hand began moving upward. The sensation was definitely not unpleasant. Nefertiti was the type of woman that would enjoy taking advantage of the situation I found myself in. But I had other things on my mind right now.

"Please, Nefertiti," I remonstrated, blocking the upward motion of her fingers, "I'm old enough to be your father."

"You are my father."

"Precisely."

"So what's your point?"

"The point is, Daughter, that I think you've been in the palace so long, and been a queen so long, that you've forgotten your origins. This would be fine if you had the god-blood in your veins. But you don't. Incest is permissible for those of the god-blood, but not for us. You know that. You've simply forgotten. Not," I added hastily, considering how badly I needed her help, "that it's not most tempting. It's a matter of time, that's all. I only have less than six days left, and I need every minute of it. Perhaps when all this is over."

She laughed, and I have to confess that when she laughs that silvery, melodic laugh of hers, she is well-nigh irresistible. "Oh my, Eye," she chuckled. "I can't believe I heard what I just heard. The god-blood, indeed!"

I looked at her, puzzled.

"Surely after all these years as vizier you don't believe in that god-blood thing, do you? And you don't have to shield me. I'm a grown woman now. Have been for a long time. I'm not your little girl anymore. You don't have to spare me from the world's truths. Believe me, by now I know all of them. The unpleasant ones at least, that's for sure."

I looked at her blankly.

She returned my look, exasperated. "Oh come on now, Eye. I was married to Akhenaten. For years and years and years. There was nothing of a god about that man. Absolutely nothing at all. If he was a god, any kind of a god, he should have been able to do *something* special, something an ordinary mortal couldn't do. But Akhenaten was as ordinary a human being as you could find. Less than ordinary, in some respects. In some very important respects. He was a very lousy lover. You'd think if a pharaoh was truly a god, he'd at least be special in that department. But the man had no stamina at all. Even when we were first married. Can you imagine a god having no stamina?"

I have to confess I was shocked to hear her saying all this.

"Really, Eye," she went on, "the myth that pharaoh is a god is fine for the peasants. It's a useful fiction, useful for the state. After all, the peasants never see pharaoh in person. But *you* saw Akhenaten all those years, too. And you've seen Tut. He's my son, but a god? I'd like to think so, but I know him too well. That's no god. You know it and I know it. So if Akhenaten's bloodline can mess around with their own relatives, why shouldn't I?"

"If my information is correct, you already have," I replied dryly.

"Oh, no question about it. I freely admit it. In fact, of all the relatives, you're about the only one that hasn't shared a bed with me."

"Even the females?" I asked, genuinely curious.

Nefertiti smiled enigmatically, shrugged her shoulders, and said nothing.

"I truly can't believe Akhenaten didn't have your head cut off for your adulteries." I meant it. They had been notorious. "Your infidelities have been an open secret for years," I continued. "Based on the reports that have reached my ears, I could raise a regiment of foot and two of horse from the men you've slept with."

Another of her lovely smiles. "You underestimate me," she purred.

"So how did you manage to get away with it?" I was truly curious. Even a mad pharaoh like Akhenaten wouldn't knowingly tolerate an adulterous queen.

"I'd like to tell you something clever, but there really was nothing to it." Her supple body writhed on the couch like a tigress in heat. The woman was sex personified. "Akhenaten couldn't get enough of me in the first few years, but after he got that insane idea that the Aten was the only god in the universe, he lost all interest in me. I swear I could have slept with Akhenaten on one side of the bed and a lover on the other and the man wouldn't have noticed—or even cared. He was obsessed with his god idea. He was consumed with the complexities of the next world. I concentrate my attention on the pleasures of this one."

Of that I had no doubt. Even as a child Nefertiti had been preternaturally precocious and amazingly adept at getting her way. A thought crossed my mind that I had had for many years, but never had found an appropriate moment to bring it up. "So, Daughter," I inquired, "is Tut truly Akhenaten's son?"

Again the eloquent, sinuous shrug of the shoulders. "Perhaps. Perhaps not. I have no way of knowing."

"And your eldest, Ankhesenamun?"

She thought about that for a moment. "Probably. In fact, almost certainly. After all, she was born less than a year after I married."

For some reason that pleased me. Although I had no regard for the dead Akhenaten at all, somehow I felt better knowing my favorite grandchild was legitimate.

"Tut has no idea he might not truly be Akhenaten's son, does he?"

"Absolutely not. None would have dared suggest this to him when Akhenaten was alive, and they certainly wouldn't dare now that Tut himself wears the double crown."

"Then do you think this charade that was played out last night has any substance to it? Was Tut so close to his father that he truly is trying to learn the truth about his death? Or is the whole thing a ruse? If he confides in anyone, it's you."

Her lips parted, and her eyes once more bore into mine. Her fingers once more began searching their way up my leg.

4

I again pushed them away, careful to conceal my mounting exasperation. "Perhaps another day, Nefertiti, when this is all over with. I really don't have much time today."

She considered that. "Well," she said after a pause, "perhaps that's right. Considering that in six days—or is it even less?—you very well may be in no condition to do anything, I can understand that you might not be in the mood. On the other hand, look at it this way. How long can it take? And if indeed you are—how shall I put it?—rendered incapable, this is an opportunity you might not want to miss. After all, what are the chances you'll be able to solve the problem to Tut's satisfaction, given the restraints he's put on you?"

Nefertiti had a point. Still, I couldn't afford to be distracted. Not yet, anyway. "I fear you're right the first time," I said. "I truly am not in the mood right now. I'm sure you understand. But if you help me, and I can get this all behind me, that will be another matter entirely." [*Translator's note: It is easy to be judgmental about Eye's— and Nefertiti's—casual attitude toward incest. But they were creatures of their time, not ours. And there is a certain logic to the acceptance of incest within the royal family, the idea being that the only way to maintain the purity of the god-blood line is for members of the royal family to mate with each other. Thus, pharaohs almost always married their sisters. Given this, the sanction against other forms of incest within the royal family would be in all probability less severe, although the historical proofs in this regard are sketchy.*]

"So what do you want of me?" Nefertiti appeared annoyed. "Obviously not my body," she went on, a smile of amused contempt on her elegant lips, "at least not right now. I'm rarely turned down. It's not the recommended way to get cooperation out of me."

I pressed on nonetheless. "Well, Daughter, let's get back to my original question." I'm sure you notice how I again brought up the word "Daughter," hoping a certain amount of filial piety might help her be a little more forthcoming. "Is this all just a device to get rid of me?"

She considered the question carefully before answering. She placed her superbly manicured fingernails alongside her face, lightly, being certain not to disturb her makeup. "I know nothing directly," she at last stated flatly. "Tut has said nothing at all to me about it. You asked if he was close to his father—the man he *thinks* is his father. That's hard to say. He was only ten when Akhenaten died. That's a very difficult age, especially for boys. Tut was always a moody child anyway. Sometimes he'd be totally withdrawn. But, on the other hand, he'd have flashes of family feeling. In fact, for Akhenaten's coronation anniversary, right before he died, Tut had sent Akhenaten's favorite servant, Narmer, across the Great Green [*Translator's note: the Mediterranean*] to gather special food for a surprise at the feast. I helped Tut in getting Akhenaten's permission for Narmer to be away from the palace. You know what a great gourmet Akhenaten was, and how much attention he paid to every detail of his meals. Anyway, Narmer was gone nearly a month, and when he came back he brought wonderful jugs of wine, wine much sweeter than any we know here in Egypt. And mushrooms. You know how particularly Akhenaten doted on his mushrooms. These Narmer brought back still in the soil, growing, so they'd be perfectly fresh. This particular variety can't be grown in Egypt. And he brought back chickens."

"Chickens?" I was truly amazed.

"Yes. Chickens. We have none at all here in Egypt, which is a great pity since they're so delicious when properly prepared. Even across the Great Green they're hard to come by. Narmer also brought back a special variety of garlic, and you know how Akhenaten loved all his food to be flavored with garlic."

I pondered this information. Something she had said caught my ear. "Tell me more about the mushrooms. How knowledgeable is Narmer? Is it possible—is there any possibility at all—that what he brought back was toadstools? Could the man have been accidentally poisoned with toadstools?"

"Not a chance. They were mushrooms. I guarantee it. You know how Akhenaten was. He not only loved his food, he was almost demented with his fear of being assassinated. And in his case, he had plenty of reason. He spent hours in the kitchens, personally supervising every meal. He was so thrilled with Tut's surprise that he prepared the mushrooms with his own hands. In fact, Tut was right there to help him."

"Tut himself?" I asked. This surprised me. It didn't sound like the Tut I knew.

"What would be so unusual about that? It was his surprise for his father, wasn't it? After all, Eye, when you stop to think about it, a pharaoh for sure is a man who has absolutely everything. What do you get him for a present? Actually, for a ten-year-old Tut showed a lot of imagination."

"It sounds like it was a nice family night. Did Akhenaten let his guard down just a little? Was he perhaps a trifle relaxed, a trifle careless?"

She snorted in derision. "Akhenaten? Never. Never. That's one thing you could count on as a given. Nothing changed. Even though he was there throughout the entire preparation of the meal, with Tut with him, he of course had everything tried by the taster. And Narmer didn't die. Didn't even get sick. You know what an exquisite palate Narmer has. If there had been anything the least tiny bit off about the food, Narmer would have detected it immediately. After all, his life is on the line at every tasting. No, if Akhenaten was accidentally poisoned, it wasn't by anything Tut had brought back for him."

I didn't know whether or not this was good news. If those mushrooms might indeed have been toadstools, would Tut have accepted the hypothesis? Very doubtful, particularly since there would be no way to prove it. All that would happen would be that he'd be extremely annoyed, if not worse, at conjecture that he himself had inadvertently caused his father's death. I was no farther along than I had been last night.

# DAY TWO

## —

# AFTERNOON

Nefertiti invited me to stay over for a light lunch. It was the expected thing for her to do—protocol and all that—but with Nefertiti you just never knew. Nefertiti was never one to be much troubled by custom—even custom hallowed by thousands of years of usage. However, even for a queen mother in the royal palace, her days were pretty much all the same. With the death of her pharaoh-husband Akhenaten, her ability to wield power from the shadows had ceased abruptly. Save for ceremony, her days were left empty. Doubtless she looked forward to whatever I might have to say to her. Women are like that in any case. They always want to be in the know about everything, and since Tut's performance the previous evening by now must have reached even the lowliest corner of Thebes, the chance for her to have first crack at my response must be well-nigh irresistible.

Her servant set my tray before me, and my goblet of wine. The plate looked as if it had been arrayed by an artist, so decoratively was the food laid out upon it. This was, after all, the palace of the pharaoh.

I took my tray, and Nefertiti's, turned my back on her, juggled them a little, and once more turned to face her. "Choose whichever you prefer."

Nefertiti laughed a rich, throaty laugh, abandoned, a laugh of genuine amusement. "Do you really think I'd try to poison my own father?"

"I haven't lived this long by taking anything for granted."

She chuckled again, sipped her wine, and picked up a morsel with her fingers, consuming it with dainty bites. "There. Your turn."

Reassured, I ate.

"Daughter," I proceeded, "as you can imagine I've thought about nothing but this problem since I left here last night. Believe me, I know exactly what you mean about how fearful Akhenaten was of assassination. Maybe you can help me. I've been able to think of only six people who might have had the opportunity to poison the man, if indeed he was murdered, which, frankly, I very much doubt. However, I have no choice but to proceed on the assumption that he was."

She raised her heavily outlined, black-bordered eyebrows in genuine interest. For me, this was literally a question of life or death. For her it was food for gossip and idle amusement. I felt no resentment. Had I been in her position rather than mine, I would react exactly the same.

"Six?" she mused. "That's a manageable number."

"Yes. And if any of the six had special reason to kill him—other than the general reason that he was a total calamity for Egypt—perhaps I can pare the list down even more. I really do need your help with this. You were in the royal palace every day. You know everything that went on. More than that, you have a head for this sort of thing. You can read people better than anyone I know. Not too much gets past you. I need your help with the probabilities as well as the possibilities."

"So who are the six on your list?"

"I imagine you can already guess. Horemheb, of course. That slimy priest Aanen. The royal physician Yuti. And, from the point of view of opportunity, I have no choice but to add Ankhesenamun."

"Ankhesenamun?" She smiled with feigned incredulity. "Your granddaughter?"

"I told you I was talking about opportunity only, at this point at least."

"And—"

"Tut himself," I answered rather sheepishly. Nefertiti smiled and raised an eyebrow in amusement, but said nothing.

I had no choice but to say it. "And Nefertiti."

This time she neither laughed nor smiled.

"Of course," she stated flatly. "If I were in your place, I'd put Nefertiti at the very top of the list."

I simply waited attentively while she went on. "I could have poisoned that idiot anytime I chose. He trusted me completely. The strange thing is, I was on the verge of doing it."

This revelation totally astounded me. Why on earth should she tell me such a thing? On the other hand, why not? She loved theatrics. This certainly was one of her better ones.

I'm sure surprise was plain on my face. "Why on earth are you telling me this?" I said, voicing the exact thought in my mind. "Even for you, Nefertiti, it's a rather peculiar thing to do."

"We're alone. And what would you do?" she responded, arching an eyebrow in elegant disdain. "Go to Tut and tell him his mother had been planning to murder his father? Particularly with no proof?" She lifted another bite to her lips and chewed slowly and with great concentration, as if her sole interest were in the taste of the delicacy she'd placed in her mouth. Then she proceeded.

"I was really very badly put out when Akhenaten died," she went on. "The timing was terrible. For me, anyway. In three weeks

I'd have murdered him myself, and taken over the throne in Tut's name, along with Antef."

Antef! The commander of the palace guard. And her lover, no doubt—one of her myriad lovers.

"Antef!" I exclaimed. "You honestly thought you could pull off a coup with Antef! Antef! The man's a complete schmuck!" [Translator's note: *The "Hebarews," as Eye would refer to them later on in this scroll, had already been in Egypt for several centuries. Doubtless many of the more colorful words of their vocabulary had passed into Egyptian, and almost certainly the Hebrew of the Bible contains words of Egyptian derivation, though we might not always recognize them as such.*]

Nefertiti's eyes narrowed to slits, and I could tell immediately that my choice of words had been infelicitous. I should have known better. Nobody likes to be called a fool—certainly nobody with the piercing intellect of Nefertiti. "Antef held the key command," she stated icily, "and our plans were well laid. Horemheb would have been on the frontier with the army, campaigning against the Hyksos. By the time he heard the news we would have already held Tut's coronation in Karnak and all the key officials would have sworn allegiance to him as the new pharaoh and to Antef and me as regents. With luck, if Horemheb was already engaged against the Hyksos, he wouldn't even be able to leave the field. Don't underestimate me, Eye. Ever."

"But," I protested, sputtering a bit I'm sure, "why would you do such a thing? You were already queen of Egypt! What could you possibly have had to gain?"

"I was doing it for Egypt's sake. To some extent for my own, of course, but less than you might think. For one thing, I couldn't stand Akhenaten. Not that he troubled me much anymore, that wasn't it. But I couldn't influence him. There are people who think he did everything I wished, that he was my puppet. There are people who think the whole concept of the one god Aten was my idea. False. Totally false. In fact, it was the Aten thing that made me do it. The man was destroying Egypt and he was so blind he couldn't even see what he was doing. Unrest everywhere. Economic ruin. Why, the new temples to Aten he was building in Amarna were enough by themselves to drain every ounce of gold from the treasury. If he wasn't stopped, there'd be a revolution. And then where would I be? And where would Tut be? No matter what else I am, I'm a mother. I wasn't going to let that man bring us all down. Not when it would have been so easy to stop him. I must say, Father, that for a long time I really resented you. You particularly. You took matters into your own hands before Antef and I could make our move. It was clever of you to let Horemheb share power, once he was able to get back to Thebes. It avoided a civil war. I'll give you credit. But you thwarted all my careful plans, and I'm not quite certain I've even yet forgiven you for that."

"Well," I retorted, a trifle miffed, "if you'd just taken me into your confidence maybe I would have stepped aside. In fact, I'd have probably worked with you, and our family would have held total power instead of having to share it with Horemheb. And you're telling me you planned it all for the sake of Egypt, and Tut? Why am I skeptical? The fact that Antef was gorgeous had nothing to do with it?"

"That too. But I was sleeping with him anyway. I didn't have to kill a king for that."

She gazed at me reflectively. "There was something else. Akhenaten was a fraud, a complete fraud, and the more I stayed with him, the less I could tolerate it."

I said nothing, knowing she'd continue, and she did.

"He knew he wasn't a god. If I knew it, he must have known it. But he acted like he genuinely believed it. You may laugh, but I'm deeply religious." I did indeed smile, and she held up a hand in stern rebuke. "The ancient gods of Egypt gave us our strength, made us a mighty power, the most powerful in the world. And that man was overthrowing every god, every god but Aten, and at the same time proclaiming himself a god too. On top of all his other foibles—I was his wife, you know, and believe me, you don't have time to hear about all his disgusting personal habits—here he was, angering the gods that had made Egypt great, and I shudder still to think what the gods might have done had the man not been stopped."

"But you didn't kill him?"

"No. I did not. But then, if I had, would I say so?"

So much for Nefertiti. Her name was still on the list. How much of her tale was true? She loved these games. She was in her element. For me, my head was on the block. For her, it was entertainment.

I sighed. "Very well. Let's continue, if you'd be kind enough. What about Yuti? He had the opportunity, no doubt about that. After all, he was the king's physician. Whatever medicine he prescribed, Akhenaten had no choice but to take. The thing is, the man's such a rabbit. He may be the finest physician in Egypt, but he has the bedside manner of a dead carp. Somehow I can't see him doing it. I can't even figure out *why* he'd do it. Still, he certainly is the one man that Akhenaten had to trust."

"Ah yes, Yuti. Not a rabbit, though. More a chipmunk, I'd say, with those puffy cheeks of his, and those tiny eyes. A chipmunk with a fat ass. And yes, he did have a reason to hate Akhenaten. A most particular reason."

I raised my eyebrows in inquiry.

"This was something even you, as grand vizier, didn't know. When it was time for Yuti's son to serve in the army he begged the pharaoh to exempt him. The men in that family are all rather timorous, and Yuti was terrified that his boy would disgrace the family. He had Akhenaten's ear whenever he chose, and he pleaded that his boy not have to serve. But Akhenaten would have none of it, and sure enough, the first time he went into combat, he flinched and ran. Now, giving him his due, he wasn't the only one that ran. His unit was badly outnumbered. But still, when they caught up with him, they executed him, along with all the others they could round up. He was Yuti's only son. It made things awkward, as you might well imagine, but Akhenaten's problem was that he had complete faith in Yuti and didn't want anyone else for a doctor. So there it was."

"Do you think the man actually could have had nerve enough to poison him?"

"You tell me. If your only son had died under these circumstances, what would you do if you had the chance?"

"You know the answer to that one. But Yuti?"

"Your guess is as good as mine."

I sighed. One more name to stay on the list.

"Horemheb?" I asked.

"Of course. No use even discussing it. True, the timing would have been bad, since he was away from the palace. Still, maybe he'd gotten wind of what Antef and I were planning, and had to strike first, regardless. I don't know. Poison wouldn't be Horemheb's style. But perhaps he had no choice. Horemheb's nothing if not a practical man, and if time and circumstance made poison the only way, then poison it would be. If he did it, I suppose I have to thank you, since I doubt if his plan would have been to rule as regent. I think he would have deposed Tut, maybe even killed him, and made himself pharaoh in his own name. I wouldn't be at all surprised if he still doesn't have that in mind."

"That makes two of us." I knew all along that Horemheb would be on my list, and that I wouldn't need Nefertiti to confirm it.

"Aanen?"

"Don't even talk to me about that slimy apostate. A high priest with all the moral convictions of a cobra. A true High Priest of Amun would have died rather than permit Akhenaten's sacrilege. Instead, he let himself be made High Priest of Aten and persecuted all the ancient gods, overthrew their images, defiled their temples. Then, when Tut became pharaoh, he was High Priest of Amun again, like nothing ever happened. Frankly, Eye, I'm surprised that you and Horemheb let that happen. You should have hanged him upside down, slit his throat, sewn him into a jackal's skin, and tossed him at Amun's feet. That's what you should have done!"

"I gather," I said wryly, "you rarely confess yourself to Aanen."

She glared at me.

"Given all that, though, why would he have killed Akhenaten? Wasn't he safer with Akhenaten alive?"

"I have to agree."

Still, I thought, and it was a thought I'd had last night, maybe Aanen wasn't the worm we all thought he was. Maybe he didn't have the courage to die for Amun, but did have the courage to kill the pharaoh in the expectation that once pharaoh was dead, worship of Amun would resume. When it comes to matters of faith, all things are possible. Regarding Aanen, Nefertiti was of no help at all.

That left only Ankhesenamun. My granddaughter. Well, it left Tut, too, but I saw no point in pursuing either name with Nefertiti. She was, after all, their mother.

"I thank you, Daughter," I said, and rose to leave. "You've been most helpful, really you have. And if I live through all this, stroke my leg again and see what happens." If you could see Nefertiti, in the same room with you, in that transparent gown that showed off every single bit of her truly magnificent body, and those queenly, slutty eyes looking as if she wanted to have you for supper, you wouldn't think so badly of me.

"You've said nothing about Ankhesenamun," she protested, much to my surprise.

"She's your daughter. I think you'd rather I figure her out for myself. Besides, I know her pretty well, too, you know."

Indeed I did. I doted on her, and truly had a hard time imagining she could do such a thing. But then, it was always possible she was impatient. As long as Akhenaten was pharaoh, Tut couldn't be. She'd been seventeen at the time, Tut only ten. Maybe she wasn't content to wait for Akhenaten to die—after all, some pharaohs lived almost forever. Maybe she'd thought I'd make her co-regent, or Horemheb would. Again, who knows? Do any of us really know anyone?

Nefertiti also rose, and gave me a long, lingering kiss, full on the lips. A father/daughter kiss, of course. She said nothing about my omitting Tut's name, and I saw no point in mentioning it again either.

Reluctantly, I pulled myself away. "One thing more I must ask of you, Nefertiti," I said as I prepared to depart. "This conversation must remain totally private. Totally between us. If I am to have any chance for success at all, none must know, lest they be alert to my suspicions. Do I have your word on that?"

"Of course you do, Father. I understand perfectly. You have my promise."

Of course I do. I knew she could hardly wait for me to leave the room before she began chittering her tale throughout the palace. Women are simply unable to keep a secret. I was relying on it. Women seem to have their own special sorority and code of conduct, and promises have no weight with them, when made to men. Maybe I don't blame them. Compared to men, they are powerless and vulnerable, and perhaps by having this code of interchange of information they can better cope with a world that has them at such disadvantage. In any case, it was essential to my plan that all those on the list knew that they were on my list. If one of them was guilty, perhaps he'd make a foolish move and betray himself. Or herself. Perhaps.

# DAY

# TWO

# —

# EVENING

I returned heavyhearted to my own palace. I could feel my shoulders slump. My eyes were cast downward. What, after all, had I accomplished? In truth, very little. I had hoped, with Nefertiti's help, to pare down the list by at least a name. No such luck. You may have noticed that I didn't push her to suggest even more names. If they existed, in a way I didn't want to know. But I do know Nefertiti, and if any had come to mind I'm sure she would have brought them up. So in the end there it was. No gain. No loss. Except for time. Time. Time, which was running out on me, which continued to slip away with each passage of the shadow down the sundial.

I was truly depressed with this stupid state of affairs. I hadn't needed Nefertiti to tell me I was on a fool's errand. It was almost certain that Akhenaten had simply had the common decency to sicken and die before having time to ruin the country completely. In fact, in the mood I was in, it was a good thing for Tut that he was as cautious as his father. If I could figure out a way to get the chance, I'd strangle the little freak with my own bare hands.

I tried to console myself with the thought that at this very moment Nefertiti was, of a certainty, already relating every detail of our conversation to the ladies of the harem, and that, before I even got back to my palace, a dozen tongues would have become a thousand, and every sentence would find its way to those whose ears I wanted to reach. For whatever that was worth. Nonetheless, it was a straw worth clutching, and at the moment the only one at hand. Nefertiti, this woman, this daughter of mine, is an amazing creature. She is ruthless as any man, and would make a better pharaoh than most. She actually thinks like a man, and what higher compliment can a woman receive than that? Her choice of Antef as a conspirator still disappointed me, but on further reflection, had her improbable plot succeeded, there's no question who the true ruler of Egypt would have been.

Yes, my daughter Nefertiti is ruthless, and tough, and intelligent, and intuitive, and one whom it would be wise never to have as an enemy. But she is a woman. A woman of very powerful appetites, yes, but no woman ever born can hold her tongue when she has in her grasp some juicy morsel of gossip. On this I rely.

My reflections grew increasingly gloomy. Now, don't misunderstand. By nature I am quite the optimist, and have a distinctly upbeat personality. Still, I have more than a little right to be downcast. The especially galling part about this whole affair is that here I am, grand vizier of all Egypt, the most powerful man in the land, in some respects even more powerful than the pharaoh himself, since I held the power of regent, and yet I'm helpless to do more than sniff and search like some peasant's hound dog. If indeed murder had been done, those that might have done it were immune from my authority.

Think about it. I certainly did. What command could I give Nefertiti, the queen mother, that she would be compelled to respect?

The same was true of Ankhesenamun, the queen. By virtue of the aura of their positions, their literal godhead, a direct confrontation could only lead to disaster if they opted to defy me. I fully agreed with Nefertiti. The blood of gods did not flow in their veins. But the myth was believed by the people. The officers of the court were people. The soldiers of the army were people. The myth was their shield, and all my writs and ordinances and commands could not touch them should they opt for defiance if it ever came to that.

As for Horemheb, he needed no myth as a shield. He had a real shield. The army. Not only that, he was co-regent, and after that little game with the palace guards, if anything, the scales were now definitely weighted in his favor. Horemheb, too, was outside my power of command. If it came to a head-to-head clash of wills, he could spit in my eye, and I would have to smile and observe that it must be raining.

Aanen was a problem too. High Priest of Amun the All-Powerful. Nobody, but nobody, messes around with the gods and gets away with it. And that includes Eye, Grand Vizier of Egypt. And though I despise him as a man, I tell you in all confidence that I truly fear him. The high priests of Egypt communicate directly with our gods. They have enormous powers, and know secrets hidden from ordinary men. Their magic is mighty and potent, and with my own eyes I have seen men struck blind, and dumb, and deaf, or even dead, by the power of their spells and incantations. A High Priest of Amun is no one to trifle with.

Of course, there's Yuti. A poor, nervous physician, who trembles if a kitten bares his teeth at him. The man is a true disgrace to masculinity. Yet by one of those mysteries of nature he is endowed with greater medical prowess than any other doctor in the land. His knowledge of potions and medicines is unsurpassed, as is his mastery of the secret formulas and magical chants and prayers that are responsible for their efficacy. It was not by chance that he served Akhenaten. And when Tut was twelve, Yuti's pharmacy produced the wonders that broke Tut's fever when he was on the verge of death. Tut will have no other attend him, and I don't blame him. Yuti is my doctor too. Although the man is so timorous I know he could never stand up to me, and although this present crisis is so critical I can't worry myself too much about the future, still, I can't help thinking that should I survive these next days, Yuti is the last man in Egypt I should alienate. Particularly at my age. I rather ruefully came to the realization that even the power to torture, which Tut had denied me, would have been useless anyway since none, with the possible exception of Yuti, would be in my power to torture. Even their slaves and servants are outside my reach. If indeed a felon exists, bringing him—or her—down will be a delicate task even if I assemble proof. Other than Yuti, all are, at a minimum, as powerful as I.

It wasn't doing my frame of mind any good to realize that my day's work was far from over. Life went on, Egypt went on, and as grand vizier my duties could not be left unattended. At least I still wore my robes of office, so I would not need to change when I reached my palace, but I knew what was in store for me. My antechambers would be scrawl with supplicants and petty officeholders and officials of the White House [*Translator's note: the Royal Treasury*] and ambassadors and minor priests and superintendents of transport and accountants and all the functionaries great and small that keep pharaoh's realm in working order.

I of course have my own staff to screen this unruly army whose demands would tax even the sturdiest constitution and who would, if they could, devour all twelve hours of the day. [*Translator's note: Egyptians divided their days by twelve, not twenty-four.*] The burden has grown so great that my personal staff has exploded beyond its capacity to contain them, and I have been forced to build an entire adjacent administrative building for the sole purpose of housing them.

In looking back at the old records, in those rare moments when I could find time to browse through them, I couldn't help but be struck by how few bureaucrats it took to run the government in the days of the ancient pharaohs. How had they done it? Despite my best efforts and those of my predecessors, every year the bureaucracy swells, and no matter how hard I try to prune the list, each and every name always seems absolutely necessary.

I fear my decision-making is not at its best this day. My mind is on other things. I somewhat pity the poor wretches whose lives will be forever altered by my ill-thought-out, absentminded judgments. But then, life is capricious for all of us.

By the time my day was done I was exhausted, and I felt like dining alone. I had little appetite, and scarce noticed what food I ate. To put it succinctly, I was in a rotten mood. I suppose you've already gathered that. I felt dusty, and weary, and out of sorts.

I find that a nice hot bath is always good to restore the spirits. We Egyptians are a fanatically clean people and normally bathe after every meal. I of necessity had had no opportunity to do so after my lunch with Nefertiti, so I was feeling particularly grimy. A hot bath was exactly the remedy for my rather melancholy spirits.

I summoned Oudah to my chamber. When the rest of my bath attendants arrived, I waved them out of the room. Nefertiti's advances had made some impression on me and, being a man, there were things on my mind other than the hot bath which also were good for banishing morbid thoughts.

Oudah eyed me warily. This was the first time I'd ever commanded her presence alone with me. I caught the worried look in her eye, the look of a fawn suddenly confronted by a leopard. I don't believe I've told you about Oudah. She's new. Relatively new. Been a servant girl here for something over a month. Since I prefer speaking the blunt truth, a slave girl, actually. I pick them all myself. And I pick only the loveliest. If you were in my place, wouldn't you?

When I was younger, and the blood ran hot, I used to mount my slave girls as quickly as I acquired them. I'm sure it wasn't a very satisfactory experience for them, but I not only didn't care, quite honestly I never even thought about it. I was a bull, a stallion, and within minutes it was done.

Gradually, as the years passed, my attitude changed. I began wanting more from these encounters. I wanted more than a swift, sweaty gushing. More than a quick release of a repetitious urge. I wanted the experience to be a communication. I wanted to get to know them, and for them to get to know me. I wanted the coupling to be in some sense meaningful. And quite often, if the girl was personable and intelligent, I preferred an ongoing relationship rather than merely a new female every time. If you are sneering, and you are male, it means that you are young.

Now I know it must seem pure folly for a man to think that when he has the power to order a woman to his bed with a snap of the finger, he can expect something akin to love from her. Yet that is exactly what I sought. I liked to convince myself that these girls really cared for me, that they had learned what a truly kind and thoughtful and considerate man I was, and that they came to my bed both eagerly and willing. This is a harmless-enough delusion. It pleases me. Sometimes it even works.

All this is by way of explaining why Oudah is as yet untouched by me. As ridiculous as it sounds given the circumstances, I was seducing her. I was giving her time to know me and to like me, and I had been plying her with attention and flatteries, talking to her, learning about her, so that when this moment came she would yield with at least the appearance of freely given consent.

That startled-fawn look when I waved the other servants from the room told me instantly that my timing was premature. Like all males, my vanity is such that I feel all women surely will succumb to me. It's simply a matter of finding the proper approach. As for tonight, too bad. Perhaps as things progressed, she'd have a change of attitude. Now, rest assured, I'm not a complete fool. I know women fake these things. But alone in my room with Oudah, and feeling the rising excitement coursing through my body, whether any responsiveness she showed toward me was genuine or false at the moment was of no concern whatsoever.

I approached her and wordlessly put my hands on her shoulders. I looked deeply into her eyes, and could see that she was totally aware of her situation. There is no woman in the world, in this spot, who would not have comprehended with utter clarity. Her breathing became rapid and her breasts rose and fell in a manner I found particularly enchanting. She truly is a lovely creature. Not the most beautiful I've ever seen, true, but certainly most attractive. Oudah is somewhat taller than most—she's from Lower Egypt, where for some reason the females do seem on average to grow an inch or two taller than the norm. I like tall women.

She wore a simple linen tunic, the standard garb for a female slave. With what I hoped was a seductive, inviting maneuver, I very slowly, very carefully, very gently pushed it from her shoulders, my fingers gliding over her silken skin, aiding the fall of the garment until it rested in folds at her feet.

This was not the first time I'd seen her body, but it was the first time I'd seen it when I was in such an intense state of arousal. Her face is a perfect oval, her eyes dark, spirited, bright. Her hair is long, black, scrupulously clean, fetchingly coiffed. Her nose is straight and clean-lined, and her carriage upright, aristocratic. Her teeth are white and even, her arms supple. Her breasts are fabulous—perfect in size for my taste, tipped by surprisingly rosy nipples for one of such a dark complexion. Have I mentioned that I'm a tit man? Most males are. Oudah's are impeccable.

How old was the girl? Sixteen? Seventeen? Whatever. She was ripe and as near perfect as one could find, and the rather shy, confused look on her face made her all the more desirable. There was something else about her that I like. She's intelligent. Speaks several languages fluently, though how she came by the knowledge I have no idea. She has that look in her eye, that look of a keen mind behind that lovely face, and by now I had become much more selective in my pick of slave girls. Years ago looks alone more than sufficed. No longer.

I nodded at her. She knew what to do. It wasn't the first time for her, just the first time in this situation. She removed the layers of clothing from me, and I sensed the trembling of her fingers. I could see the troubled calculation in her eyes, as she tried desperately to evaluate her situation. Should she try to dissuade me? Should she feign eagerness, to try to reach a favored station among my slaves, perhaps—unlikely thought—to become an officially recognized concubine? The confusion and indecision in her eyes inflamed me even further. Every impulse in me urged my mounting her on the spot, but I knew that prolonging the evening would raise the pleasure to a literally unbearable peak. For this I could spare a few extra minutes from my day.

As you will note, up to this point conversation had been at a minimum.

"The hot water, Oudah, please," I said simply. Note the "please."

Note the lack of command in my voice. I wanted this creature to want me as much as I wanted her. I wanted at least the illusion of consent.

"Of course, master," she replied demurely, and prepared the water and oils in the same manner she had this morning. Now, you might think, under the circumstances, I might have said something like, "that's all right, Oudah, you may call me Eye." I was too experienced for that. There are rules, even in these matters. In the morning I would still be the master and she the slave, and overpermissibility in matters of address breeds insolence.

Oudah was well experienced in the art of bathing, and I certainly didn't rush her. Knowing what was to come, her hands were more caressing, her touchings more intimate. I knew I would not be her first, and found that somehow oddly disappointing.

She looked down at me, giggling, and said shyly, "Oh, master, you're a monster. A bull. An elephant. You're so huge. What on earth will I do?"

They all say that. Clearly, Oudah had opted for cooperation, sensibly concluding that any attempt at dissuasion would, at this point, be quite futile.

In what I knew she would find to be an unexpected turn of events, I then bathed her. All of her, with particular attention to her breasts. They weren't at all dirty, you understand, but nonetheless I lathered and laved them at great length and my fingers never ceased their caressings and squeezings. Nor did my fingers, anointed with slippery, scented oils, ignore other favorite parts of her body.

We attended to each other until the water in the urns grew cool. She was becoming more relaxed. I felt maybe she was even growing eager. I knew better, of course, but men are all vain in circumstances of this sort.

We dried each other with huge, fluffy towels, Oudah giggling all the time. Quite frankly, I don't much care for giggly women, but at her age I suppose it was to be expected. It was a minor flaw. In all other respects I found Oudah eminently satisfactory.

I held her at arm's length, again drinking in those fabulous feminine delights. I've long ago lost count of all the women I've possessed, but a new female body always has the power to seem in some manner like the very first. Some men say if you've seen one, you've seen them all. I disagree.

I took her hand and urged her to my bed, where I bade her to lie down. She complied, but to be honest, I didn't sense any eagerness on her part.

I went over to a bureau drawer and extracted a curved, bronzed razor, impeccably sharpened. Oudah looked at me, puzzled, and more than a little alarmed. This certainly wasn't what she was expecting next.

"Don't worry, my dear," I said soothingly. "This is just a little . . . eccentricity of mine. It'll be fine. Just stay as you are. Don't move."

Oudah's eyes remained dubious and wide, but she lay still. I came over to her and kneeled by the bed. "There, there," I said, as calmingly as I could. "You're doing just fine."

I took the razor and, with infinite patience and care, shaved the tightly curled hair that grew at the charming spot where her legs join. She literally held her breath until I was finished. And believe me, I took my time. I wanted it all, and I got it. When I was through, she was as smooth there as a newborn child, which was exactly what I preferred. It made her look totally innocent, totally new, and as intense as my desire was, this always served to heighten it even more. These things are all a matter of taste, and this was mine. I sleep on a pillow stuffed with hair from the countless women I have shaved in similar fashion. All right, so I'm a pervert. I admit it. All men have their proclivities. I think this one is relatively benign compared to many I know of. And be honest. If you could always have as many lovely females as you wanted, whenever you wanted them, wouldn't you too seek variety, lest the whole process become depressingly monotonous? If, however, a surfeit of nubile females is not your present problem, I shall understand your lack of sympathy.

Oudah's look was more wary now. And with reason. I had a few other oddities—nothing painful or depraved, you understand, but things that transformed encounters like these into something out of the ordinary. I brought paints and brushes from the bureau drawer.

"Just lie still, Oudah," I commanded.

She looked doubtful. "What are you doing now, master?" She tried to keep her voice steady, but she was getting really nervous.

"Don't worry, dear," I soothed once more. "You won't mind this at all."

I took the brushes and water-based paints and knelt over her. Slowly, and with care, I painted her body. The brush played over her breasts, and as it toyed with her nipples, they grew taut. I drew my designs on her stomach, over her navel, down her thighs. The light touch of the brushes obviously excited her, and her lips were parted, and her legs, involuntarily, began to spread.

It took me perhaps twenty minutes before I was done. The calligraphy wasn't my very best work, but under the circumstances it was rather well done, if I do say so myself. What I had done was to cover her entire body with hieroglyphics, filthy, obscene hieroglyphics, describing every part of her anatomy and every act I was preparing to commit with her in the most graphic, coarse manner my mind could invent. It would have given me even greater pleasure if I could have her stand and see herself in the mirror, but I knew she couldn't read.

Now, tell me, where's the harm in it? I know for certain there are masters who do things to their slave girls with whips and subject them to truly painful, unspeakable atrocities. I'm not like that. But I do have my own rather imaginative variations on the standard theme, and they greatly amuse me. A man with no imagination in these matters is a man with no imagination for anything. [*Translator's note: If you are a woman you probably feel Eye to be a disgusting rogue and bounder. I, on the other hand, being a man, feel chagrin that he, living 3,400 years earlier, displayed so much more erotic creativity than has yet come to my own mind. When I tell my classes how much we can learn from the ancients, little did I know.*]

In growing impatience I extinguished all the oil lamps but one. I like a certain texture, and have found that the light of a single lamp provides exactly the atmosphere that delights me most. I had wanted to restrain myself even longer, but by now, drinking in this intoxicating creature lying on my bed, body all washed and oiled, shaved smooth, covered with my handiwork, I could contain myself no longer.

Most times, I prefer doing things to the woman that gives her her pleasure first. I know it's unmanly and a weakness, and I would blush to confess it to any living human being, but by the time this is read I will have long been in my House of Eternity, so what difference will it make? In any event, this time there could be no more waiting. I forced myself upon her, and she yielded readily. She tried to make some show of pleasure, of passion, but it was all over too quickly. When I was done, totally spent, I slumped over at her side. The vixen tried to coax more from me, to no avail. After all, I'm fifty-seven. [*Translator's note: In regard to Eye's encounter with Oudah, I freely admit that I've loosened up a little on the original hieroglyphics in translation, but the essence of it is quite accurate.*]

As always, sex leaves me thirsty. "Oudah, dear, please pour us some wine. There's a good girl."

She pouted prettily and rose from the bed, still naked, still covered with my artwork. I gave her a patronizing whack on her lovely round bottom. She gave me a look, then went to comply with my instructions. In a moment she was back with a goblet for me.

"For yourself, too, Oudah. Pour yourself some wine. You've earned it."

She laughed lightly and did as she was told.

"Please be a dear and light the lamps again."

"Ooh, master," she sighed, "do I have to? Couldn't we just wait a little while, then . . ."

"Not tonight, dear," I answered indulgently. "There will be plenty of other times." Whom did she think she was kidding? I've heard this routine hundreds of times. If she thought this was going to get her favorable treatment, she'd learn that she was dealing with a man who knew women. I was a little disappointed in her, actually. I'd expected a little more subtlety.

"Well, if I must," she said with a great show of reluctance, and with a candle went the rounds, reigniting lamps. She returned to sit by my side.

I took the goblet and signaled her to raise hers. We touched rims. "To other nights, and other delights," I toasted.

"Whenever you wish, master. Gladly."

We tilted our cups and drank. Now that the act was completed, I couldn't wait to get her out of the room. Still, even though she was a slave girl, and even though I was a little annoyed at her transparent efforts to appear enthusiastic about her situation, I felt that ordinary courtesy demanded that I spend a moment or two with her after lovemaking. Women seem to have a thing about that.

I drank rather quickly, hoping that she would do the same so I could get her back in her tunic and usher her out of the room. I was really tired now, but definitely in a nicer humor.

She downed her goblet, and as she did I saw a peculiar look in her eye, and that lovely face began contorting in a strangled grimace. In absolute horror, helpless, I watched as her hands grasped at her throat. In a matter of moments her face took on a bluish cast. Terrible, animal grunts began bursting from her mouth. She writhed in agony. She tried to speak, but all that came from her throat were those awful grotesque sounds. And foam. Bubbly, dripping foam, that gradually started turning pinkish in color.

I knew what I was seeing, knew instantly. I knew there was nothing I could do for her. Nothing anyone could do for her. She was doomed, and swiftly. I seized her roughly. "Who did this?" I demanded. "Tell me now, and I'll avenge you. WHO DID IT?"

She tried to speak, but it was useless. I wasn't even sure she heard, or understood. She looked into my face. She put her hands to her head in an odd, compulsive gesture. She then took her hands and savagely clawed at her breasts in a fierce, peculiar manner. She dropped her arms into a pose of prayer, and she died.

I looked down at her, where she was lying on the floor, her body naked and covered with my painting, the intimate part of her body shaved. It would be a definite embarrassment for her to be found in my room this way. You might think me callous to have this as one of my first thoughts, but there was nothing I could do for the girl. She was dead.

I found a towel and, using the cold bathwater, scrubbed the water-based paints from her body. About the shaved portion I could do nothing. I pulled her tunic back over her head and laid her back down. Her body now had some semblance of dignity. I knew full well that these peculiarities of mine must be common knowledge throughout my palace, and beyond. Every girl who had shared this room with me had been warned upon leaving that, upon pain of the most extreme punishment, she must say nothing about any unusual things that had taken place. I knew it was futile. Might as well demand that the Nile cease flooding every year. Still and all, for the sake of her honor, and mine, far better that she be properly washed and clothed before I called anyone in to take her away.

I knew, instantly, precisely what had happened. How many times have I said that I'm wise in the ways of a royal court? When I had her get up to light the lamps, I switched goblets. If she had poisoned mine, her fate would be just.

I felt sorry for Oudah. I knew that what she had done, she had done at the command of another. I felt certain she held no animosity toward me, certainly none strong enough that she would attempt to murder me. I was a good master, and all my slaves felt themselves lucky to be in my household. No, she had been compelled to act upon the order of one she could not refuse. But who? What a pity the poison had acted so swiftly.

As I thought about it I realized that, in a way, it was well that this had happened. For me, of course, not Oudah. I now knew that Tut was right, that his father had been murdered. My ploy with Nefertiti obviously had worked. One of those on my list had heard that indeed he *was* on my list, and rather than risk my searching out his guilt, had opted to strike first. So. There was a murderer after all.

That part was good. What wasn't so good was the knowledge that this probably wouldn't be his only attempt. Next time, no matter how careful, I might not be so lucky. Look what happened to

Akhenaten, and he'd been fanatic about his personal safety. Still and all, I couldn't help but feel a certain sense of satisfaction that the seed I'd planted with Nefertiti had borne such swift fruit.

I rang a bell for my servants and after a few words of explanation had them take Oudah away. Although she had tried to kill me, I felt no animosity toward her. In fact, I would provide a House of Eternity for her far above her station, so that in the Netherworld she would know the peace and comfort that had been denied her in this one.

I extinguished the lamps and fell exhausted into bed. My mind was spinning with a thousand conjectures. It had been an interesting day.

# 7

## DAY THREE —

## MORNING

I did not rest well that night. Even with my head buried into my special pillow, sleep came fitfully. Since I'd also had a troubled night's sleep the evening before, I awoke in the morning not the least refreshed. Normally, I'm the sort of man who can turn his worries off as soon as the body hits the bed. I had what I confess are mixed emotions about Oudah. I am—or at least once was—a warrior, so the sight of death wasn't the least bit new to me. Still, when death comes so unexpectedly to one so young and charming, it's a shock. I won't try to say that I truly *cared* in any meaningful way for Oudah. She was simply there, and had it not been Oudah, it would have been someone else. Still and all, she was a human being, a person, a person I'd in a certain sense caused to die, and this troubled me. On the other hand, I couldn't help being human enough to be annoyed at Oudah too, considering that she'd tried to kill me. I knew she must have felt she had no choice but to do it, but still . . .

Setting all that aside, knowing someone is most seriously trying to make you dead is the worst possible cure for insomnia. For the second night in a row, instead of getting the sleep I now so desperately needed, my mind kept churning, desperately seeking to squeeze new solutions out of the meager facts in hand. Like dirty water squeezed out of wrung laundry, what was coming out was less pure than what went in. I was getting nowhere; my futile speculations became more and more fanciful and absurd.

I fear you are gaining the impression I am of a morbid and melancholy disposition. I again assure you this has no element of truth whatsoever. I have a robust and hearty nature. Truly I do. I enjoy life and take full and unapologetic advantage of the station which, by brains, by talent, and by the fortunate marriage of my daughter, I have been able to achieve. My appetites remain sound, and if evidence is needed, gaze upon my impressive girth. It's just that the prospect of reaching my House of Eternity so much earlier than I would voluntarily prefer makes it difficult to maintain a jovial frame of mind.

Regarding appetites, considering that I was having trouble falling asleep anyway, I did give passing consideration to sending for one of my concubines. I had nothing as elaborate in mind as the games I'd played with poor Oudah. Really, it was the companionship I had in mind more than anything else. In fact, I even considered summoning Tey, and when a man seriously considers asking for his principal wife you know he's of a troubled mind indeed.

In the end, I decided against it. One thing would lead to another, and although, I hasten to assure you, I still had the capacity, the prospect of expending all that energy again seemed scarcely worth it. Thus I spent the balance of the night alone.

Shortly before dawn I must have dozed off, for when next I opened my eyes the sun was full bright in my bedroom. I hauled myself out of bed, reluctantly, and called for my morning servants. Oudah of course had to be replaced. I gave the choice to Sentib, my majordomo, and he suggested Yennah, a recommendation I accepted without comment.

I felt sorry for Yennah. She wasn't the ordinary slave girl. Most of them are from the peasantry, sold by their parents to get rid of a mouth they are ill-equipped to feed. That's the bulk of them. As workers they're docile and tractable, but from this pool one rarely finds any fit for harem duty.

Many slaves arrive as booty, the survivors of sacked and ruined cities. This of course depends entirely on the fortunes of war, and slave prices rise and fall depending on the successes of our armies in the field. Yennah came from neither of these sources. She simply had the misfortune to be on a sailing ship seized by pirates, with the pirate ship in turn seized by a swift war galley of our fleet.

She is a rarity, Yennah. A Greek girl. We get few of these in Thebes, and they cost a fortune. She's comely—that should go without saying. I'd otherwise have had no interest in purchasing her. In a world entirely inhabited by dark-skinned, dark-eyed, black-haired humans, both male and female, Yennah is a most welcome contrast. She has thick, glossy hair the color of ripened corn, and it flows down her back in entrancing swirls and waves. Her eyes are dusky blue, and her skin so fair that in our brutal climate it burns bright red and peels away if she is exposed to it unprotected for more than a very few minutes. I've been saving Yennah for a special occasion, but with Oudah gone I have to move up my timetable a bit.

How old is she? I haven't asked. Younger than Oudah by a year or two. Whether she has the other qualities I find so delightful in my females—warmth, spontaneity, intelligence—I have yet to learn. I'm sure I will in time. Yennah has only been in my household for a little over a week, and I've been too heavily engaged in these other things.

In addition, I'm in no rush. You know my style. I want her to get to know me better, to be able to converse with me, to, well, to *like* me before I proceed further with her. This ridiculous mode of thinking remains my weakness, and I'm stuck with it.

For these reasons, and because my mind was occupied elsewhere, I didn't even have her undress before assisting me with my morning bath. In one corner of my mind I made a note to discuss with her, when I had the chance, the unwisdom of attempting to poison me, even if the party forcing her to act had apparently crushing power over her. My own power was still formidable, and had Oudah come to me for protection rather than crumbling under the force that must have been applied, she would not this very moment be in the hands of the embalmers, and I would not be out the outrageous slave price I'd paid for her.

I wasn't looking forward to this day. I was floundering, a blind-folded man shooting arrows. With the attempt on my life I knew there was a living target out there, but the knowledge brought me no closer to the discovery of who he was. So all I could do was pursue my inquiries, inventing as I went, since my investigations and thought processes had led me to the handful of people in all Egypt over whom I did not hold sway. All I knew was that one of them had killed Akhenaten, and wanted me dead too.

Today I'd tackle Horemheb. Might as well get it over with early. It was possible, I told myself, that he'd be cooperative. We'd been fellow soldiers for many years, on many a hard-fought campaign. I'd saved his life once. Well, maybe that was a stretch. My cavalry had charged the flank when the Syrian army was on the verge of breaking Horemheb's infantry. It won the day for us. Maybe by judiciously reminding Horemheb of our past comradeship and talking over old campaigns, he'd begin seeing me again as a fellow warrior, a fellow comrade-in-arms, and perhaps could give me a tidbit—anything—that might be useful to me. It was possible. And eunuchs might sire babies.

# DAY THREE

—

# AFTERNOON

The day was hot and dusty. This part of Egypt is always hot and dusty, so that was no surprise. It annoyed me considerably, nevertheless. General Horemheb was with his troops in the desert, so there was nothing for it save for me to go there to him. In the desert. Miles and miles past the green, irrigated fields of the Nile.

It was pure affectation. This is what I felt. If I didn't know better, I would swear the man had taken himself into the desert just to spite me. He could quite easily have stayed in Thebes, enjoying the privileges of his rank and the pleasures of the city. Who would think anything of it? After all, at the moment Egypt is at peace with its neighbors. Sharing the hardships of the desert with his troops might make him look good with the pharaoh, but by Toth, he was co-regent already, so what was Horemheb trying to prove?

Normally I would have traveled with a much larger contingent of guards. Since I hadn't been able to sleep much anyway, I'd given considerable thought to just the right note to strike when I entered Horemheb's camp. Too many mounted guards might look threatening. It might also make me look fearful and timid. I'd die before I'd give Horemheb that satisfaction. On the other hand, I was co-regent and grand vizier, and my rank mandated an impressive retinue. And as of now, I regarded my guards as guards, not theater. Someone wished to hasten my journey to the Netherworld, and it could well be Horemheb. A reasonable band of guards was certainly prudent. After much thought I decided on a reinforced platoon as being just about the proper size—forty mounted soldiers, all bedecked in their fine parade uniforms.

Now, you might protest, under my current circumstances walking into the armed camp of the mightiest general in the army might not be a career-prolonging move. You might also reasonably suggest that no matter how many guards I brought with me, they'd be useless compared to the regiments of Horemheb's veterans that would be surrounding me. As usual, you'd be right.

However, think about it. Would Horemheb murder me in his camp, in broad daylight?

He might. But it was unlikely, even if he was Akhenaten's murderer. A military camp miles out in the desert is no place to commence a coup, and if he killed me so openly and brazenly he'd have no choice but to overthrow Tut and seize the throne. Or such was the line of thinking with which I tried to reassure myself.

Remember, Tut himself was no fool. With the nation at peace, he'd dispersed the army. Although Horemheb was the highest-ranking general, he wasn't the only one, nor was this camp the only one. There were many more regiments than these, scattered about the frontiers, and whether they'd support Horemheb against Tut was by no means a sure thing. In addition, I'd managed to keep the bulk of my cavalry concentrated at Thebes. Admittedly, if I were dead, the outcome of a coup would only be of trifling interest to me. Still, I'd given my second-in-command strict instructions that, in the event of anything peculiar happening, he was to take his orders from Tut, and Tut alone. He was a good lad and I felt certain he'd obey. Much as I disliked my grandson, if Horemheb meant to kill me, I wanted to do everything in my power to thwart whatever plans he might have.

There was a point to this, other than sheer pique. My cavalry was a formidable force in its own right, and I doubt very much that Horemheb would instigate a coup without having a clear picture of which way they'd hop. In fact, I was betting my life on it. What choice had I? This was the third day.

Horemheb's camp was about forty miles outside the city. Normally, forty miles is an easily manageable distance. That's forty normal miles, not forty desert miles. I'd abandoned my chariots and opted to make the journey with horses alone. It was brutally hard on my hemorrhoids and I was in agony after covering scarce a tenth of the distance. Regrettably, chariots are short-endurance vehicles and tend to break down in rough terrain. They also get their wheels stuck in deep ruts or drifts of sand, and when that happens the entire column halts until they're manhandled out. Right now, time was my most precious possession. I couldn't afford to waste it. If I went by chariot it might cost me an extra half a day, and I didn't have those hours to squander.

My mounted force was considerably bedraggled by the time we reached our destination. My men were sweating and disheveled; their gorgeous parade uniforms terribly the worse for wear. We had looked so fine when we left Thebes. I should have opted for field dress. How stupid of me. On the other hand, it wasn't as though I hadn't given the matter thought. I knew the sight of my splendidly garbed cavalry guards would affront Horemheb—they were bound to be a sore spot with him. But if I showed up with my men in ordinary field uniform, it would make me look apologetic and weak. Oh well, it can't be helped now. In the end, I wind up looking foolish. Luckily, a rather minor matter, and if it's the worst mistake I make this day, I'll settle for it.

Horemheb's camp was unprepossessing. There was nothing whatsoever of pomp or show about it. An army camp in the desert, nothing more. Horemheb had always had a marked distaste for pomp of any kind. I, on the other hand, reveled in it. Oh well, to each his own.

We entered with little ceremony. No blare of trumpet or tattoo of drum. Nor were honor guards awaiting us. First of all, they didn't know we were coming, so they could hardly have been expecting us. Second, if Horemheb had known it was me, he wouldn't have put out an honor guard anyway.

As we straggled into Horemheb's camp, a single soldier eyed us with a bored, indifferent look. He was completely bare save for a loincloth and the spear he rested on, but he was heavily muscled and his skin burned nearly black by the sun. A towel-like device wrapped around his head and draped over his neck offered some protection, but not much. He had a low, beetling brow, and his body, glistening with sweat, bore many scar-tissue ridges, some probably from battle and others from camp brawls. He stank.

Houy, my troop commander, dug his heels into his mount's flank and cantered over to the man. "General Eye," he said sharply, "here to see General Horemheb. Call out the guard. Commanding officer entering."

The man looked at Houy with an air of mild bafflement. It wasn't insolence. It was more like puzzlement. "What guard?" he said in a thick, slurred voice, the accent betraying his origins as a man from Nubia or thereabouts. "I'm the guard. Just me. And lucky at that. Nearly everybody else is out in the field on maneuvers. Rotten day for it. Of course, that's the only type of day we get out here."

Houy looked at me in exasperation.

I trotted over to the man. My rear end felt as if it were being devoured by alligators. "Never mind, Houy," I said. "I'll take care of this."

I dismounted, thanking all the gods of Egypt for finally being able to get off the animal's back, and walked up to the soldier. "I'm General Eye," I barked imperatively. "Take me to General Horemheb. At once, you disgraceful pig."

The man, and the entire camp, were indeed in my opinion a disgrace. If I were in command here, things would be in full military order, shipshape, you can bet on that.

The soldier looked me up and down for an instant. There was no way he could have any doubt about my rank. He waved a half-hearted salute at me. If I hadn't been in a hurry, I would have paused long enough to give the pathetic excuse for a soldier the truly rough side of my tongue, and a prod in the ribs with my saber. Instead, I just shook my head in disgust and let him lead us, at a leisurely pace, down the dusty camp street to a large tent which clearly marked itself as Horemheb's.

I was lucky Horemheb wasn't in the field with his regiments. It would have taken another hour or two to track him down, and I doubt very much I could have endured that much more time on the back of a horse.

We were a jingling, clattering bunch, considering all the paraphernalia a troop of mounted cavalry carries with it, and Horemheb must have heard our approach. When we reached his tent he was standing at the entrance, leaning against a tent pole, waiting.

Horemheb was scarcely a more impressive-looking sight than the guard who had led us there. He wore no badge of rank or uniform, and was naked to the waist. A caplike device perched on his head at an odd angle, from which extended a yard of cloth, shielded his neck from the burning sun. He wore a baggy, shapeless garment that covered him from the waist down. That was it.

But even if you didn't know Horemheb by sight, you'd never for an instant doubt that this was a commander. The man had presence, I can't take that away from him. He dominated. He had bulk, massive bulk, but you couldn't call him fat. He stood at least four cubits tall [*Translator's note: Six feet. Remember, I told you a cubit was roughly eighteen inches.*] His eyes were deep-set into his heavily bearded face, and his face bore a perpetual scowl, as though he'd never seen anything in his life that had pleased him. There was menace about the man. His nose was broad, and the smallest portion of the tip was gone, slashed off in that fight with the Syrians I told you about. He had a certain piglike quality—definitely not the sort you'd think of first to invite to a dinner party—but I knew Horemheb well, and if ever there was a man I'd want beside me in a fight, he was it.

His reputation for courage was legendary. I will say nothing to disparage it. This he had earned, in fullest measure. There is no man on this earth I would rather not have for an enemy, and I genuinely regretted that circumstances had come to make us so. Still, whatever is, is.

Horemheb looked at me in scowling displeasure. Since he always scowled, I had no way of interpreting his mood.

He glanced at my troops. "I see you brought those faggot guards of yours with you," he growled contemptuously. "They don't look so pretty now, do they, after forty miles through the desert. For that matter, I've seen you looking better yourself, Eye."

Horemheb made a gesture with clenched fist and thumb. "Soldier," he spat, indicating the Nubian who had greeted us, "take these girls"—indicating my guards—"over to the commissary and get them something to eat and drink. When they're done, ask the quartermaster if he can find them some dresses in their size."

I was off to a bad start. Score one for Horemheb.

He turned his face back to me.

"So what brings you here, Eye?" he demanded. "Only real soldiers are here. You must want something from me real bad to get those little dollies of yours in their pretty clothes all sweaty and dusty. I pity Tut if those pansies are the best you can scrape up to guard him."

Normally I'm at my best in this sort of give-and-take, but I bit my tongue and took his heavy-handed humor because indeed I did want something from him.

When I failed to needle him in turn he grunted and, which seemed impossible, his face took on an expression that was even more disagreeable. "I see," he stated flatly. "This must be about that business of Tut and his father. Serves you right, Eye. You've had it coming for a long time. I'm surprised Tut's waited." He laughed, but the laugh had little mirth in it. "I'm really going to enjoy this. So you have to find a murderer that doesn't exist, eight years after he didn't do it, and without using torture, no less! Serves you right," he repeated. "Remember when you ordered those slaves in Pithom to make bricks without straw? Same deal here. What goes around, comes around."

"Not the same deal at all!" I shouted indignantly, wagging my finger in the general direction of his face. "Those Hebarews had it coming. The worst slaves in Egypt, and believe me, if there's one thing I know about, it's slaves. With most slaves, you order them to make bricks, they make bricks. Not the Hebarews. Always arguing. 'How long should the bricks be? How wide? What size? What shape? What color? How many? We never used to make them that way. The straw's no good. The mud's no good. The sun's too hot. The water's too warm. Our blankets are too thin. How many hours do we have to work? Our tribe had the excavation work last time—it's Levi's turn.' Always something.

"And on top of it, they're so weird. That seven-day week of theirs. Now I ask you, Horemheb, be honest. How can anyone make a decent calendar out of a seven-day week? And the one they come up with is lunar, on top of everything else—they have to keep dropping in extra months to make the thing work right. After all these centuries in Egypt you think they'd at least pick up some of our modern ways, but they don't."

"It was your problem, Eye, not mine. Thank Osiris."

"Yes!" I exclaimed, picking up on the theme eagerly. "That's another thing. That god of theirs. That absurd one-god idea of theirs. I honestly think that could be where Akhenaten got it from. You know, I can't believe they still worship their god, considering that they've been slaves here for centuries now. You'd think they'd finally figure out he has no power here. And another thing. Can you imagine it? They believe he actually ordered the men to circumcise themselves. The men! Now, I could understand it if they circumcised their women. Women are faithless creatures at best. Female circumcision makes sense—keeps them from straying. But the men actually do it to themselves!"

"At least, if they run away, it makes it easy for us to identify them when we catch them."

"You're right about that, Horemheb, absolutely right," I agreed eagerly. "You'd think after all these years they'd have figured that one out, but no, they just keep doing it to themselves. And then," I said, really warming to my subject now, "there's that cheeky leader of theirs. Actually demanding we give them three days off for some sort of desert festival. Said their god demands it. Three days! In a row! Can you imagine what things would have been like if we'd given in to them? Every slave in Egypt would be clamoring to convert to Hebarewism!

"And then, to top it all off, that lunatic leader of theirs kept demanding to see pharaoh in person. 'Let my people go!' he kept screaming. 'Let my people go!' Go where? I ask you. Go where? I got so exasperated I finally told pharaoh we should take him up on it. I still think so. We ought to drive them out into the Sinai or somewhere. They're more trouble than they're worth."

"Is this why you came here, Eye, to complain to me about the Hebarews?"

Horemheb was right. I'd gotten off the track.

"Well, no, Horemheb, the truth of the matter is that I thought— I hoped—that you might know something that could be of help to me in this little problem Tut dropped in my lap. Anything at all you know would be a big help to me. Any little thing. I'd really appreciate it."

Horemheb looked me directly in the eye. "Fuck you," he said coldly. [*Translator's note: What Horemheb actually said was, according to Eye's hieroglyphics, "May you eat rat vomit and drink your own urine for eternity. May the gods rip off your head and piss down your throat. May they cut off your penis and stick it in your ass. If you had one. A penis, that is. May they turn you upside down, stick your head in the sand, and forever beat your balls like gongs." I would give the rest of Horemheb's surprisingly creative invective, but in the hieroglyphics it runs on for several pages. I believe that "fuck you" captures the essence of it.*]

I took Horemheb's reply to mean that he was unwilling to let bygones be bygones. Nonetheless, I'd come all this way, so I figured I might as well see if I could perhaps still accomplish something.

"Now look, Horemheb," I pleaded. "I know you're angry with me about those new horse guards at the palace. But you'd have done the same thing in my place, and you know it. We're really on the same side, whether we like it or not. Tut's starting to feel his strength. You've seen it too. We've been co-regents now—for what? Seven years? Eight years? Unless we work together, it's all going to come to an end. For both of us. I'm just his first target. When I'm out of the way, it'll be your turn."

"Watch it, Eye," he warned brusquely. "It sounds like you're on the verge of talking high treason."

Has anyone ever heard of low treason? I thought to myself, but felt I'd better not say it. Horemheb had an iffy sense of humor.

Instead, I simply plunged on. "Look, man, I'm not proposing a coup or anything like that. We've both of us gotten used to power, and I know neither of us wants to give it up. But you've watched Tut growing up, same as I. Do you like what you see? There are pharaohs and there are pharaohs, but if you ask me, Tut's going to turn out to be as crazy as his father. In fact—and I swear to you, Horemheb, I'm not making this up—he's been saying things lately that make me think he might even try to restore that ridiculous Aten-cult that Akhenaten nearly ruined Egypt with."

This Horemheb took seriously. "Don't mess around with me, Eye," he said flatly. "You're at the palace all the time. Do you mean it?"

"Yes, Horemheb," I said with all the sincerity I could muster. "I really mean it. Honest." I was lying. Tut hadn't shown any inclination whatever to restore Aten. Quite the opposite, actually. Still, I needed something to get Horemheb's attention, and this was the best I could come up with on short notice.

"I thought we put all that behind us when Akhenaten died," Horemheb mused, and I could almost literally see the thoughts circulating through his mind. "Egypt couldn't take any more of that. What man in his right mind could actually believe that there is just one god, and one god only? Who could believe that the same god that rules the day rules the night?"

"Exactly," I agreed solemnly. "And who would be mad enough to believe that the same god that rules good also rules evil?"

"True." Horemheb nodded. "Absolutely true. And could the god of plenty also be the god of famine?"

"Ridiculous. Makes as much sense as believing the god of peace is the same as the god of war."

"Or life and death," he opined.

"Or light and darkness," I said.

"Health or sickness."

"Sound or silence."

"Truth or falsehood." I had no idea Horemheb would be so good at this.

"Left and right!" I exclaimed. "Up or down! In or out!" Horemheb stared at me frostily. I'd gotten caught up in the spirit of the thing, and gone much too far.

"Well," I went on hastily, talking fast before he could explode in anger, "you understand what I'm talking about. We can't take the chance of having another pharaoh trying to restore the Aten-cult. We've been through all that. All I'm asking from you is a little cooperation, for old times' sake. I'm not plotting treason here. I'm not suggesting overthrow of the government. Not yet, anyway. All I'm saying is that we're natural allies, and neither of us can afford to let Tut pick us off one at a time. We have to hold on to our power until he matures. You must see that. If he gets rid of me now, you can bet he'll give command of the cavalry to some relative completely under his thumb. And remember, I'm a relative. By marriage, anyway. You're not. So if he's willing to be rid of me, what chance will you have? With the cavalry in his hands, if he orders you to step down as regent, what'll you do? Start a civil war? On what grounds? Think about it, Horemheb. I'm not asking for a lot. Maybe there's nothing you can help me with anyway."

Horemheb did think about it. "We did have some good times all those years ago, didn't we?" he said, relaxing. I let out the breath I'd been holding. "Remember the campaign in Nubia? The one we fought down by the second cataract, down by Abu Simbel? By Anubis, that had to be some of the most awful country I've ever fought in. We lost nearly half the army to disease and those horrible poison insects before we even got near the enemy. I'm surprised we survived, let alone won."

"Yes," I agreed, relaxing. "Those were days. Good days. We were young then, you and I. I was a soldier then, a real soldier, a fighting soldier. I miss all that. You're lucky, Horemheb, to be out here in the desert, away from the palace, from all the intrigue, the back-stabbing, the corruption. You're out here with honest soldiers, good sturdy boys, loyal boys. Stinking ones, too. I know water's scarce, but isn't there any frankincense or something in the camp? Regular incense? Anything at all?"

Horemheb roared and slapped me on the back. "I can't believe you've gotten this soft, Eye! I guess you're an old man after all. Back in those days down at Abu Simbel you smelled like all the rest of us, and didn't complain about it either."

Fair enough. But that was then. This is now. And so far, all this conversation had gotten me nowhere.

"Look, Horemheb," I pleaded, but tried to keep the pleading out of my voice, "I don't have much time. If you do know anything that could possibly help, it's in your interest as well as mine to let me know. I tell you quite openly, so far I've made hardly any progress. I remind you one more time, you and I are balanced off against each other, but together we balance against Tut. Think hard about what it will be like with me gone and Tut itching for full power."

I could see Horemheb's eyes cunningly pondering this very question. "It's all been so long ago," he mused.

"Eight years."

"That's a lot of years. I do remember one thing, though. Maybe it means something, maybe not. About a month before Akhenaten died, Aanen came to me and struck up a private conversation. I remember being surprised because Aanen isn't the type for small talk—neither am I, for that matter. Anyway, after rambling on aimlessly for a while—it seemed like hours but it probably was only fifteen minutes—he dropped a rather pointed hint that it might be better for Egypt if some other pharaoh were on the throne. I didn't pick up on it, and he didn't push it. I don't know if it means much. After all, just about everybody in Egypt felt we could use a new pharaoh. But there it is. For what it's worth.

"Aanen said that?" I exclaimed eagerly. "Aanen, the high priest?"

"Of course Aanen the high priest, you idiot!" Horemheb exploded. "What other Aanen would I be talking about?"

I very deeply resented his speaking to me that way. He didn't have to be so huffy about it. There was, after all, more than one

Aanen in Egypt. Still, under the circumstances, I had to bite my tongue and keep from snapping back at him.

What I said was, after a dignified pause, "I thank you for the information, Horemheb, truly I do. Is there anything else you might remember?"

Horemheb pondered the question briefly. He shook his head. "Nothing I can think of right now. If something else comes to mind, I'll send you a letter."

"By fast courier. I've not much time."

"You've made that clear more than once."

I took a deep breath, paused, then took the plunge. I felt I had to do it, even though I felt utterly foolish.

"You know, Horemheb, just between the two of us, there's something I have to ask you. Even if you tell me, there's nothing I can do with the information. There are no witnesses here. By chance, did it happen to be you who murdered Akhenaten?"

Horemheb roared with laughter till I thought his face would turn purple. His sides shook, and tears streamed down his face. "Eye," he gasped, between explosions of mirth, "do I have the 'glyph for 'stupid' painted on my forehead?"

# DAY THREE

—

# LATE AFTERNOON

The return back to Thebes was far worse than the journey to Horemheb's camp. For one thing, I was discouraged. What of value had I learned? Very little. Almost nothing. And I'd had to humiliate myself in front of the man to glean even the one tiny and probably useless scrap he'd thrown me.

On top of that, with my rear totally inflamed, another forty miles through the hot desert loomed unendurably. If I'd had the time I'd have stayed in Horemheb's camp overnight, but I didn't have that luxury. I really would not be able to stand the return trip on horseback, so I commandeered a chariot. It would slow the homeward journey somewhat, but it couldn't be helped. I made certain Horemheb wasn't around when I took it—I'd taken more than enough ribbing from him for one day.

Regrettably, my feet weren't in the best of shape either, despite the daily ministrations of my chiropodist. I of course had to stand all the way, and after a few hours the pain in my feet equaled the burning in my hemorrhoids. All in all, I'd had better days.

Suddenly, unexpectedly, while my mind was on other things, the chariot took a violent lurch, flinging me unceremoniously to the ground. The horses reared in confusion and dragged the damaged vehicle nearly forty cubits before coming to a halt. Luckily I was thrown completely clear and struck soft sand or I might have been seriously injured.

I dragged myself up and brushed some of the sand off my face, my arms, my uniform. It made little difference—by now I was pretty much papered in sand everywhere, so the extra scarcely mattered. I walked over to the chariot, limping a little from the fall, and inspected it carefully. Broken wheel. Bad luck. But I'd taken the precaution of bringing along spare axles and wheels. It would cost us a little time fixing it, but my men were experts at this sort of thing and it shouldn't slow us up for long.

Maybe I should have done the same thing on the outward journey—taken a chariot instead of riding horseback—but I had no way of knowing what might transpire at Horemheb's camp or how much time I'd need, so I sacrificed my bottom for the good of my country.

As the chariot wheel was being tightened on its axle, I glanced backward and my heart came to a full stop, or so it seemed. Ahead of me the sky was bright, the day clear and hot, the sun burning. Behind me was utter darkness. A wall of black—deep gray might be closer to the truth—but darkness, sheer darkness. In all that heat of the desert, I felt my skin turn cold and clammy. A few of my cavalrymen saw it too. The whites of their eyes, large in their sand-encrusted faces, grew even larger, even whiter. Their terror transmitted itself to their fellows as one by one each turned and pointed back in the direction from which we'd come.

For several moments I simply stared at the wall of darkness, transfixed, as paralyzed with fear as the least of my soldiers. The wall was moving inexorably toward us, and despite the fact we were cavalry, clearly there was no way we could outrun it. As the dark mass approached closer, it howled and shrieked. If ever I'd heard the implacable curse of an avenging god, this was it.

The hand of a god—which one, I could not know or guess, but nonetheless the hand of a god, reaching to grasp me and bury me namelessly in this pitiless desert. And nothing in this world I could do to stop it. My mind ceased functioning. If I was buried here, unknown, unmarked, there would be no House of Eternity for me. No goods or possessions to sustain me in the afterlife. I would truly, utterly perish, like the most miserable slave. Eye, Grand Vizier of Egypt; Eye, with power of life and death; Eye, whose palace held wealth beyond inventorying, would come to this. Would come to nothing, would exist as nothing. It was a thought that never before had crossed my mind, but cross it now indeed it did, as I watched the howling mass roar relentlessly closer. [*Translator's note: I fear I may not have been able to convey the full extent of Eye's terror. As opposed to our bleak religious convictions, the Egyptians believed quite strongly that indeed you can take it with you, if you're rich and powerful enough, and their elaborate tombs were filled with all the necessities for a long and comfortable afterlife. But to secure this pleasant existence, everything had to be done according to proper ritual and formula, and one's House of Eternity had to be properly provisioned. As Eye contemplated this preternatural wall of darkness closing in on him, understandably he panicked in superstitious dread.*]*

Who among my enemies has such power? I thought to myself. Who among them can raise this terrible apparition to strike me down? What magic have they been able to invoke? What spells have they been able to cast, what god have they bribed, to wreak this terrible plague upon me and upon the poor men I brought with me?

I felt helpless. Yet I knew I had to act, even if action in the face of a god's wrath must of necessity be futile. I could see that what was coming at me was the dreaded khamsin, the horrible desert sandstorm that obliterates and buries everything in its path. [*Trans-*

lator's note: I have used the word "khamsin," which is Arabic in derivation, to describe this storm. Obviously, Eye used an Egyptian word for it,
but "khamsin" is better known to Westerners.]

Then another emotion took over. Anger. If my enemy had cast
a spell to overwhelm me with this khamsin, I could relate to that.
I'd disposed of a few enemies myself in my lifetime, albeit without the aid of magic or spells. But whoever my enemy was, he had
no right to take my boys down with me. Particularly not these
boys, the very finest, the very flower of my cavalry.

It was this thought that galvanized me, that allowed me to cast
off the fatalistic lethargy that without question would have meant
my doom—meant the doom of all of us.

I had no idea if anything I could do would be any use, particularly with the thought still in the forefront of my mind that if, indeed, this khamsin was the work of a god, all resistance would be
futile. Still, I had to try. If I was going to die, it wasn't going to be
passively.

We couldn't be in worse shape. Our journey to Horemheb had
been planned as but the work of a single day. We had no tents, no
supplies of any kind save the very little ration of food and water
we carried on our persons, and nothing whatsoever that could protect us from the fierce onslaught bearing relentlessly down on us.
And though I was beginning to recover from my initial panic, I
could tell from the look on my men's faces that they had not. I
saw terror there. I felt horrible guilt. They were looking to me for
leadership, and in my self-absorption I was giving them absolutely
none.

"Houy!" I shouted, "We have no time to waste. Turn the chariot over on its side and tether the horses to it. Now!"

Houy looked at me in bewilderment. The leathered skin of his
face was still contorted in an expression of total fear, and his eyes
gazed, wide with dread, at the rapidly advancing black wall of sand
that was perhaps no more than a half mile away.

"Do it!" I shouted again. "We've no time to waste! The chariot
will anchor the horses, and we can shelter behind them. We can
use them as a windbreak!"

Houy stared at me without moving. He was still caught up in his terror, a fear with which I sympathized. On the battlefield Houy was as brave as they came, but this was different. Everyone knew what it meant to be caught in the desert in a khamsin without shelter, without provisions, but there wasn't a moment to spare and I had no time for indulgence.

I took my sword from its scabbard and with the flat of the blade struck him savagely across his ribs. "You're the leader of this column, Houy!" I exclaimed savagely. "Act like it, or by Osiris I'll kill you before the sand does!"

This he understood. He pulled his own weapon, and prodding with the point, quickly got the platoon to work. Houy was intelligent as well as brave. Now that I'd recovered my own sense of command, he responded to it like the fine soldier he was. With remarkable swiftness he prodded his men into action. It was impossible to tether all the horses to the chariot. They tied up as many as they could, then tied the rest to whatever portion of the tethered horses was most convenient, so that all the animals formed a single compact mass centered on the overturned chariot. It was a start.

I tore a portion of my formerly gorgeous cloth-of-gold tunic into a long strip and wrapped it around my mouth and nose, and with a gesture indicated to Houy that all the men should do the same. The storm was almost on us now, and the roar of the wind was making it nearly impossible for voice commands to be heard.

"Form the tortoise!" I shouted at the top of my voice. "Make a wall with your shields! Drive them into the ground as solidly as you can, twenty in the bottom row, and lock the other twenty in a second row above them. Hurry! Now! We're running out of time!"

My men were well drilled. They understood the tortoise maneuver, and in a matter of a moment they had this shield-wall locked and assembled, facing the oncoming storm, their bodies braced stoutly against the protective shields, muscles straining to hold against the violent wind that was already reaching for us. By the gods, I was proud of my boys. I couldn't blame them for their

initial panic—I'd panicked too. But in an instant, as soon as I'd recovered, they too found their discipline returned. They were soldiers of Egypt, and no higher praise can be given any man.

I had never been in a khamsin before. I had heard about them,
of course, but nothing had prepared me for the experience. The
sound was overwhelming. A thousand demons shrieked and
moaned in our ears. I strained my ears to see if I could hear any
identifiable words, any voice of a god calling my name, but I heard
nothing but the wind. The sound was unendurable, but endure it
we must since our hands and bodies were straining to keep our
shield-wall intact and there was no way we could cover our ears.
Our eyes we could only keep closed. Despite the protection of the
horses, the chariot, the shields, the sand was scouring our faces,
our arms, our legs, every part of our bodies that was exposed. The
shield-wall was only an imperfect barrier. The wind remorselessly
drove the gritty sand through every crack and crevice of our in-
terlocking shields. Whenever a man's arms wavered, a fresh torrent of grit spewed over us.

How long could we hold out? It was only a few minutes, and
already my muscles ached beyond endurance. As the storm overwhelmed us, the sand began piling up behind the shield-wall, and
the weight of it and the force of the wind made it harder and
harder for human muscle and sinew to resist.

I tried to keep hope. We'd covered about half our return journey from Horemheb's camp before the khamsin overtook us. It
was late afternoon. In another hour the sun would set. With sunset, the khamsin would cease. At least it *should* cease. If it was a
normal storm. If this storm was magic, there was no reason to expect a mere sunset to stop its blowing.

I wore an amulet around my neck, a scarab given to me by my
mother when I was but a child. It too had magic properties; my
mother had most solemnly assured me this was true, and I had always most earnestly believed it. I prayed with frantic sincerity to
the god of the amulet, prayed that its power counter the magic of
the storm, counter its spell, and if it could not cause the storm to
cease, at least force it to behave like a normal storm and die with
the setting of the sun. I desperately wanted to finger the amulet

to give greater force to my prayers, but my arms and body were fully engaged with pressing my shield back against the force of the wind and the sand.

We held out against the power of the storm. It flung itself with supernatural power against our pitiful barricade and we held out against it. For how long? Fifteen minutes? Half an hour? It was impossible to tell. But we were human and could only stand so much. The sand was piling up ever higher against us, and with it the weight. We were reaching the limit of endurance. Our throats ached for water, and the inside of our mouths filled with dirt and grit, despite the cloth covering our faces. Even had we been able to open our eyes, we would have been able to see nothing. We were entombed in a howling, shifting mass of darkness.

If we could but retreat a few yards yet keep the shield-wall intact, we could free ourselves of the weight of sand which by now was threatening to pour over the top. Yet it was impossible to give the command, for no one would be able to hear me. Even if they could, in our weakened condition it was totally unlikely we'd be able to pull the maneuver off.

In any event, it mattered not. The end was inevitable. A single soldier faltered, one whose shield was forming the top tier, and thus was least able to bring his full body weight to bear against the force of the storm. His shield wavered, then collapsed away. This was all it took, a single breach. In an instant the entire wall broke down. The sand that had built up behind the barricade poured in over all. Discipline vanished. Instinctively, I pulled my shield over my head as waves of sand engulfed me.

# 10

## DAY THREE

## —

## EVENING

I have never known such utter terror, before or since. I knew I was dying. I felt the enormous weight of sand pressing down upon me, and with my body and strength already weakened by the enormous exertion of maintaining my place in the shield-wall, lethargy overwhelmed me. I am not a young man; my muscles and sinews, long unaccustomed to strenuous physical activity, were totally spent. The collapsing sand buried me nearly to my nostrils, and it was incredibly tempting simply to admit defeat, to cease to struggle, to let whatever was going to happen, happen.

The life-force is truly amazing. I was too tired to live, too stubborn to die. Too curious, too. Despite my exhaustion, I simply wasn't ready to die without the answers to the questions I'd been wrestling with. Even more important, I wasn't going to accept entombment in this desert sand, not when my House of Eternity was nearly ready for me but would remain empty should I be buried here. I'd lived too long to accept this anonymous death, to abandon the joys of the abundant afterlife which would be mine only if I rested in the abundantly stocked place prepared for me. I wasn't giving all that up this easily, not if I could help it.

I genuinely needed to know who this enemy was who had the power to conjure up the khamsin. I simply wouldn't die before knowing. I summoned the will, for that is what it was—will, for truly I lacked the strength, to force myself up and out of the mountain of sand that was burying me. The howling wind never ceased its shriek, and every fragment of my flesh exposed to the biting sand-tempest was quite literally being scoured from my body. I could no longer breathe. My nostrils were filled, clogged, and breathing through the mouth was an agony. There was no possible way to open the eyes without having them sand-polished blind in an instant.

Every instinct told me to place my back to the wind. But in that there could only be death. Somehow I knew I had to force myself forward, into the wind. To stand was impossible. I somehow found the strength to claw myself free from the mass of sand covering me, and I rolled, eyes tightly closed, forward, into the wind. It was my only chance. Somewhere, but a few yards in front of me, was the overturned chariot, with the tethered horses. If I could reach them, perhaps, with luck, or the efficacy of my amulet, I would find a shelter, a tiny pocket of concealment.

A few yards may not sound like much, but try it in the teeth of a howling sandstorm when your body is already in a state of total exhaustion, your mind paralyzed, your throat coated and parched, your will to live nothing but a last defiant flicker. Try it when your muscles are paralyzed and you can't even draw a deep breath lest your throat choke with sand. I do not recommend it.

How long it took, I do not know. It seemed an eternity. Probably it was ten minutes, perhaps a bit more. Each turn of my body was an agony of effort. To this date I don't know where I found the strength, or the will. At last, almost despairing of success, I felt myself bump into something solid. It was a horse, down on its side. Dead. Three-quarters buried in sand. I reached out my hand and felt its contour. Near as I could tell, I was somewhere near the animal's front legs. Using my fingers as a guide, I forced myself forward a little more, pressing firmly against the beast's inert body. I reached the neck, and with strength I didn't have forced it upward and stuck my nose underneath. It was shelter. Temporary, insecure, but shelter. I kept my nose pressed against the animal's underneck, pressed into the tiny protected airpocket. My nostrils filled with the odor of stale horse sweat. I won't say it smelled like nectar. It stank. But it was air, uncontaminated with sand. I gulped in all my lungs could hold, and grateful enough for it.

And then it happened. Again, I can't say how long, but it couldn't have been but five or ten minutes later. It stopped. The storm stopped. As suddenly as it had materialized, it was over. The quiet was eerie. At first I thought I'd gone quite deaf. It took me a while before I realized that indeed the khamsin had died.

Cautiously, I lifted my head from under the horse's neck, and even more cautiously opened my eyes. I could recognize nothing. My eyes smarted from the grains of sand that immediately ground themselves under my eyelids. Squinting, I looked out on the desert. All I could see was rolling, shifting dunes. The road was obliterated. All landmarks were gone. The overturned chariot was completely buried under sand, and the horses were dead. Most of them. A few made piteous noises and were struggling to their feet. Not many.

My command was wiped out too. Or so I at first thought. Then, little by little, one by one, I saw apparitions struggle up out of the sand, gasping, choking, reaching for the water bottles at their sides, greedily draining the contents at a single gulp. I pulled the scrap of tunic away from my nose and mouth and instantly followed their example.

Of my original platoon, barely half were left alive. The rest were somewhere under that sea of sand. For the first time I felt anger against my enemy, visceral, implacable anger. When I found him, whoever he was, I would kill him. Up until now I'd been strangely

dispassionate, even after Oudah's attempt on my life. I'd had a lifetime of palace intrigue, and understood how the game was played.
I'd played it often enough myself, and won. But this was different. These were my men lost somewhere under the desert. They
didn't deserve to be dragged into what was a private war between
me and my unknown enemy. If my foe had the power to raise a
khamsin, he doubtless had the capability of striking at me personally in some magical way without killing close to twenty fine
young men needlessly. Whoever had caused this storm to be raised
against me was going to pay, and pay in full measure.

I was immensely relieved to see that Houy was among the survivors. I would be needing him this night. The sun was almost set,
and I again remembered that time was still my most pressing problem. We must be some twenty-odd miles from my palace, and it
was absolutely essential that I get back this very night. I would be
able to do nothing until morning, true, but I'd need every minute
of the next day, and if at all possible, I'd need a few hours' rest before tackling it. The road was gone. Soon the stars would be out.
If I traveled east, I'd inevitably reach the Nile somewhere, and once
there I'd find settlements, and directions home.

I now had to give one of the hardest orders I can remember. Perhaps it wasn't all that big a thing, but nonetheless it bothered me
immensely. I have always made it a point of honor, when in the
field, to endure all hardships with my men and to make no exceptions for myself. I eat what they eat, sleep as they sleep, go as
they go. Under these circumstances, however, this was a luxury I
simply couldn't afford. For the first time in my military career I
was compelled to give an order for no reason other than my own
personal advantage.

With extreme regret I summoned Houy to me. "Houy," I stated
flatly, "I must return to Thebes as swiftly as possible. There are only
six horses left alive, and I'll need every one of them. Pick five men
to accompany me, and you follow on foot. Be sure to mark your
path very clearly, for tomorrow, after you've rested, you must
come back with pack mules and retrieve the bodies of our dead. I
want every single one of them recovered. Every one, mind you. I
intend to give each a burial fit for a noble."

Houy looked at me with a questioning expression on his sand-plastered face. He raised an eyebrow, or at least I sensed that's what he raised, since his face was so encrusted I could see nothing but eyes and mouth. He looked upon me as though I'd somehow lost my senses. Perhaps he felt that the ordeal had somehow unhinged my mind. "That's most generous of you, General," he drawled slowly and carefully, in a tone of voice one usually reserves for a child or an idiot, "but, sir, do you really think it's wise? It will set a very lavish precedent. We've lost men in battle before many times, and for certain will lose others in the future. Their burials have always been simple, as befits simple soldiers that have merely done their duty. To do more for these men might cause awkward expectations in the future. With all due respect, General, I think perhaps you should give this a little more consideration once you've had time to rest and recover."

Houy had a point, an excellent one, but I was in no mood to be crossed. "This is different," I snapped. "These men didn't die in battle, Houy. I understand what you're saying, and I appreciate it. But these men died because of me personally. They died under a spell, under the curse of a god, and but for their misfortune at being chosen to be with me this day, they'd all still be alive. They didn't die for Egypt. They didn't die *for* me, either. Only because of me."

Houy wouldn't leave the matter alone. We'd soldiered together a long time, and Houy had long ago reached the point where he felt he could talk to me bluntly, rank or no rank. No doubt he felt I still hadn't recovered from the sensation of being nearly buried alive. "There was no curse, General," he said stubbornly. "No spell. Just a khamsin. Just bad luck. I'm positive others are dead under the sand too. We're not the only ones."

I sighed wearily. I was neither of a mind to argue nor to reprimand. "Do as I say, Houy," I sighed. I'm in no mood to argue with you. Just do as I say."

The return back to Thebes was terrible. For one thing, I was discouraged and exhausted, and guilty over the fate of the men who had died in what, after all, was my own private battle. And I'd had to humiliate myself in front of Horemheb to glean even the one tiny and probably useless scrap of information he'd thrown me.

On top of that, my entire body was raw. And to make things even worse, with the chariot totally buried in the sand and with no spare animals to pull it, I'd have to make the journey back to Thebes on horseback. I really didn't know if I could endure the pain from my hemorrhoids, but I had no choice. Endure I must. If I'd had the time I'd have stayed where we were and sent a rider back to Thebes to fetch new mounts and a replacement chariot, but I clearly didn't have the time. The only good thing about the entire situation was that it was night, and other than for thought, the night hours were of no value to me in solving my problem. With luck, I should be able to get back to my palace around midnight, assuming we made no stops and that the horses survived. That was an iffy proposition in itself. The beasts were in as bad a shape as we were. Maybe worse. I could only hope they had another six hours left in them.

I was abominably filthy. I'd of course been unable to bathe in Horemheb's camp, and even if I had, it wouldn't have made any difference. Not after the khamsin. My robes were laden with sweat and underneath the encrusted layer of grime and sand the smell of my own body was easily perceptible in my nostrils. I don't know which smelled worse, the horse I'd been pressed up against, or I. I'm personally most fastidious, and as we made our slow way toward Thebes, the vision of my evening bath became obsessive. It drove all other thoughts from my mind. And with the thought of my bath, thoughts of Yennah came floating into my head. Yennah. Yennah of the corn-gold hair, of the lissome limbs, of the as-yet-unseen body.

You may be surprised that I would be having thoughts like these, considering what I'd gone through and the condition I was in. Don't be. First of all, you haven't seen Yennah. Second, men have a habit of using thoughts such as these to divert themselves from matters that for the moment they simply prefer not to cope with. Obviously, what I felt wasn't lust. Not with my body hurting and stinking the way it was. No, what I was doing was simply playing a mind game, but if it served to make the miles pass more swiftly, where was the harm? [*Translator's note: Thirty-four hundred years later this would be called a "defense mechanism." Eye clearly didn't need Freud to figure that out for him.*]

After an eternity and a half we finally reached my palace, luckily striking the Nile less than half a mile from the departure point of our original route. A bright moon had lit our path for the last eight or ten miles, making our journey home immensely easier. I dismissed my exhausted guard and they promptly and gratefully clattered away. In their haste, they failed to make the usual farewell salute. It had been a hard day for them too, and I didn't bother with a reprimand.

I dragged myself into my quarters. I'd nibbled little on the road—in truth, there had been little enough to nibble on, just a few scraps I'd carried with me. I wasn't hungry anyway. I just wanted to get clean. I was pleased to find the night doorman on duty and alert. He looked at me in considerable surprise. Never before had he seen me in such disreputable state. But he was wise. I'm sure he could tell from the look in my eye that I was in no mood for any questions or comments, and he was absolutely right. For my part, I didn't even know the man's name. I have a very large retinue attending to the wants of my palace, and I almost never had occasion to enter the palace when the late-shift night doorman was on duty.

I summoned my bath staff and bade them attend to me at once. They were sleepy-eyed and annoyed, but too bad. They had a good deal in my palace. Far better than most, and if they didn't know that, they should. For what it costs me to maintain them, a little inconvenience now and then is something they'll just have to put up with. I resolved to stop being so lenient. They were beginning to forget their station. A popular master usually has a sloppy operation.

I made it a particular point to summon Yennah. I was more bone-weary than I could ever remember, and never more in need of a bath. If I was going to bathe at this hour of the night, there wasn't a reason in the world I shouldn't do it with Yennah.

Yennah looked especially fetching. I couldn't take my eyes off her. However, I had one of the manservants remove my robes and undergarments—I didn't want Yennah close to me just yet, not the way I smelled, and I had him carry the filthy clothing at once to the laundry.

The hot water felt delicious and I reveled in its soothing warmth. It cascaded over my naked body. I nearly purred with the feel of it. Even better were the soothing oils and ointments applied to my scoured flesh and buttocks. I took my time, and when the normal routine was finished, had them do it over again. My skin in the places exposed to the wind was red and raw, but the mild balms and lotions had an amazing healing effect and the luxurious, perfumed hot water had amazing restorative powers.

I was starting to feel closer to my normal self. I was in a strange mood anyway. It had been a truly awful day, and tired as I was, I felt the need for distraction. For my age I do have a robust constitution, and even though I rarely get the sort of exercise I'd had this day I still normally don't require a great deal of sleep. I dismissed the staff, but commanded Yennah to stay. There was no frightened-fawn look in her eye. I rather liked it.

"My dear," I said to her unctuously, trying to put her at her ease, and for the moment setting all other concerns aside, "you truly are a lovely creature. Just how old are you? Fifteen? Fourteen?" I tried to keep my eye from wandering over her form, still concealed under a single loose, flowing gown, but Yennah was so comely that it was a near impossibility. I could see from the wary look in her eye that I wasn't fooling her for an instant. She knew where things were headed. She could see I was aroused.

"I'll be fifteen in two months," she said quietly, turning her head somewhat away from me. Her voice was surprisingly husky and sultry for one so young, and though she was clearly alert to my intentions, she had a certain air of confidence about her that I found positively delightful.

"Fourteen! What an enchanting age! We really must be getting to know each other better, you and I." Forgive the redundancy— I wasn't paying too much attention to grammar.

I looked firmly and meaningfully into those exotic blue eyes of hers. I put both hands on her shoulders, and wordlessly pushed down the straps of her gown until it fell to her hips. Usually I'm not this direct, but this night, for some reason or other, I wanted to come right to the point. My hands reached out and grasped her lovely breasts, and I gasped at the sight of them. Her skin was so white, her nipples so pale-rose, that there seemed but the merest delicate change in shading.

She looked back at me, jaw set, without fear, and slapped me hard across the face. My head jerked violently to the side.

"Just what do you think you're doing?" she demanded.

"Squeezing your tits," I answered lamely, my head ringing from the force of the blow.

"I know that," she replied in exasperation. Her lips were grim and taut. "It was a rhetorical question."

This was a totally unexpected and unprecedented turn of events. I tried to gather my wits. The girl was making me feel an utter fool.

"I—know—what—you—want," she proceeded, each word clipped and spaced, her nostrils flared. "Well, you're not going to get it. You don't own me."

What an astonishing thing for her to say. "As a matter of fact," I stammered rather ridiculously, "I do."

You won't believe what I did next. I actually went to my bureau and began searching through scraps of papyrus, hunting for the bill of sale. As you can tell, the wench had completely thrown me off my stride. Or maybe I simply hadn't totally recovered from my ordeal in the desert.

I found it and showed it to her. She crumpled it up and threw it on the floor. "That doesn't mean anything. You don't own *me*. I'm a princess of Corinth. No man owns me!" I never did understand feminine logic.

"A princess? Really? From Corinth?" What an astonishing revelation! "I had no idea!" At this point I suppose I was babbling.

"Yes. And my name's not Yennah, either. That's the closest those fool servants of yours could come to it. No matter. They can call me anything they like. But my father is Jason, King of Corinth."

I pondered this surprising bit of news. Was she telling me the truth? Even grand viziers don't usually get princesses for slave girls.

"If he's King of Corinth, why didn't he ransom you?" I asked suspiciously. "Pirates are in the ransom business. Surely they must have sent your father an offer."

"Kings of Corinth *never* pay ransom," she flashed proudly. "Not even for their own flesh and blood. But I don't envy the pirate fleet that took my ship, after my father hunts them down." She had a look about her, a manner of carrying herself, that made me believe she truly was a princess. It was a certain hauteur, something one has to be born with. I'd never bothered to study her that much before, but now I could see it.

I felt I was losing command of the situation. This little slip of a girl was absolutely defying me. It was intolerable. I grabbed both her wrists. "You may be a princess in Greece," I snarled, "but here you belong to *me!*"

I tried to drag her to my bed. With surprising ease she put one leg behind mine and flipped me to the ground. I couldn't have been more shocked if a piece of the moon had fallen from the sky and hit me on my head. She was strong for her age. I tried to console myself with the thought that if I weren't so weakened from my exertions in the storm she never could have succeeded in tossing me aside, but in truth I'm not so sure.

She stood over me, triumphant, a tight smile on those luscious lips. I pulled myself up, with a certain difficulty, and came at her again. She held up her hands defensively. "What are you going to do, old man?" she sneered. "Rape me? Just try it. It takes more than you to do it. Go ahead, call in your servants. Then maybe you can. That'll make great gossip, won't it? The mighty vizier can't rape one fourteen-year-old girl without calling on his servants for help!"

I was totally dumbfounded. What should I do next?

"You're nothing but a fat, dirty old man!" she screamed harshly.

"I am not fat!" I protested. "Maybe a little paunchy, but not fat!"

"And," she went on contemptuously, gazing downward, "stop pointing that thing at me. It's not the least bit sexy. You look absurd. If you need it so bad, why don't you send for your wife Tey?"

I felt myself shriveling up. I grabbed a towel and wrapped it around my waist to conceal my embarrassment. Obviously, when

I bought this girl I got more than I had bargained for. In more than one sense of the word. A princess! Imagine that.

One thing was certain. The girl had certainly gotten me out of the mood. "Oh well," I sighed, trying to console myself. I really had only been doing this for the sport of it, not out of any really urgent desire. There would be other evenings. I again went over to my bureau and pulled out a game board.

"Do you play draughts?" I asked.

"A little."

I set up the pieces on the alternating black and white squares. I pointed to a chair and motioned her to sit. "Your move."

# 11

# DAY

# FOUR

# —

# MORNING

It had been a most peculiar evening. I had beaten her five games out of five. Tired and distracted as I was, five games out of five. She really wasn't a very good draughts player. Or maybe she was, and had simply let me win. Yennah obviously was no fool, and young as she was, perhaps she nonetheless knew it would be unwise to humiliate me further.

In the morning I awoke totally befuddled. Actually, once I went to bed I'd slept remarkably well, deep, dreamless, untroubled sleep. Maybe it was simply overdue, since I'd slept so badly the two nights before. Maybe it was fatigue from the unusual exertions of the day. Whatever it was, I felt surprisingly refreshed, although my body ached all over from the battering it had endured in the desert.

I awoke totally unable to make sense of my own actions. The episode with Yennah truly baffled me. It just wasn't the ease with which she had rebuffed me, although it did strike at my male pride. It was the why of it. Why had I bothered with her, when I truly wasn't in the mood? It was bad enough to be made a fool of, but even worse when your heart hadn't been in the enterprise in the first place.

And what was I to make of my experience in the desert? Only Horemheb knew I was in his camp. So only Horemheb could have raised the khamsin against me. For a moment I felt I had my answer. If Horemheb had raised the storm, then Horemheb was the guilty party. Yet of all my possible adversaries, Horemheb was least likely to have the magical power to raise such a spell. And as I thought of it, I realized that indeed others knew, or might have known, of my destination. I'd made no effort to advertise it, but also none to conceal it. Of necessity I'd had to let certain of my subordinates know where I was going so I could be reached in the event of emergency. I'd seen no reason to enjoin them to secrecy. So maybe others knew after all.

Or maybe Houy was right. Maybe the khamsin had simply been bad luck. After all, the storm indeed had died at sundown, as khamsins usually do. Perhaps it all was just bad luck, or coincidence. If so, the timing was certainly most suspect.

I rose from my bed and yawned. I slept alone. Although Tey was my principal wife and the palace filled with my concubines, I preferred it this way. What man would sleep in the same bedroom with a woman if he was rich enough to afford not to?

Once more it was time for my morning bath. Once more I looked forward to it. Bath-time of late was turning into the most interesting time of day.

Again Yennah was there, and performed her duties admirably. I looked at her closely, trying to sense if there was an expression of triumph on her face, of glee at my discomfiture. There was not. She was completely professional.

I tried to turn my mind once more to the single most pressing problem I had to deal with. Having Yennah in the room was difficult. She was a distraction. The ease with which she had rebuffed me was a distinct embarrassment, and her presence intruded on my concentration. She was becoming a nagging problem for me, secondary to the more important one of keeping myself alive, but nonetheless intruding. I definitely would have to do something if for no other reason than to recover some of my pride, but I couldn't afford to waste too much time contemplating it.

Sometimes, when faced with an overwhelming, compelling problem, the solution will come to you in a dream. So far, I hadn't been that lucky. I had the feeling, though, that vague bits and pieces were assembling somewhere out there, if only I could put them together. I had an impression that I was learning more than I knew, that each day was bringing me knowledge if I had but the wit and skill to assimilate it.

Horemheb had reminded me of those poisonous desert insects that had decimated our army when we'd served together all those years ago. Was there something significant in that? Had Horemheb caught some of the little things in a jar and used them to poison Akhenaten? Not very likely. What about desert scorpions? Not likely either. I was really grasping at almost anything now. Getting a trifle desperate. Still, I had to keep an open mind to every possibility. The one certain fact I had was that someone had tried to kill me. Once for certain, and depending on how one viewed the khamsin, perhaps twice. I was on the trail of someone. If only I could use torture, I'd have the answer! But that was exactly what Tut wanted me to do, to panic and defy his very specific orders. Whether I found the right man or not would be beside the point. When a pharaoh gives orders in open audience, even a grand vizier, even a regent defies them at peril of his very life. And this not even mentioning that those who might be implicated were for the most part torture-proof by virtue of their exalted positions. Torture solved nothing. But old habits are hard to break.

My mind kept returning to Horemheb, possibly because of the unsatisfactory interview with him in the desert. Horemheb had indeed gained great power upon Akhenaten's death. More so than anyone else. Except for me, of course. I had to admit that, objectively speaking, my own name should be the one at the very top of the list. I'd tried to schedule another audience with Tut, a private one, to do anything I could to prove to him that I had nothing to do with his father's death. What I could have said that would be absolutely convincing, I truly didn't know. Still, I felt that this was the crux of it all, that Tut believed I was his man, and this was his devious way of making me suffer, like a worm wriggling in a frying pan. Perhaps telling him that Oudah's death proved I couldn't have been the murderer might have some weight with him. Probably not. He'd think I'd simply poisoned her myself. The feeling of time slipping away like water dripping from a water clock grew increasingly oppressive.

I was in this somber mood when Yennah approached me and whispered in my ear, "Dismiss the servants."

I looked at her in astonishment. Who was she to give me orders? Particularly after last night? And in that peremptory tone of voice. I was starting to feel certain she indeed was a princess. No slave girl would speak to her master that way. She repeated her admonition. "Dismiss the servants. Get rid of them."

She had an eager look in her eye. What an odd girl! After last night's little episode I would have thought that being alone with me would be the very last thing she'd want. I looked her over carefully to make certain she carried no concealed weapon in her tunic. It was quite obvious she didn't. Intrigued, I did as she suggested.

The servants left the room, with knowing smirks on their faces. Once more we were alone. I decided I could spare a few minutes to find out what this was all about. "I really don't have time for draughts this morning, Yennah," I said. "Besides, you're not that strong a player. I honestly prefer more of a challenge."

"You know it isn't draughts I have in mind," she replied, and this time the look on her face was different from that of the Yennah I'd had to deal with the evening before. She was being openly inviting, seductive. Nothing subtle. Every woman born knows how to do it. In a way it's insulting. Women think men are such pigs that all they have to do is crook their little fingers and men will come panting after them. The galling part is that they're right.

I said nothing and waited for her to go on.

She didn't beat about the bush. "Do you want to fuck me?" she

110

stated flatly, and her hand reached for me. I let it. But I was put off by what she said.

"I don't like young girls to talk foul-mouth."

She shook her head in exasperation, and her golden-yellow curls undulated in a most delectable manner. "All right," she said. "Do you want to be intimate with me, in a manner akin to marital relations?"

"That's better."

"Well, do you?"

I moved eagerly toward her, but she held out her hands and held me back. "There's a condition."

Of course. That's the way it always is with women. The price. One way or another, there's always a price. I raised an eyebrow and waited.

"Guess."

"I don't have time for games."

"Guess anyway."

"Yennah, get on with it. What's happened between last night and this morning to make you so . . . accommodating?"

"Nothing, actually, except that after last night I gave the situation a little more thought. For a princess of Corinth, being a scullery maid is quite a comedown. The more I've pondered it, the more I realized that maybe this was an opportunity for me after all."

"I'm beginning to see. You'll be nice to me and I'll be nice to you. What do you want? To be an official concubine? Consider it done." I reached for her again, because in spite of my residual annoyance with her, my desire was getting urgent and the light strokings of her fingertips weren't alleviating the situation any. I didn't know what her game was yet, but, being male, I was already half of a mind to let her win at it. Provided she won quickly.

Yennah snorted at my suggestion. "Concubine? I'm a princess of Corinth, remember. That's not at all what I had in mind."

"Aha," I said. "I'm beginning to see. You want to be a wife."

"Not *a* wife. Principal wife."

Principal wife! I was utterly dumbfounded. Fourteen years old! Amazing! I was struck nearly speechless by her audacity. "Sorry,

Yennah," I replied stiffly, pushing her away and reaching for a towel, "but I already have a principal wife. I've had one for forty years."

"So what? What good is she to you?"

"What do you mean by that?"

"When was the last time you fucked her?"

"Yennah!"

"Oh, all right. You know what I mean. When was the last time . . ."

I raised my hands. "Yes, I know what you mean."

"Well?"

"Well what?"

She put her hands to her shoulder and pushed down the straps of her gown. With a little urging it fell to her feet and she stepped daintily out of it. At last her naked body was directly in front of me. She braced her arms behind her back. The sight was truly awe-inspiring. "What would you rather have in bed with you? This, or Tey?"

Yennah was one hell of a saleslady.

It was, as you can imagine, getting increasingly difficult to deal with the situation. We have an ancient saying in Egypt, "A prick has no brains," and it was getting extremely difficult to keep mine from doing my thinking for me.

"What you have in mind is impossible, Yennah." I was still thunderstruck by her outlandish proposal, and considerably affronted by the cool, assured way in which she presented it to me. "You're not Egyptian, or you'd know what you're talking about is completely absurd. Even if I wanted to—and I don't—there's no way in the world it can be done."

She took my hands and placed them on her breasts, and other places too. "You're the grand vizier," she breathed. "You can find a way."

How do women do it? How do they know? I'd had who knows how many hundreds of women in my time, but by withholding herself, this one was driving me insane. What she wanted was out of the question. Still, promise them anything . . .

I tried to think, though under the circumstances, coherent, logical thought wasn't easy. "Why is it so important that you be *principal* wife? Wouldn't wife do? After all, Yennah, I'm old enough to be your father. Old enough to be your grandfather, actually. What difference does it make whether you're principal wife or not? It's really all the same, one way or another. I promise I'll treat you well—you'd be treated like a principal wife in everything but name." Despite myself, she was getting me so excited I was ready to say anything. Luckily, there were no witnesses, so I could always say she misunderstood.

"Principal wife or nothing."

"Why?"

"Because I want to be queen of Egypt."

The utter brazenness of that statement took my breath away. "You're out of your mind!"

Her eyes narrowed dangerously.

"I say that in the most loving way," I added hastily. The girl truly had me totally off balance. "But, Yennah, you know I'm not pharaoh and I'm not going to be."

"You can be if you want."

"How so?"

"Kill Tut."

I couldn't believe what I was hearing. This naked goddess was actually standing there in front of me, urging me to murder the king of Egypt, as calmly as though she were asking for a drink of water. I'd like to say that her utter, barefaced boldness—wickedness, actually—suddenly cooled my ardor, but in truth it did not. I really wanted this woman. Despite the perverseness of the situation, I really wanted her.

I was absolutely speechless, so she went on. "Of course," she continued coolly. "Kill him. It's what you have to do, you know. If you don't know it, everyone else in Thebes does. Even I know it, and what am I? A new slave girl that's barely been in your palace a week. He's out to kill you. I can't imagine why he's playing his little game with you, but you're lucky. He could have just done it. This way, he's giving you time. Use it. If you want me, use it."

"Don't overestimate yourself," I said, regaining a certain amount of composure, but still astonished at having this kind of conversation with a fourteen-year-old slave. "There are thousands of women in Egypt. I can have any of them I want. And I don't need your advice about Tut. I can handle that myself, thank you. You've gone too far with me. Way too far. I'll have you whipped raw for this. I'll do it myself."

She ignored the threat. In fact, she gave me a look that indicated that, young as she was, she knew about the possibilities inherent in whippings. "Maybe there are thousands of women in Egypt," she persisted. "But look at them. How many of them look like this?" And she ran her hand lightly up her body, through her hair. She had a point.

I took my own hand and ran it through those thick, wonderful, cascading tresses. Without genuinely willing it, I heard myself murmuring, "Your hair. It's like"—I found myself groping for words—"it's like melted ingots of gold pouring from the crucible. Like that special sand from the shore of the Great Green tumbling down through opened fingers. It's like moonlight shimmering on the wine-dark sea."

"It's blond," she said flatly.

"Blond?" I inquired, puzzled.

"Blond!" she exclaimed triumphantly, fingering her thick, golden curls. "You don't even know the word! Look at all your wives. Look at all your concubines! They're ugly! Dark skins. Dark eyes. Dark hair. That's all you have here in Egypt."

"They're not ugly at all," I replied defensively. "They're quite attractive, actually."

"If you say so. But none of them are blondes."

She had me there.

"So you want to be queen of Egypt," I mused. "Astonishing. Positively astonishing. And considering your age, commendably audacious on your part."

"So?" she purred, and rubbed that fabulous body against mine. "What do you think?" She really wasn't playing fair.

"Let me think about it," I said, playing for time. I put my arms around her and pulled her to me. She felt fantastic.

She lightly slipped out of my reach. I was, after all, still quite wet and slippery, so wriggling away was easy. I wanted her so bad I thought I'd explode.

"All right," she said. "Think about it." Her fingers once more played with me.

"That's just a sample," she cooed. "That's just a sample." She kissed me lightly on the cheek. "Think about it, Eye. Think about it. I know you will."

In my confusion of mind I completely overlooked the impertinence of her calling me by my name. One thing I could say for certain. My days were more interesting of late. In truth I had no time for the astonishing brazenness of this amazing slave girl Yennah. Not with my life on the line and the days growing short. All that is true, but it's also true that you haven't seen Yennah. As she said, she's blond. I should be concentrating on the more pressing matters, but already the thoughts she put into my mind were crowding out my other concerns. Life is full of complications.

# 12

## DAY

## FOUR

## —

## LATE MORNING

I would have bet my very considerable fortune that nothing like Yennah could ever happen to me. It certainly couldn't have happened at a worse time. I did, after all, have a quite literal, quite personal life-or-death matter to deal with.

To state it baldly, I'd conceived a totally irrational lust for Yennah. In a mere day's time. And at my age. It was ludicrous, but there it was. I was obsessed with the woman—woman-child, to be more accurate. I absolutely couldn't get her out of my mind, and I desperately wanted to. This was no time to have sexual passion interfering with my search for the slayer of Akhenaten. Time was growing scarcer and scarcer, and every minute spent pondering how to possess Yennah's delectable body, and what terms I could negotiate to acquire it, could very well be the minute that, were my mind not so concupiscently engaged, might be needed to solve Tut's riddle and thereby keep my head attached precisely where I longed for it to remain. But that's how an obsessed mind works, and there wasn't a thing I could do about it.

Now, as I hold my brush in hand and paint these hieroglyphics on this scroll, I full well understand how, at your remove, you might find this predicament intensely unlikely for a man of fifty-seven years. You'd be absolutely right. So would I feel, if it involved anyone else but me.

Not only was I a man of, let us say, mature years, but also it wasn't as though I'd never had a woman before. I've lost count. In fact, the truth is that by now, for me, sex was more a matter of power than passion. It wasn't that the fires of passion were extinguished, just they no longer burned as fiercely as once they had. The pleasure was far more in the conquest than in the act itself.

Perhaps "conquest" is the wrong word. With female slaves, I suppose my first choice of words was better—power. Then this Greek girl comes along. She defies me, and I for the life of me can't figure out what to do about it. She manipulates me with a skill and deftness that would make Nefertiti ache with envy.

As I thought about it, I realized that Nefertiti was an apt comparison. Yennah was a blond Nefertiti. I'm certain her blondness was a part of my obsession—blondes, particularly gorgeous ones, are a rarity in Egypt. Blond princesses are quite unheard of. Still, I had no illusions about Yennah. I saw her precisely for what she was. She was ruthless, ambitious, aggressive, tough, determined. She should have been a man, but considering how beautiful she is, that would have been a pity. And in my entire life, though my acquaintance of her was but a day old, not counting some incidental sight of her when she first was brought to my palace, I've never known anyone, male or female, to have such incredible chutzpah. [*Translator's note: Here it is again, another of those remarkable "Hebarewisms" in the text. This should not be considered all that remarkable, considering the events related in this scroll are very close in time to the Exodus.*]

Principal wife! Unbelievable. Here she is, a slave girl, totally subject to my command, and she manages to have me actually considering—fantasizing, actually, about acceding to her request. I've long since forgotten the names of the numberless slave girls like Oudah who have passed through my bath or my bed, and this one has me panting like a sixteen-year-old. Her game is breathtakingly clear. It's the selfsame one I used on Akhenaten when I saw how obsessed he was with my Nefertiti. I insisted Akhenaten take Nefertiti as principal wife, and Yennah thinks she can play the same game with me. I tell myself there's no way that will happen, but there's a part of me that thinks perhaps otherwise. Yennah sees herself as more than queen of Egypt. She sees herself as pharaoh. She sees herself ruling Egypt by ruling me. That, I absolutely assure you, will never happen. Even for Yennah, it's an unattainable ambition. Regardless of this unexpected, irrational, blind obsession, should Eye ever be pharaoh, no woman, not even Yennah— perhaps *certainly* not Yennah, would ever wield true power in my stead. That I guarantee. I am a normal, mortal man, and whereas I concede that a woman may, on rare occasion, blind me with her charms, no woman, never, will dictate my actions. My flesh may be malleable, but my decisions, never.

Still and all, I had to give her credit. That one in her position could reach so high and actually have a grand vizier of Egypt toying with certain thoughts is an astounding feat. Particularly when you consider she's gotten this far in just one single day. Tell me I should dismiss this whole thing out of hand. Tell me it's insanity. I agree. But those of you who've been there yourself will understand.

It took every ounce of willpower I possessed to drive the image of her body from my mind, but I forced myself to do it, knowing full well that it was but temporary and that, unbidden, her tantalizing form could at any time once more rise like a vision before my eyes. With regret I admit I am a man much bedeviled by women. I always have been. In past years, many times I felt a woman would be the death of me. Right now, that may well prove to be the literal truth.

With my mind still occupied, however reluctantly, with this

subject, another, darker thought suddenly intruded. Yennah had shown her hand last night with remarkable boldness. Given her now known temperament, and her familiarity with intrigue as a princess of Corinth, could she have poisoned Oudah in order to expedite her access to me? If that was true, was I back to where I started, with no evidence whatsoever that there was an actual murderer to discover?

As quickly as the thought surfaced, I banished it. Impossible. The poison had been meant for me, not Oudah. I'd switched the goblets. Besides, if Yennah had intended to kill Oudah, she could have accomplished it with much less risk to herself than having the murder take place in my presence.

I sighed, deeply, and sighed again. It only went to show how fevered and suspicious my mind had become, and in how many different directions it could fly. The strain was becoming more than I could bear. So many problems! So many troubles! Once more I reflected that Tey had been right. I should have resigned gracefully years ago, when I might have been able to do so in safety. I was the envy of every man in Egypt. I was grand vizier. I was powerful—depending on how you looked at it, arguably the most powerful man in the nation. To a large extent the power of the Egyptian crown was mine. Yet what joy was there in it? What pleasure? I could not help but reflect upon how uneasy lies the head that wears a crown. [*Translator's note: Do you think that each and every one of Shakespeare's lines was original? No doubt he ran across this one when he was doing research for* Antony and Cleopatra.]

It was thus wrapped in dark and conflicting thoughts that I made my way toward Karnak, this time garbed in my ceremonial robes as Grand Vizier of Egypt. My uniform as General of the Palace Guards wouldn't be appropriate, not at the Temple of Karnak. Besides, my things wouldn't be back from the laundry yet and were probably ruined beyond repair, considering what they'd been through in the desert.

And so I traveled, this time accompanied by but a half-squad of guards, and these dressed in field uniform, toward Aanen, High Priest of Amun. Again, in all likelihood a waste of time, but what more was there to do? I couldn't help but think that I'd made a terrible mistake yesterday. I should have stayed with Horemheb and done everything in my power to persuade him to join me in a plot to kill Tut. In this regard Yennah, too, quite remarkably, had been right, although I still couldn't believe she had the absolute, utter gall to make the suggestion. Kill Tut. There was at this point no doubt in my mind, none whatsoever, that she was precisely what she said she was, a Greek princess. Only one raised from childhood in a royal court could understand this type of situation so promptly and come up with the solution so matter-of-factly.

I'd wasted my day with Horemheb, and now it was too late. He was off deeper in the desert on maneuvers, and by the time I could find him, even if he could be persuaded, it would be too late to concoct a plan that would have a reasonable chance for success. I tried to console myself with the thought that it probably had already been too late yesterday, but in all honesty I'm not all that sure.

One thing I could do. I could keep my word about the burial of my poor lads who even now were doubtless being dug out of the sand by Houy. Before the day was done he'd have their bodies back. What Houy had said about setting a bad precedent was true, but it no longer mattered. Within a few days my whole personal situation would be irretrievably altered one way or another. I gave some thought to making my own House of Eternity available for the journey of my fallen soldiers. Considering the way my nephew was botching the inscriptions, having the carving rechiseled might be an excellent solution. On the other hand, I myself very well might be needing my House of Eternity in just a few more days, so, bad spelling and bad grammar and all, now wasn't a good time to start work on a new one.

I took a certain grim satisfaction in the solution that came to hand. Akhenaten had had an uncle who was, not to put too fine a point on it, an incompetent, overbearing, pompous, insufferable ass. I could obliterate his name from *his* House of Eternity and inscribe in its stead those of my boys. I'd have him removed and my boys entombed there in his place. It would serve him right. If ever a man didn't deserve a luxurious afterlife, it was that intolerable uncle of Akhenaten's. [*Translator's note: The practice of obliterating*

1
2
◊
·

names on tombs and using them for later occupants was not at all un-
common in ancient Egypt. There is little written record of the exact reasons
why this was done, but based on the archaeological findings it appears
evident that in many cases it was a form of revenge upon the dead. In others it may simply have been a matter of sheer convenience. We may disagree with the seemliness of such actions, but these were Eye's times and
not ours.]

After all my failures to make progress I had little hope for this
journey to Karnak. What was the likelihood I'd learn anything significant there? Little. Still, I had to do *something*, and this remained
all I could think of, this mindless interviewing of the people on
my list, in the hope that, in Horemheb's words, one of them had
"stupid" painted on his forehead. Oh, how I wished I had some
precedent to go by, that someone else had been given this type of
conundrum and had come up with a successful procedure. "No
torture! No torture! No torture!" Tut's words rang ceaselessly
through my head like the very voice of doom.

I dreaded this day. I'm a deeply religious man—I believe I've told
you that already—and Karnak filled me with awe and something
akin to terror. Now, I'm not a coward. Whatever else you may
think I am, I'm not a coward. I have scars on this somewhat over-
weight body of mine, scars from enemy warriors, to prove my
courage.

I absently fingered the scar tissue on the inside of my left arm,
the still-raised ridge running from just above my elbow to just
below my armpit. The old wound had healed imperfectly. I was
lucky it had healed at all, considering how deep the enemy soldier had driven his sword into me.

He was a Hittite, and a brave one. The day is now nearly thirty
years past, but I remember the man as if I'd just seen him a moment ago. He was huge. A giant. This isn't just battle-induced exaggeration. He was nearly a foot taller than I, and I am no small
man. He was younger, too—heavily muscled, well-armored, with
the fierce look of the warrior in his eye, the blood intoxication. But
my blood was running hot too that day.

He was a leader of some sort—whether of a platoon or of a regiment I have no idea, but he had a Hittite medallion of rank around

his neck and his sun-wrinkled face bore the print of a man others would follow to their deaths.

My chariot was in the van of the charge. I always led the charge. Personally. Clouds of dust boiled up from my chariot wheels, and I could hear the thundering hooves of my cavalry pounding fiercely, relentlessly behind me, to a man following wherever my chariot might lead. I was striking straight for the chariot of the enemy king, and his personal cavalry guards stormed out to meet us, fully prepared to die to save their monarch, as indeed was their duty. This was the Hittite elite corps I faced, their king's personal bodyguards, the picked men of their entire army.

The Hittite came at me shrieking that murderous, savage, ululating yell that makes blood curdle in the veins. I saw his face but for an instant, but the memory of it is burned into my mind and I will forever take it with me on my eternal journey, for a million years to come. I will forever remember every feature and detail of that enemy, down to the tufts of hair spraying out from his flared nostrils.

He slashed at me mercilessly with his saber, and I was certain my left arm was totally severed from my body. But at the same time my lance caught him full in the eye, and the terrific force of our steeds charging full-tilt in opposite directions sent the point of my lance clear through his skull, through the back armor of his bronze helmet, and out the other side. Before the battle was over I'd lost so much blood from my wound that I nearly perished, but oddly enough I felt no pain whatsoever until the enemy was driven from the field.

Yes, I've faced enemy soldiers, man-to-man, face-to-face, and left more than one dead from the blow of my sword or the point of my lance. But courage in battle is one thing. Courage before the mysteries of the gods is something else entirely. I believe with all my heart in the ancient gods of Egypt, and Karnak is the holy of holies, the home of the Hidden One, Amun, who reigns there and performs his miracles in his Divine House, his House of Life. I have seen his miracles with my own eyes, and no man who has seen them could ever doubt the holy power of Amun. I clutched at my amulet for protection. If it proved indeed that Aanen the high priest was the murderer, I knew that my little amulet would avail nothing against the spells that he could conjure. Still, Mother's amulet was all I had.

You of course know Karnak. How could you not? There is no Great House in all the world anywhere near its like. Its vastness is beyond belief, and any man entering its sacred courtyard is like a fly, a mosquito, a gnat. I tell you with great pride that as grand vizier I personally have been responsible for much of the elaborate work that has been lavished on this magnificent edifice, and that I personally inspected every stone, checked every hieroglyph, approved every statue, whether small or colossal, to make certain it was completely free of any flaw or imperfection. By now you know that I am but a man, flawed in many respects, perhaps more so than most, or perhaps I am simply more honest about myself than most, but when it came to Karnak and to the sacred residence of the Hidden One, I approached the task with reverence and purity. I cleansed my body seven times before entering the sacred precincts, and I cleansed my soul with prayer and fasting, so that all the great work that was done by my order and by my hand would be acceptable and pleasing to the Great Lord Amun. [*Translator's note: Eye speaks the plain truth. The expansion and adornment of the magnificent Temple of Karnak is largely his work.*]

I reached the outskirts of the temple precincts and paused at the Avenue of Sphinxes, removing my headdress and drawing my chariot to a full halt for a minute of respectful silence. The day was hot—what day isn't in the Valley of the Kings? Yet despite the fierce heat of the sun, I suddenly shivered and my skin felt cold and clammy. I felt—what? Something. A premonition, if you will. A sense that here, if anywhere in Egypt, the solution to my puzzle would be made known to me. This sense, this perception, this vague, unfocused feeling was surprising considering that at the start of the journey I'd had such an opposite feeling, such a certainty that this would all be a mere waste of precious time.

As you know, the Great Temple of Karnak is perhaps eight miles from the royal palace, taking into consideration all the twists and turns of the road. This day's journey, through the broad and pleasant streets of Thebes, was a delight, particularly compared to that terrible sojourn through the desert I was forced to endure yesterday. Also, this day there was no need for either my dignity or my body to suffer. I was able to stand in my chariot, and eight miles was not sufficiently arduous to cause any unacceptable discomfort to my feet. I was virtually alone, accompanied by but four of my cavalry guards. The terrors of Karnak were quite differnt from those of Horemheb, and four bodyguards at Karnak were quite sufficient. In point of fact, they were more ceremonial than functional, but four was the minimum number I felt I needed to sustain my dignity and stature.

As long as I'm being honest with you, I have to tell you that facing Horemheb yesterday was like petting a kitten compared to what I felt about facing Aanen today. The high priest terrifies me. Not physically, of course. I could break him like a dried papyrus reed. It's who he is, and what he can do, that scares me.

I don't like him as a man, but as the high priest of the Hidden One, I quail in his presence. If, indeed, he is the guilty one; if indeed he murdered Akhenaten, he did so by magic and incantations and there would have been nothing anyone could do to save the pharaoh. Still, I must learn all I can learn, and if Aanen is responsible for sending Akhenaten to his House of Truth [*Translator's note: to his tomb*], it will be up to Tut to decide what to do about it.

I urged my horses forward through the Great Gate, past the sacred lake, and forward down the hypostyle hall until I reached the entrance to the sacred sanctuary, beyond which the horses could not go. Everywhere I went I saw the work of my own hand. All was new, and I prayed Amun was as pleased with my handiwork as I was. With pride I read the perfect hieroglyphs, etched deeply into the stone and perfectly painted in the sacred blues, reds, and greens, attesting that it was Eye, grand vizier of Akhenaten and Tutankhamen, that had caused this magnificent temple to be expanded for the greater glory of the gods.

I felt this day a peculiar sense of timelessness, of unreality. I felt I was feather-light and floating. The great door to the sanctuary loomed before me. I needn't describe it to you. You've seen it, all gilded and carved and breathtakingly immense, with the winged god gazing serenely down upon his subjects, creating the most astonishing aura of peace and tranquillity. Sweet purification enfolds all who come to stand there, and without thinking it, without even sensing it, the Spirit of Eternity enwraps a man as though those all-encompassing wings have already lifted him from the woes of this world into the perfection of the next. My own workmen made that door.

It was here, I reflected, that Tut, a child of ten, became king. His coronation was held here, and I had arranged it all. It was here that he received his coronation name Nebkheprure, but to me he will always be Tut. I see him now, naked to the waist, his feet bare, clad in only a simple pleated loincloth. The interior of the temple was badly scarred then, and there had been no time to complete repairs despite the vast army of architects and craftsmen I had assigned to the task. It had been essential that the coronation take place swiftly. Essential for Horemheb and me, if we were to consolidate our power.

I had ordered every sign, every hieroglyph, every image of the hated Akhenaten excised, and the stonemasons had chiseled away from dawn until last light, and on the day of coronation it was as if the pharaoh Akhenaten had never troubled our world. The marks on the walls and pylons were raw and ugly, but all trace of Akhenaten, all his names, all his images, had vanished, never again to pollute and insult and offend the mighty Hidden One.

I still see in my mind, eight years later, the procession of the priests, accompanied by the highest dignitaries of the court, foremost among whom of course was Eye. And Horemheb. The temple priests, heads shaven and bowed, eyes averted lest they make contact with those of their pharaoh, led him to the center of a shallow pool into which Tut stepped for the rite of purification. Four priests stood at the four cardinal points, recalling the division of the world into four parts according to the ancient liturgy. Upon their faces were masks, different masks. There was Toth with his ibis beak, falcon-headed Horus, Seth with his curved muzzle and square ears, and the one other falcon-god Dunawy.

After many baptisms and lustrations, the priest Inmutef, wearing a wig of plaited hair drawn to one side and a heavy leopard skin that covered him from head to foot, placed upon Tut's head, one after another, the many crowns confirming him as Amun's chosen one. They placed upon his head the white miter and the red mortar-shaped cap; they placed upon his head the crown of the Two Powerful Ones, they placed upon his head the diadem of two tall plumes, they placed upon his head the *atef* crown of the great god Re.

The ceremony continued all day. It was exhausting, but each and every god had to be honored, and it was nearly sundown before at last Tut was granted the five names selected by the scribes of the House of Life, and Egypt had its new pharaoh, its new King of North and South.

This was no idle reverie on my part, no daydreaming. If I failed in my quest—and there were but three days left—two stark choices remained before me. I could announce my failure and await my fate, hoping that it might be no worse than banishment. Or I could kill pharaoh and with luck and skill and daring stand here once more with all those crowns being placed, one by one by one, on *my* head.

I stood there in my chariot, deep in thought. I bowed my head in silent prayer. With lips moving silently, I recited the timeless invocation to the great god Amun before moving forward, deeper into his holy sanctuary.

Totally without warning I felt an enormous blow to the chest, a blow that bent me backward and nearly flipped me over backward. In fact, it would have flipped me entirely out of the chariot had I not instinctively grabbed for the reins. My driver gave a shout of warning, much too late to do me any good. I felt all breath pass from my body, and it was several moments before I could draw another. I had been stricken by the fist of Amun.

"Master!" my driver shouted. "Are you all right? Are you hurt?" I could see genuine concern in his face, although whether that concern was for my safety or fear that I'd have him cudgeled for failing in his duty to protect me, I know not.

"I'm fine," I replied, though I wasn't all that sure. My voice was raspy. "What happened?"

"You were shot, master. An arrow. Look!" My driver left his post on the right side of the chariot and leaped nimbly to the ground, sweeping up in his grasp the broken shaft of a giant arrow. He passed it to me and I examined it carefully.

"Not the usual military-issue arrow, is it, Artouf?"

Artouf examined it carefully. "No, master. It definitely is not. I've never seen one like it."

Perhaps he hadn't, but I had. It was a ceremonial arrow, very long, very thick, and fletched at the end with falcon feathers. It was an arrow from the quiver of the palace guard. Not my cavalry guards. Horemheb's infantry guards. Were I not wearing my body armor concealed underneath my robes, it would have passed clear through me. Whoever fired that arrow at me had very powerful arms and a very accurate eye, for the bow must have been drawn back to the maximum. My chest still ached from the force of the blow.

My first thought, of course, was Horemheb. But immediately I recognized that even though one his guards had apparently loosed the arrow at me, it proved nothing. In fact, with Horemheb in the desert and me here, I couldn't imagine how he would know I'd be at Karnak this day. That was assuming, of course, that Horemheb was still in his camp and hadn't returned to Thebes unknown to me.

No, any of my potential adversaries—save perhaps Yuti, and even he was rich enough for bribery—could have recruited the assassin. What concerned me every bit as much was that this meant someone in my own palace, someone of my own staff, was betraying me. The information concerning my whereabouts this day could only have come from my own household. I would say that it was a sobering thought, save that my thoughts already were about as sober as they could get.

I held the broken arrow firmly in my hand, trying to glean more from the splintered shaft, and failing. I motioned Artouf to proceed forward. He paused, and I don't blame him. Were there more assassins waiting inside these sacred premises, concealed in the gloom, hidden behind pillars, arrows drawn, daggers ready? Well, if this was where death would find us, there could be no better place than in this greatest and holiest temple in all the world.

I took a deep breath and strode forward. As I was about to pass through the great door and enter the holy of holies, I sensed some-one behind me. I didn't hear anyone, I simply knew someone was there. I turned involuntarily, and there stood Aanen, fully garbed in his glorious robes of office. It gave me quite a start, I tell you. How had he done it? I hadn't heard a single footfall, a single swish of a single robe, yet there he was. Perhaps now you know why the man makes me uneasy.

As I had described before, Aanen was purse-lipped and sour, with such a grimness to his face that it made one certain it would take one of my stonemasons to carve a smile. He was exception-ally tall—taller than Horemheb, even—and exceptionally thin. He had all his hair, and of this I was extremely jealous, yet even the hair, tightly close-combed to his head and heavily pomaded, looked angular and severe. He wore no beard, and his eyes were dark and hooded, concealed even more by the deep blue—almost black—makeup with which they were encircled in an almond shape. If one wants a high priest who looks like the wrath of god, Aanen is your man. He certainly frightened *me*.

In his right hand he carried a jewel-encrusted miter of office, and his left was heavy laden with golden rings adorning each and every finger, and the thumb. The richness of his garments and the quality of his gems attested that being a favorite of Amun brought its rewards in this world as well as the next.

"Well, Eye," he said without preamble, "here to see me about that Akhenaten matter, I presume?" You would have thought his voice would be sepulchral. It was not. The voice was deep and melodic—how he produced it from such a slender frame I have no idea—and when on holy days he sang the sacred psalms you thought you were hearing the voice of the god himself.

"You're exceptionally well informed, Aanen. And it's good to see you, too."

He ignored my little dig. "You go nowhere these days without the news of it both preceding and following you. You're the best entertainment Thebes has had in years. People—people in the streets even—are making bets on the outcome."

"I'm sure the odds must be heavily in my favor."

"The odds, as we speak, are three to two that you won't be alive by this time next week."

Aanen didn't smile when he said this. Aanen never smiled. And he never jested. If he said the odds were three to two, they were three to two.

"I appreciate your telling me, Aanen. When I leave I think I'll lay down a bet myself."

"I'd suggest you bet everything you have. What have you got to lose?"

I thought about that. The man was right.

While I was thinking, Aanen kept talking. "It's a pity you didn't arrive yesterday. The pharaoh was here. I'm sure he would have liked a report from your own lips, bringing him up-to-date about your findings, as it were. He and Yuti and I came here right after that amusing audience he held with you—it's the Feast of Buto, you know. A minor festival, but the pharaoh never misses a one. Most commendable of him. He's one of my most steadfast parishioners."

"Did Yuti go back too?"

"No. He's still here. Today is the anniversary of his father's death. Yuti is a devoted son. He spends the day in prayer and sacrifice for his father's soul. It's a pity more men aren't as steadfast as Yuti. The custom isn't observed as scrupulously as it was in years past. Such a pity, too. Everybody too busy making money these days to take off even a single day for the repose of their father's soul."

Finally, a decent break. With the time left reaching the point where I was beginning to count it in hours rather than days, I wouldn't have to waste any of it tracking Yuti down. Yuti was right here. And Tut wasn't—another bit of good fortune. After what I'd been through, I'm entitled to a bit.

I had dozens of questions for Aanen. Questions about his recollection of the events surrounding Akhenaten's death. Questions about any knowledge he might have of the event that had just occurred. I thought these were what I was asking when I opened my mouth. I was aghast at what came out. To this very day I can't believe what I actually said, or why. What came out was, "Aanen, I have this—this friend that has a serious problem, and I thought maybe you could help me with it. He has this principal wife with whom he is having certain difficulties, and he was wondering if there was any ecclesiastical way he could . . . [*Translator's note: At this point Eye goes into a long, convoluted explanation of what he had in mind. The word he was searching for was "divorce," but in Egypt at that time there was no divorcing a principal wife after she'd borne children.*]

Aanen pondered the question. I stood there thunderstruck. Where had that come from? Do you see what I mean by magic? I wasn't even *thinking* it, yet out the words came. Here I'd just been struck by an assassin's arrow; here I had urgent questions for Aanen about any possible knowledge he might have of the episode, and *this* is what came out of my mouth. The Hidden One knew thoughts I didn't know I held myself, and Aanen could see into my soul.

Another thought whirled darkly to mind. Other than the obvious spell of her charms, did Yennah have the power to work a spell of another sort on me? I swear I never once consciously considered, even for an instant, the idea of ridding myself of Tey. Yet out of my mouth the question popped. I could feel the blood draining from my head and I nearly fainted.

Aanen, unperturbed, pondered my question at length. He gave not the slightest impression that he found it the least bit odd. "A— friend, is it? You're inquiring for a friend? It's an unusual question. Let me study upon it."

# 13

## DAY

## FOUR

## —

## AFTERNOON

Aanen put the tips of his fingers together, making a little, prayerful temple of them as he continued to ponder what I had said. What *I* had said? What had come out of my mouth, which is nothing like what I felt certain was on my mind. Yet clearly it *had* to have been on my mind, or I wouldn't have said it. How can something be on my mind that I myself don't know? A true puzzle. Amun the All-Knowing lives in this his temple, and once more I could but bow my head in awe at his incredible and mysterious powers.

"It's a most unusual request you put to me on your friend's behalf," Aanen continued, and he sat for a moment deep in thought, though his brow remained unfurled. He looked at me—or rather, looked into me, or about me, or beyond me, for it was impossible to tell. One of his eyes didn't quite remain in synchronization with the other, which gave the uncanny effect that although he was talking to you, you weren't even there.

"Was there adultery involved?" he inquired unctuously.

"I'm not certain," I mumbled, averting my eyes. "I was just passing along a question."

"If there was, there's no problem at all. For adultery the wife dies. That takes care of the problem. Of course you already know that, being chief magistrate. I presume your friend seeks an ecclesiastical remedy rather than a civil one. Some men do. They feel it more fitting, more sealed by the gods, if it has the imprimatur of the temple."

He pursed his lips in that familiar pursing. "With adultery, it's simply a matter of preference. Stoning. A poisoned cup. Burial up to the neck in the desert. It's entirely the husband's option. My personal preference is stoning. I think it's more satisfying, somehow. Time-honored and all that. Still, I never attempt to press my preferences on others." This last he said with a certain sanctimonious self-satisfaction which I found exceptionally annoying. I had no quarrel with what he said, just with the insufferable oily holiness with which he said it.

I said nothing further. I hadn't consciously intended to pursue this line of conversation, but Aanen seemed intrigued by the problem and wouldn't let it go.

"Now, if there's no adultery involved, it's a much more complex matter," he continued, warming to the subject. "I would guess in your friend's case there's no adultery, else he'd already know the answer. If there's no adultery, your friend must have another woman in the picture. That's almost always the problem. And your friend must be very highly placed, else he'd either make the female a secondary wife or concubine or mistress. Whatever."

As long as Aanen was chewing on this bone I might as well learn what I could learn. No harm in that, is there? So I continued to say nothing, sensing that he'd continue to delve into the subject without further encouragement from me. "Sensing" is perhaps the wrong word. I absolutely *knew* he'd keep going. Like all clerics, once he started showing off his erudition, nothing in this world could stop him. If I dematerialized in a puff of smoke he'd still go on talking until he'd totally unburdened himself of his total store of knowledge on the subject.

"You know," he mused, confirming my thoughts, "I had a case like this once before. It was a number of years ago. It involved an august personage, and I instigated a truly prodigious amount of research."

A burst of light exploded in my brain. "Akhenaten!" I exclaimed. "You worked on this for Akhenaten!" Whatever had caused me to open up this line of conversation, of a sudden it appeared likely to bear fruit.

I should have kept my lips tight. To interject at this point, particularly on such a sensitive subject as the former pharaoh, could easily be the one thing that would make Aanen shut down his dissertation. And of a sudden it appeared that if Akhenaten was the subject of Aanen's prior researches, the information could be of vital import to me. Yet out of my mouth, unbidden, his name had sprung. I am both by nature and experience the type of man who thinks carefully before ever uttering a word. Amun's powers must still be working.

What a frightening situation—to be unable to conceal your innermost thoughts even against your own conscious will. I trembled to think what might come out of my mouth next. In fact, how could I even know, since the words seemed to emerge before I even had a chance to think them?

Aanen started visibly. He looked at me closely—well, one eye did. The other was a near miss. "I know you're deeply involved with this Akhenaten thing right now, Eye," he said, slowly and carefully, clearly taken aback by what I knew must be the accuracy of my deduction. "It must be all you have on your mind. Don't leap to conclusions."

"It's Akhenaten! I know it's Akhenaten!" I didn't, of course. But then again somehow I did. Aanen's sudden confusion simply confirmed it.

"Really, Eye, you know I can't reveal more to you. Such information is privileged, and I'm sure you wouldn't want me to violate my oath and my conscience." I wanted to hit him in his straight, patrician nose. He was so oily he nearly oozed into a puddle.

"I have to know!" I snapped. "I'm running out of time, and what you can reveal might be critically important."

Aanen knew what I was talking about, but he simply sat there and shook his head. "I wish I could tell you more, Eye, but you know I can't."

I looked back at him. I presumed both my eyes were in focus, because I wanted to look at him as intently and meaningfully as I could. "I understand, Aanen," I replied calmly. "Truly, I do know your position. You are compelled to keep such matters completely inviolate. I commend you on your rectitude. However, now's as good a time as any to mention another subject. I haven't been to Karnak for a while. I didn't realize how many improvements have been made, new ones over and above the work I'd originally authorized. It's all simply magnificent. But I don't remember seeing the property reassessed on the tax rolls. That's one of my departments, you know. I really must look into it first thing when I get back to Thebes. The treasury," I said, looking at him as purposefully as possible, "is missing out on a truly huge source of additional revenue. I shall have to locate the assessor and punish him severely."

Aanen looked at me. I looked at him. We did a lot of silent looking.

Aanen flinched first. "Well," he said, with genuine reluctance, and a very plain look of distaste on his face, "perhaps I can continue in a general way. Without naming names, you understand."

"I understand."

"Anyway, there was this most august personage who came to me with much the same problem your friend posed."

I sat on the edge of my chair expectantly. "No adultery involved, I presume?"

"Strangely enough, there was."

"Then I don't understand."

"This very august personage had ample proof of adultery. His wife—and of course I can't name her either—seemed to have a predilection for bedding down with anything male. Based on this personage's descriptions and evidences, I wouldn't be surprised if that might not have extended beyond mere human males."

"Then," I said, scratching my head, "what was his problem?" When I say scratching my head, I mean that literally. I'm quite bald, you know, and one of my fingernails had a little snag. I scratched my pate deep enough to draw blood.

"Well," Aanen went on, dragging out his words, "this—this personage was in a most awkward position. If he had her executed for adultery, he would cast a pall over the legitimacy of his children. And in his position, this was an absolute impossibility. It would shake the sta—— it would simply be an impossibility. Every bit of his prestige would have been shattered. Every bit of his dignity destroyed. That's all I can say."

Nefertiti! For absolute certain sure, Nefertiti! Maybe at last I'd struck a vein that would lead me to the mother lode!

Aanen shifted in his chair uneasily. I waited him out. "So," he commenced again, "you can see his dilemma. He wanted to put her aside, which is why he came to me. To find out how to do it. There was something else to it, too. The man truly was a gentle person. He really didn't want to kill his wife, despite her many crimes. He was quite content to exile her. But he very much wanted to strip her of her title of principal wife. This would strike deeply at her vanity and would totally destroy her social position. That much punishment he very much wanted to inflict."

"So what could you do for him?"

"Not a thing, I fear. Now in matters such as this there's usually a way. The trick is to find it. Here at Karnak we keep temple records of immense antiquity. I felt that if we began working backward through them, at some point we'd find a precedent and would know what to do. One mustn't trifle with the gods in matters like this. Putting aside a principal wife is truly a grave matter. Many oaths have been sworn and many ceremonies conducted. Far better to be unhappy with a wife than to have a god unhappy with you."

I recognized the problem.

"So what did you learn?"

"Nothing. Nothing at all. It was a most difficult and laborious task. Most time-consuming. We had only managed to search our records back for three centuries before the personage died. That of course brought the entire matter to a close. Except for the research fee he owed us, which to this day remains unpaid."

I tried to retain my composure, but very much doubt I succeeded. So Akhenaten had been trying legally to rid himself of Nefertiti, and then he died! And because he died before the temple had found a legal way to accommodate the pharaoh, she retained her social standing and prestige as queen mother. Fascinating!

As I pondered this information, I felt my elation subside slightly. I turned all I knew over in my mind. Did this revelation truly have significance? Nefertiti had told me from her own mouth that she had been plotting a coup with that intelligence-challenged dolt Antef. The coup attempt had been within mere weeks of taking place when the "personage" died. Any coup takes co-conspirators, and the more tongues, the more talk. Why risk plotting a coup if poison could take care of matters more quickly and surely?

Good question. I wish I had an answer. But still and all, it was very obvious that Nefertiti felt she absolutely had to do *something*, and quickly, or else she'd find herself banished to some hovel in the Nubian desert with scorpions instead of gorgeous guard commanders for companionship. Reason enough for her to be desperate. Reason enough for her to strike, whether by poison or by coup.

My mind was thus distracted while Aanen picked up the thread of the conversation without missing a beat. "If your friend is interested, we could continue our researches," he continued, clearly oblivious to the fact that I no longer was all that interested in pursuing the subject. "I have to warn you, it's extremely expensive. And of course, he'd have to pick up the cost of the work we've already done."

"Of course," I answered abstractedly.

Without change of expression or tone, Aanen stated matter-of-factly in that magnificent, molten-silver voice of his, "You don't like me, Eye, do you?"

"You want the truth? No."

Aanen sighed, and again his fingers touched in that prayer pose. "A pity," he breathed. "All men wish to be liked. Still, I thank you for your honesty."

"I'm in a holy temple."

"Oh yes. Certainly. Well, I hope if you don't like me, you at least respect me."

An odd line of conversation. Still, so far, everything about my conversation with Aanen was odd, including my blurting out an inquiry I hadn't the foggiest notion I was going to make.

"Regrettably, Aanen, since you've chosen to ask, I must answer that question 'no' also. I freely admit I'm in great fear of your powers, your ability to tap the source of the mysteries and to converse with the gods themselves, but as for respect . . ." I shook my head.

He looked genuinely hurt and puzzled. "I'm sorry to hear that. Not to be liked can be borne. We all have our natures, our personalities. We are who we are. Not to be respected is something else. Any man, however unlikable, can earn respect."

"Why are you asking me these questions?"

Aanen thought about that. "I'm not certain. I wasn't planning on it. I thought I was going to ask something else, but that's what came out."

Believe me, I could relate to that. I would have thought Aanen immune, considering he was high priest and spent nearly all his days here at Karnak.

"Does it happen often?" I inquired, genuinely interested.

"Not often. Sometimes. We sit in the middle of the mightiest temple of the mightiest god in the universe. Nowhere is the god's power stronger than in his own house. Perhaps Amun works on the minds of those who pass through his portals in ways we cannot comprehend, and here in his very house exposes the truth of our minds and our hearts without our volition." [*Translator's note: Perhaps indeed he does. Or perhaps ordinary men, even temple priests, in the presence of their god blurt out words they'd prefer to keep hidden, unconsciously feeling that the god must know their minds, thus involuntarily making their innermost thoughts manifest. This certainly would be the* facile, modern explanation. Personally, this translator would prefer to think it truly was the work of the gods. Many things happened in ancient Egypt which remain inexplicable to this very day.]

"As long as I've broached a subject which even ordinary good manners should have kept concealed, I'd really like to know what you have against me." I looked at Aanen's face, and I could see that he genuinely wanted to know.

I thought about the question awhile. It was certainly an interesting one. At length I answered, truthfully, "It's because you're such a hypocrite."

Aanen pondered that. "Ah," he said simply. "Ah." He thought about it a bit more. "Isn't that somewhat like the viper calling a cobra a snake?"

The unexpectedness of this assault made me bristle with outrage. "Who are you calling hypocrite? Me? Grand Vizier of Egypt? I'm not the man who betrayed my oath and my gods just so I wouldn't lose my post as pharaoh's high priest! You, on the other hand, seem to change gods as easily as you change clothes. I fight for what I believe in!"

"Do you now indeed, Eye? Do you? Good for you. If that's true, however, how come there are still the most absolutely gushing inscriptions on temples and statues in Thebes and Amarna and Memphis and everywhere else in the land, praising Akhenaten as the most wonderful ruler to wear the double crown in all of Egypt's history? There are so many of them that they'll all probably never be obliterated, though I know you're doing the best and fastest job you can. Curiously enough, all those fawning dedications are signed by a certain Eye. Eye, Grand Vizier of Egypt."

"That's different," I retorted sullenly. "I'm not a high priest. I'm a mere government official."

"And did you really believe Akhenaten was so wonderful?" Aanen pursued relentlessly. "All your inscriptions say you did. Be honest, Eye, here in the Temple of the Hidden One. When Akhenaten ruled, weren't you one of his very staunchest supporters?"

He had me, but there was no way I was going to admit it. If I could help it. "Of course. I had no use for Akhenaten. Who did? But what difference did a few inscriptions make? It's the custom, that's all. And besides, I would have been nobody without Akhenaten, without his marriage to my daughter." Now why did I say that? I swear I didn't have those words on my tongue. What was going on here?

"Ah, yes," Aanen observed, not unkindly. "Your high position. Believe me, I truly understand."

"At least I wasn't a high priest," I shot back, but the steam was going out of my thesis. "We expect more of high priests. We expect them to be true to a higher standard. We court officials deal in the real world. The very nature of our jobs make us deal in compromise, in give-and-take. But you. You were High Priest of Amun. Of *Amun!* Then, when Akhenaten commanded his heresy, you calmly became apostate and continued as High Priest of Aten. Then when Akhenaten died, back to High Priest of Amun again. For a priest your convictions are suspiciously flexible." That last was perhaps uncharitable, but no man likes to have his own honor impugned, particularly by one who has shown even less.

"Ah," he said once more. "There it is. The usual. Priests are supposed to be pure, without sin, ready to be martyred for the faith. I suppose that's true. We're not supposed to be human, but we are. And I freely admit, when it came to reality, to the pure choice of accepting the Aten as the one god of Egypt or giving up the high priesthood, which for me meant giving up everything, I failed the test of courage. Most in Egypt at that time did. But consider, if you will, something else.

"Consider what I was able to accomplish by converting to Atenism. You know those terrible times, when the man commanded the destruction of all gods but Aten, all those gods that have ruled us for a million years. The very gods that gave us knowledge, that made Egypt great. Had I not accepted the reformed high priesthood, a less resourceful man would have. Remember this, Eye, it wasn't just the gods he tried to destroy, he tried to destroy the way they're approached. Before Akhenaten, all men could approach the gods directly. Akhenaten demanded that the Aten could be approached only through him. The pharaoh's power as man/god is great enough as it is. But as gatekeeper to the sole god, to whom none may have access save through him? We're talking power raised to an entirely new dimension! In Akhenaten's hands it would have made little difference. The man actually was benign, and kindly. His only vice was that he was mad. But what about that power in the hands of a successor? What of Egypt then?"

"Are you telling me, Aanen, that you're a true believer, a true believer in the old gods, and not a mere opportunist?" Despite myself, I was beginning to have a better feeling for the man.

"That's precisely what I'm saying. I'm flawed and I confess it. But I protected our old gods every possible way I could. I memorized the Book of the Dead. Try it sometime—it's quite a lengthy document. I memorized others of the scriptures. Luckily I have the type of mind that can do it. I performed the ancient rites in secret, and protected as many ancient images as I could. I passed down the ancient ceremonies to the priests that stayed true to the old belief. I waited for the storm to pass. And it did."

I nodded and made a waving half-salute. "If you've told me true, then I withdraw my prior words."

"For that I thank you. And I mine." I nodded in acceptance, although in truth I had reason to alter my opinion, and he none.

"The gods exist," he went on firmly. "Without the gods, nothing on this earth would have any sense or meaning. It has taken us a million years to learn the ways of the gods, their mysteries. To learn, slowly and painfully, by signs and by portents, which gods rule the earth and which the sky, which rule love and which hate, which control each and every portion of our daily existence. This knowledge was long in the coming. The gods are eternal, and are in no rush to reveal their truths to us. How many thousands of years must have passed before we came to know the ways of the cat-goddess Bastit and her son the crocodile-headed lord Min, protector of fertility? Who among us was first to fathom the mysteries of Osiris or the prayers required before Seth would listen? All that knowledge, gathered so painfully by generations without number, Akhenaten tried to sweep away. Yes, I was young and ambitious, and yes, I quailed at the thought of being dispossessed from my high post, yet I feel the gods themselves placed me where I was for a purpose, and that had I not been the man, our ancient religion would have disappeared and our beloved Egypt forever destroyed."

He smiled a self-deprecating smile, the first I had seen. Quickly it fled his face.

"Enough of this," he said. "I truly don't know how we even got on the subject. It is mealtime. We have your food prepared. Would you care to join me in the courtyard? It's a pity that the pharaoh wasn't able to stay longer. It would be nice if he could dine with us too. I so much enjoy his little visits. He's quite deeply religious, you know, and has a very keen mind. When it comes to fine points of theology, he really keeps me on my toes."

Was the man sincere? Did he really *enjoy* Tut's company? I had to know. "Aanen, let's be honest. Just between you and me. What do you really think of Tut? Forget I'm his grandfather. Forget he's pharaoh. What do you *really* think of him?"

"I like him," Aanen replied flatly, without the slightest trace of irony in his voice. "Oh, he's still young and like all young men needs some polishing, some maturing, but all in all I think he'll make a splendid pharaoh."

Aanen saw the look of incredulity on my face, and held up his hand before I could speak. "Now, Eye," he continued, "let's be honest about things. We are in Amun's temple. Aren't you taking advantage, when you come right down to it? Tut is past the age where he can rule in his own right. There's no need for a regency anymore—no legal need. I know power is the most voracious appetite of all—one that can never be slaked, never satisfied. But it's past time for you and Horemheb to give it up. If Tut has placed you in this impossible position, given you this impossible problem to solve, in all honesty to a large extent you've brought it on yourself. You're going to have to relinquish the regency sometime. In my view, you've waited too long already. If you and Tut are at odds, can you blame him?"

Aanen was right. Horemheb and I *had* already extended our co-regency to the absolute limit, and still hadn't found a way to turn it loose without putting ourselves at risk. Neither of us would step down without the other, and neither of us trusted each other enough to believe that if we jointly relinquished the regency, the other would not by some treachery seize control unilaterally. So there was more than a kernel of truth in what Aanen said. Maybe my animus toward Tut had more than a little self-justification in it. But still and all, I didn't like the boy.

"Did Tut speak to you at all about any of this when he was here? Anything at all you haven't told me? *Anything?*"

The corner of Aanen's mouth turned up in a wry, amused smile. "No, Eye, we exchanged no confidences on the subject. I've already given you my assurances. But I have eyes that see beyond these temple precincts. I'm aware of the situation at court. But I have no hidden knowledge. So perhaps now you'll join me for the meal?"

"Thank you no," I said hastily. "I appreciate your kind offer, but I've had a series of very wearying days, and if you don't mind, I'd like to take a simple meal and then rest. I've brought a box lunch."

[*Translator's note: When Eye said "a box lunch" he meant a box lunch. He goes on to describe a huge box, lavishly ornamented, containing a mind-numbing assortment of foods. I rather doubt you want to hear his detailed description of each and every item.*]

To my amazement Aanen actually laughed. Laughed out loud. The rich baritone reverberated off the farthest walls of the great temple. "Do you really think I'd try to poison you? Here in this god's own house? Do you really think I *need* to poison you? I know ancient spells and incantations that can make you infertile or make you sick or make you blind or make you dead. Would you like me to show you a sample?"

"No thank you, Aanen," I replied in some haste, and I felt the hair on my arms stand straight up as he said those words in that calm, matter-of-fact voice. "That won't be necessary. Thanks all the same." Nevertheless, I preferred to dine on my own food, and as diplomatically as possible I told him so.

"As you wish," Aanen conceded. "A pity, though. I assure you upon my word as High Priest of Amun that nothing in food I serve will do you harm. Still, I'm certain that your own kitchen is every bit the equal of mine, so that whatever food you've brought will be enjoyable to you. And as long as you've brought it, you might as well eat it. It's a sin to waste food when so many people in the world are starving."

Thus, in this rather peculiar fashion, we dined, he on his food, I on mine. "You're sure," I inquired after a moment's pause, "that Yuti remains here in Karnak?"

"Of that I'm positive," Aanen responded. "Would you care to visit with him?"

"How long is he staying?"

"Until tomorrow at least. Believe me, he won't want to miss his morning bath. And, speaking of baths, would you care to be attended by some of our temple maidens this evening? You'll find them truly enchanting creatures. You have my personal word on it."

Now, I knew that "maidens" was a polite euphemism—temple prostitutes would be more accurate. Still, I also knew they'd be stunning—none but the best would do for the Temple of Karnak, the House of the Hidden One.

I demurred. After Oudah and Yennah, my ardor for additional females was slaked for the time being. Enough was enough, particularly now. A nice, undemanding hot bath would do me quite nicely. In fact, it was something of a relief to be here and not at my own palace where Yennah, much as I lusted for her, would be more of a challenge than I felt like facing at the moment.

I couldn't help laughing out loud at the thought of that pitiful creature Yuti being attended by beautiful temple maidens—whores—whatever, and when Aanen asked what I found so amusing, I told him. "I just can't imagine," I said, chuckling, "Yuti being bathed—and presumably serviced—by beautiful females. The poor things. How awful for them. And how awful for Yuti, having to see them cringe and pull away every time he reaches for them."

Aanen raised a knowing eyebrow. "As a matter of fact, Eye, that's not the way it is at all. The girls love it. They fight to see which will be the first to bed him. They pout and cry and scratch each other if they're taken off bath duty. It's really most remarkable."

This was more than I could believe. There are some things sim-

143

ply impossible, even here in Karnak. "Yuti!" I exclaimed. "Are we talking about the same Yuti? Yuti the physician? Yuti, that bald-headed, bottom-heavy, weak-eyed excuse for a man? With those prominent front teeth of his and that twitchy nose, he looks like a rabbit but without nearly as much personality."

"Well, Eye, you know what they say is the most noticeable proclivity of rabbits."

It was the only funny thing I'd heard Aanen say all day. The whole thing was mystifying, incomprehensible and, let me be honest, humiliating. Deep in my heart—well, not all that deep, in fact, right on the immediate surface—I knew that temple girls, prostitutes or not, wouldn't be falling all over each other to get a crack at *me*. What could Yuti possibly have that I didn't have? Women had *never* fallen all over for me, unless, of course, they wanted something, and that didn't count.

Another mystery. And one of the worst sort. Could it be conceivably true that women actually found Yuti more appealing than they did me? Just what I needed, more mysteries and humiliations. I was dealing with more than I could handle as it was, thank you.

# 14

## DAY

## FOUR

## —

## EVENING

After dining with Aanen, and trying to cope with the impossible image of Yuti as a sex god, I excused myself from Aanen's table and spent the afternoon wandering the vast precincts of my great temple of Karnak. I thought of it precisely so. My temple. Everywhere I looked, my name was inscribed as the architect and builder, and as long as I was here I inspected my handiwork, or, to be more precise, that of my craftsmen and masons, with a close and critical eye, and was most pleased at what I saw. The workmanship was superb, and the Hidden One would reign with pride in this his house for a million years to come, and my name would endure alongside his.

I couldn't help smiling at the signs of improvement on what I'd ordered. In spite of the molten river of gold I'd poured into this place, obviously it hadn't been enough. I suppose nothing is ever enough. Throughout the enormous temple I noted works I'd never authorized, works paid for by the temple treasury, and conveniently kept off the tax rolls. I would have been indignant but for the fact that I kept my own palace appraised at a ridiculously low figure.

It was impolite of me to excuse myself from Aanen, but I needed time alone. I'd done much investigating, but now, with time running down, I was becoming increasingly desperate. No matter how hard I pondered the matter, or what additional scraps of information I was able to glean, I was nowhere near an answer. I knew my pharaoh wanted me out of office—perhaps wanted me dead. I knew that someone else wanted me dead too. And that someone obviously wasn't counting on the failure of my mission to bring me to my doom. Whoever he was, he was more impatient than that. The attempt through poor Oudah had failed. The arrow whose blow I could still feel on my chest had failed too. But these attempts could certainly be repeated again—in fact, they almost certainly would—perhaps in such a way that all my cunning could not prevent, nor all my watchfulness avert. Power is an illusory thing. As grand vizier I held it in abundance; as co-regent of Egypt no man was more powerful. Still, even a slave can kill a king. It had been done before, and could happen again.

Oudah had tried. I still thought of her as "poor Oudah," for I felt certain that she bore no personal malice toward me. In fact, after a rather hesitating start, I felt certain that in the end she had rather enjoyed our one encounter. I certainly hoped so, since it had been her last. No, Oudah had been placed in an impossible position by someone powerful enough to exert threats upon her, credible threats, enough to force her to go through with his demands. Or hers. Somewhere in the back of my mind I had to concede that maybe it had been a matter of some indifference to Oudah whether I died nor not, but that wasn't the point.

The arrow which would have extinguished my life but for my prudence in donning concealed body armor was in its way even more troubling. Obviously someone was subverting my household with consummate ease, and every move I made was being reported almost the instant I made it. I was under surveillance even in my own palace.

The matter of the desert sandstorm was a trifle more conjectural, but no matter how I viewed it, each of the last three days had seen my life in deadly peril. What would tomorrow bring, or tonight, for that matter? Regardless how alert I tried to stay, or how many bodyguards I surrounded myself with, the odds were overwhelming that whoever was after me would succeed long before I could discover the slayer of Akhenaten. The thought left a sour taste in my mouth.

I opted to retire early and to eat my evening meal alone. I wasn't in the mood for small talk, most certainly not with Aanen, and needed to go over in my mind how I might approach Yuti tomorrow. I took my bath with the aid of male attendants, and for the life of me couldn't conjure up a picture of Yuti being fought over by nubile, sex-obsessed females. If any save Aanen had told me the story, I would have dismissed it as a feeble and impossible joke.

I prepared for bed in this melancholy frame of mind, and requested that the servants leave the lamps lit in my room. I have, I regret to say, a rather weak bladder, and I didn't want to stumble around in strange quarters when I would have to get up in the middle of the night. I suppose it is an inevitable consequence of a lifetime of dining on rich foods, or maybe it's just a natural consequence of being fifty-seven years old.

This of course wasn't the first night I'd ever slept in this great temple. But before, it had always been a work in progress, and although services were constantly carried on even during construction, somehow, before, it had always seemed more of a building project than a holy place. It was different now. It was fully complete, and fully belonged to Amun. On top of that, I was still unsettled by the spell that had so peculiarly unlocked my tongue.

As I lay down on my bed in my sleeping garments, Yennah, unasked, came floating into my mind and her sinuous form and captivating face danced tantalizingly before my eyes. I tried to banish her from my mind, but could not. As she reached out with her long, supple, sinuous limbs, I felt interest stirring in me once more. I could not rid my mind of her; I desperately wanted to . . . to . . . I tried to strike the word "fuck" from my mind. I like to think of myself as a cultured man. I rarely even think this particular word, and never say it out loud. It was a horrifyingly sacrilegious thought to have here, of all places, in the supreme temple of Amun. Yet there it was, unbidden.

How does one keep a thought from coming to mind before one knows one has thought it? I hastily got up from my bed, got down on my knees, placed my head on the floor, and humbly begged Amun's forgiveness. Amun knew my very thoughts. I needed all the help I could get. The last thing I wanted was to alienate the All-Powerful by defiling his holy place with these impure fantasies. The strain of Tut's impossible demand, and these repeated attempts on my life must be driving me mad. These last three days I've scarcely been able to recognize myself. Somewhere around the edges of my mind I was beginning to disintegrate. I felt it.

I returned to my bed, very deeply troubled by the possible consequences of my inappropriate thoughts and even more highly troubled that I was even having them, when I noticed near the closed door of my bedroom a kitten pawing itself playfully. Odd. What was it doing there?

It was a winning little creature, pure black save for a touch of white at the front paws, with a lively, alert look in its eyes. It gazed at me with great interest, and kept staring at me in a somewhat unsettling fashion, direct, unblinking, in a manner unlike that of most kittens in my experience.

The kitten continued to stare at me, and I at it, until I noticed motion from the corner of my eye. There, in the corner of the room, sat a baby crocodile. This wasn't entrancing at all. I hate crocodiles. I've always hated them. This was really most peculiar. It was more than peculiar, it was downright annoying. How had that little crocodile gotten into my room? How had the kitten gotten in, for that matter? There were no obvious gaping holes anywhere. The entire temple is virtually brand-new, and if I knew anything at all, it was that my workmen weren't sloppy. I freely admit I don't mind cutting a corner here and there when it comes to building a royal palace or an administrative building—what's the point of being grand vizier if you can't make an extra coin or two now and then?—but on the construction of a sacred temple, never. I revered all the gods much too deeply for that, and for that matter feared them much too deeply, too. I'd never fill an extra coffer with gold by shoddy workmanship and subcontractor kickbacks, not on a god's temple. I knew what the gods could do to me if they chose, and being on a god's shit list for eternity was a prospect for which I had no stomach whatsoever. [*Translator's note: Again, forgive the mild obscenity, but this is the nearest I can come to properly conveying Eye's words into the modern vernacular, while still retaining the sense of his hieroglyphics.*]

This did not resolve the problem of how these animals had been able to get into my room. How had they gotten in? What were they doing here? I was on the verge of getting up to locate their source of entrance when, to my utter shock, as well you may imagine, the kitten began growing right before my eyes. When I say growing, I mean *growing*. And growing. And growing. I cowered back in bed, transfixed by the sight, until in what amounted to but the working of a few instants I knew with horror who stood in this room before me.

It was Bastit—the goddess Bastit. She towered over my bed, with her feline head and her human body. Her cat's eyes burned brightly in her head, and her tongue licked at me menacingly, hungrily. She was draped in a filmy robe from the waist down, and she wore nothing at all save a necklace around her neck from the waist up. Thus I could tell for certain this was indeed a goddess. She had fine tits. Men notice these things, even under extremely peculiar circumstances. In fact, were it not that she seemed exceptionally angry at me for some unknown reason, and had very sharp teeth, she would have been a rather fetching being. Her cat's head didn't bother me all that much—I felt this was no big impediment, since the head isn't one of the parts of a woman's body in which I have the greatest interest. In fact, since cats aren't known for being all that conversational, this particular configuration might well prove to be a net advantage.

Involuntarily, I found myself shrinking backward. For, although the creature was in some respects beguiling, I didn't like the way she was looking at me. I kept my eyes locked on this apparition. It was impossible to tear them away. This goddess—this Bastit— had a very nice figure, but I'd seen nicer. Yennah, for example. I freely admit these things are subjective and a matter of personal preference, but still and all, one would think that a goddess ought to have a figure far superior to that of any mere mortal. It was an odd time to have these theological musings, but there they were.

Bastit snarled and hissed, and she began making menacing, scratching motions toward me with her arms. Her arms were human, and her hands, but her fingernails were exceptionally long and sharp. They looked tough and strong, too—claws that could cut like razors if they reached my skin.

All of my attention had been fixed on Bastit. I'd taken my eye off the baby crocodile. This was a major mistake. It too was growing, growing, and the taller it grew, the meaner, the more threatening. And I knew who it was. It was, without question, Min. It was the god Min, at the height of his powers. Now, even as babies, crocodiles don't draw any oohs and aahs for cuteness, but when you're suddenly confronted with a full-grown freak, an entity with the head of a crocodile and the muscular body of a powerful man, there's nothing comforting about the situation. The feeling of menace and peril is even worse when confronted with two ravenous monsters, both of them looking at you with obviously hostile intent, not to say appetite.

Once Min confronted me, I dropped all thoughts of Bastit. Min was disgusting, with no redeeming qualities whatsoever. His enormous, bloodshot eyes bulged obscenely. He slavered and drooled. There was nothing of pity in him. His arms were enormous and powerful, his barrel chest all scaly and clammy, and if there was anything at all positive about the situation it was that his legs were grotesquely short. With luck I could outrun him, if I could find a way out of the room before Bastit cut me off.

I was, I freely confess, panic-stricken. My breath came in short, spasmodic gulps. I had a short, sharp dagger at my waist but knew it would be futile even to draw it. All it could possibly do would be to anger these apparitions even further. I couldn't imagine what to do or why this was happening to me.

I was totally speechless. I wanted to shout, to cry out for help, but my voice choked in my throat. I watched, paralyzed, as the two creatures began advancing on me. I wanted to run, but my feet felt nailed to the floor.

Suddenly my room, dimly lit by the lamps, began glowing with a strange, unearthly radiance. It blinded me. I threw my hands over my eyes to shield them from the dazzling brilliance. I knew if I didn't protect my eyes my vision would be permanently damaged.

Within the core of that brilliance I could, for just an instant, make out the apparition of the god Re-Horakhty, god of the sun. I couldn't tell much about him. He shone far too brightly for me to look upon directly. Was he there to protect me or to devour me?

I would never know, for at the very instant of his appearance he was set upon by Min. Min devoured him. It was an ugly, nauseating sight. Crocodiles aren't known for their table manners, and the horrifying, crunching and chomping sounds sent violent chills down my spine. Re-Horakhty, almost as soon as he appeared, disappeared into Min's cavernous stomach. With each bite the brilliance in the room diminished. I was able to take my hands from my eyes. I watched as more and more parts of Re-Horakhty were consumed, until at last the final morsel was gone and the room returned to its dim, lamp-lit state. Min glared at me in evil triumph, the last remnants of Re-Horakhty clinging to his teeth and dripping from his jaw.

It took a few seconds for my eyes to readjust to lamplight. Luckily Bastit and Min as yet made no move. I knew not what to do. I was doomed if I did nothing, but my brain simply ceased functioning. As my eyes regained their focus, I noticed that Bastit held in her hand a water clock and Min a sundial. My mind registered these peculiarities, but they were of no useful significance.

They took a step toward me. Both of them. I bolted away from the bed and pressed my back against the wall. My feet had finally decided to move, but whether or not to any useful purpose I hadn't a clue. They again advanced, in no hurry, taking their time. I slithered away from them, keeping my body glued to the brick of the wall. I saw a brief opening, a moment's chance, and I took it.

My bedroom door was barred from the inside, and with a flip of my arm I flung the bar upward, wrestled the door open, and fled madly screaming down the hall. I thought to myself, somewhat irrelevantly under the circumstances, that considering how little exercise I'd been having of late, I really was making remarkable speed. Also, not to put too fine a point on it, I was scared shitless.

My escape from the room enraged Bastit and Min. Min seemed particularly annoyed. I don't recommend to anyone having an enraged Min pursuing you. I'd hoped his appetite would have been satisfied by consuming Re-Horakhty, but clearly that had been but a snack. The crocodile-headed monster chased me furiously, screaming in a deep, reptilian, rabid voice, "Unfair! Unfair! Unfair!"

I sat upright in bed, drenched with sweat. Not only were my bedclothes soaking, the bed itself was heavily damp. My heart beat so wildly I could feel its thumping battering the inside of my rib cage. I breathed heavily, gulping air greedily through my mouth. My clammy skin shivered uncontrollably.

It took a few moments to convince myself that Bastit and Min were gone, that all had been but a dream. Dream? A nightmare, and one I would never, ever forget.

I couldn't seem to get enough air. I truly didn't feel well. It took at least five minutes before my heart began beating at a normal rate.

After a time I became reasonably calm again. Shaken, but reasonably calm. I felt morally certain that this dream must have some meaning, that it directly related to the problem Tut had set for me to solve. But what? Was there any sense at all to it? I pondered that question with all the intensity I could muster. The waterclock in Bastit's hand and the sundial in Min's? Were they trying to tell me that time was running out? Thanks a lot. I didn't need a nightmare to tell me that.

Useless, I thought to myself, after perhaps a half hour's reflection. There's no way in the world I'm going to figure this one out myself. I need a dream interpreter. Perhaps one of those Hebarew fellows? I seemed to remember that one of them, a fellow called Jesaph or Josep or something, had reputedly interpreted one of pharaoh's dreams a long, long time ago. Something to do with fat cows and thin cows. My dream was a lot better than that. But then, could I trust one of these Hebarews to give me a true interpretation? I wasn't exactly on their "A" list for social invitations, after the bricks-without-straw episode. They'd just love to give me an interpretation that would terrify me directly into my House of Truth.

So who? What about Aanen? What *about* Aanen? He had a reputation for being the finest interpreter of dreams in Egypt. Deservedly so, I had absolutely no doubt. That was one of the things high priests were paid for. And I was right here in the same temple with him. Still, what if he was the murderer of Akhenaten? After our conversation today, he remained as strong a possibility as anyone. Perhaps he'd felt he couldn't simply wait out Akhenaten's reign, but had opted to bring it to a premature end. If that was the case, and the meaning of my dream indicated Aanen as the culprit, what might the man do, having me in his power in his very own temple?

No, I'd have to look elsewhere. The Hebarews weren't to be trusted, nor Aanen. It would have to be someone else. Who? Just what I needed. Another problem.

This temple I'd built was one spooky place, let me tell you. First those odd conversations with Aanen where words came to mind unthought and unexpected, and now this. It had been a mistake not to have seen Yuti this afternoon and gotten out of here. Well, too late to do anything about that.

I was unable to get back to sleep. With an effort of will I forced the nightmare from my mind. No use thinking about—I knew I lacked the ability to interpret it. My powers as grand vizier were enormous, but they were temporal. In the realm of the metaphysical I had no more competence than the lowliest slave in my palace.

With sleep out of the question, I began to think once more of those strange words of mine. Was I really, seriously, considering deposing Tey and installing Yennah as principal wife in her place? I found that impossible to believe, yet there it was. Tey and I had been married forty years, give or take one or two. Forty years. I was comfortable with her, like with a well-worn sandal. I trusted her advice. I knew she'd always be in my corner. Could I know that about Yennah? In truth, never. She'd already revealed herself to be an ambitious, ruthless bitch. An irresistible one, but a dangerous bitch nonetheless. I still had to have her, I was still obsessed with her body. I've never been a man given to irresistible compulsions, but there it was, the truth of it. In my head I saw things clearly, saw Yennah clearly, but none of it mattered. I knew this irrational passion would burn itself out once I possessed her—Yennah was a mere child, after all, and there was nothing in common between us—but that knowledge was useless until the fever for her ran its course.

Well, once this was over, once I'd sorted everything out; if I ever did, I'd try to make it up to Tey. She'd done nothing to deserve any of this. I'd go to the royal jeweler and commission the finest necklace in Egypt, finer even than any Tut had had made for his queen, Ankhesenamun. For a man, remorse is an expensive emotion.

Despite my fears, I really felt I needed to get to sleep if I could, although the thought of those monsters coming at me again made the prospect terribly unsettling. I could send to Yuti for some powder that might help me get my rest, but obviously another sleepless night was preferable to accepting whatever prescription he might choose to prepare for me. And I certainly wasn't going to get anything from Aanen.

I sent for servants and had them bring me a full, sealed jar of the wine I'd brought with me. I inspected it most carefully, to be absolutely certain that the seal hadn't been tampered with. Satisfied that it hadn't, that it bore the imprint of my very own signet, I unstoppered the jar and, without bothering with a goblet, poured the entire contents down my throat in what amounted to a single, uninterrupted gulp.

Within fifteen minutes the wine did its work and I fell into a deep, untroubled sleep. I definitely needed it.

# 15

## DAY

## FIVE

## —

## MORNING

I awoke in the morning very much surprised. I was surprised at having been able to sleep at all. Even with the help of the wine, on the whole the sleep hadn't been all that restful. I sincerely hoped that the Lord God Amun who had sent that dream to me would find no necessity to repeat it. Or anything like it. I remembered it very vividly. I absolutely had no wish to find myself once more pursued by demons. Unlike normal dreams that vanish on the instant of waking, this one was so permanently burned into my memory as to need no repetition.

I of course continued to puzzle over the meaning, making no progress whatsoever. The crocodile-god Min had chased me with mealtime on his mind, screaming, "Unfair! Unfair! Unfair!" What could that possibly mean? If anything, *I* should have been the one shouting "Unfair!" I was the one who had to solve a capital crime without resort to torture. I was the one being chased by the demon-gods. I was getting nowhere with the dream, and it seemed to me I was getting nowhere with anything else.

I opted to eat no morning meal. I wasn't the least bit hungry. I rarely breakfasted anyway, and considering that another attempt on my life might well be made at any time, eating or drinking anywhere save in my own household was the absolute height of folly. And even there I couldn't feel all that secure.

It was dawn of the fifth day. I picked up my bronze mirror and stared at my reflection. It was totally unsatisfactory. It's lucky it's the fashion to paint the eyes. Mine had huge dark bags sagging from them that would require considerable art to conceal. Was it my imagination, or did I look older? And forgetting the dark circles, did my eyes have a peculiar, somewhat dazed look about them, a sort of vague, unfocused daftness? I could see by my reflection there was a limit to how much more of all this I could take.

Unfortunately, I had no choice. I'd have to take whatever came. I didn't know whether to wish for more time or less. I'd reached the point where I just wanted the whole thing to be over.

With great solemnity and as concentrated a mind as I could manage I performed the ritual of the triple bath and donned my holy ceremonial robes. I followed every step of the procedure with utmost fidelity. Nothing was more important than this. Today I would make obeisance to Lord Amun, who would save me from my peril if any force in this world could do it. If I expected Amun to protect me, it was only right that I observed each of the proper forms and procedures, recited every prayer, made every offering in the proper fashion.

I entered the holy sanctuary, my saffron-and-maroon robes resplendent even in the faint glow of first light. Aanen awaited me. Arising at dawn was routine for Aanen. His gown outshone mine as the sun the moon. It was of some shimmery, almost insubstantial material, and the colors changed as the full-draped arms stirred with every movement of his limbs. The entire garment was elaborately embroidered with imagery—the sun, the moon, the stars, the signs of the zodiac, the images of the gods. His angular face was of a somber and foreboding mien, befitting a man who took his faith with utmost sincerity, as in truth did I also.

The holy inner sanctuary of my Lord Amun is magnificently gilded, elaborately decorated, and completely empty. There isn't an image anywhere, only intricate, magnificent carvings and sworls of geometric design. In this solemn place lived the Hidden One himself, the All-Powerful, the All-Knowing, and only the most devout of his priests and the very highest of the court could set foot in these sacred precincts and live.

The temple choir began to sing, to chant the godly mass of Amun, and the voice of Aanen rose clear above all others. In such a place as this it is impossible not to feel the power of our ancient faith cleanse one's very soul. I was struck dumb with reverential awe as that magnificent voice, so deep, so fluid, so powerful, resonated off every golden, enameled panel of this inner sanctum, and I could sense, could feel, the emerging presence of the great god Amun himself. He was here, in this room, with me, and as the solemn words of the sacred mass washed over me I felt my mind open to receive the blessing of my Lord.

Reverently I fell to my knees, and reverently touched my head to the polished floor. "Lord Amun," I intoned, "be with me now and in these my days of testing. Guardian of Truth, sustain me. Holy Protector, send me wisdom. Knower of Hearts, cause thy dream to be made clear and manifest to me. Send me the wisdom to find perfect understanding. And if I lack the wit, send me one to interpret, O Keeper of Secrets. And if I should prove unworthy, O Mighty One, spare my name so that it not be excised from this your holy temple that I worked so mightily to build for your everlasting glory. If all should fail me, permit my name to live here in your holy place, so that when for a million years men come to worship here they shall see the name of the man that created this your home, for your eternal adulation."

In this vein I prayed for the better part of an hour, without pause, without looking up, knowing that upon the sincerity of my words my life and fate depended.

At last I rose. I had not brought my cudgel of office with me, and Aanen assisted me. He looked into me deeply, his dark-set, brooding eyes attempting to see into my very soul. "You have prayed most eloquently, Eye, and Amun will heed your words. So says Aanen his high priest; so says Aanen keeper of his sacred mysteries."

With that we solemnly departed the sanctuary, and I felt a lightness of heart unknown since Tut first sprang his little surprise on me, which now seemed eons ago. I was purified, restored. I felt serene. I had passed my fate into better hands, and would trust Lord Amun with the outcome.

"Will you wish to see Yuti now?" the high priest inquired, his tone of voice considerably less liturgical now that the services were over.

"Yes. As quickly as possible."

"He's at breakfast now. Would you care to join him?"

I followed Aanen, and he, with his retinue, led me to the dining area. I made no mention of the fact that I preferred not to eat, nor did Aanen refer to it.

Yuti was seated at a small, ornate table, finishing the last of his repast. I shan't describe the table—everything in the Temple of Karnak is magnificent, and even a small, ordinary breakfast table a major work of art.

I looked at the man and shook my head. He was exactly as I remembered him. Yuti was definitely bottom-heavy, and totally bald. His weak, myopic eyes gazed at me, desperately trying to see, and his prominent incisors conveyed that unmistakable rabbitlike impression by which all who knew him described him. He was an albino, and there was something unhealthy-looking in his paleness. There was a flabbiness about the man, and his skin was smooth and almost womanlike in texture. Yes, this was the Yuti I well remembered.

Aanen motioned me to sit. "I'll be leaving you now, Eye," he said magisterially, and with an almost invisible motion of the hand signaled his retinue to follow. "I presume you'll want to visit with Yuti in private, and I have no wish to intrude upon your confidences." He disappeared from the room, his retinue following in perfect step.

I looked at Yuti more closely. It was almost impossible to imagine that this forlorn specimen of manhood was the finest physician in Egypt.

Yuti was the type that relished small talk, and I wanted to put him at his ease, so for the better part of an hour we discussed trivia, aimlessly, pointlessly, until I felt Yuti might be sufficiently relaxed to carry on a meaningful conversation. That rabbitlike quality gave the sense that he would bolt and run at the first hint of any unpleasantness.

I could not resist broaching one topic first. "Yuti," I inquired, and this time I eagerly and most sincerely waited for the reply, "I understand your powers over the women of the temple are well-nigh irresistible. I've never had that talent myself. Tell me, if you would be so kind, please tell me, just exactly how do you do it? Just between the two of us, of course. It will go no farther."

Yuti blushed red, and the flush rose from his toes until it engulfed the very top of his pate. He glowed like a lighthouse. "It's— it's—" he stammered, his nose twitching nervously, "it's just something I've learned about, that's all." He was already beginning to perspire freely, and he wiped his brow with his napkin. "I'd really prefer not to go into it."

But I knew he would, if I insisted. And I insisted. Yuti was one of those who cave in the presence of authority. He had no power to stand fast, to hold his ground. I knew that in my presence—I, the grand vizier—his nervousness would steadily compound. If I had any hope of learning anything significant, it would be from this man, who had no ability whatsoever to lie convincingly and who simply lacked the ability to tell anyone, particularly one of high station, that certain questions were simply none of their business. In a way I felt sorry for him, but I didn't have the luxury of sparing his feelings. Whatever I wanted to know Yuti would reveal to me, and about every topic.

"Learned about? Interesting," I pursued. And though it was at the moment a distraction, I truly was interested in learning more about his remarkable abilities. "Perhaps you could teach me. I admit to you I could use the instruction."

He never made eye contact if he could avoid it. Averting his gaze, and clearly uncomfortable at this intensely personal line of questioning, he muttered, "Well, perhaps "learning" isn't the right choice of words. It actually doesn't work quite like that."

Obviously, he desperately wanted a change of subject. I, on the other hand, wasn't about to let this one go until I had an answer. With luck, I'd survive long enough to make use of whatever Yuti could teach me.

I pressed on. "If there's nothing to learn, then what *is* your secret? Whatever it is, every man in Egypt would give his entire inheritance to know it." That was scarcely an exaggeration.

"It has to do," Yuti replied with a resigned sigh, attempting to maintain some measure of dignity, "with my practice as a physician." He mopped his brow again, and his face, if anything, grew redder. I actually felt a little sorry for the man, but I absolutely wasn't going to drop this until I had my answer.

"And?"

I waited. He waited. This truly was none of my business, but it was an opportunity I couldn't let pass by, and I was determined to pry the answer out of him.

"It's nothing. An accident, really. A part of my pharmocopoeia. Nothing more." The man was as uncomfortable as a fish in a frying pan, and gave every appearance of being just as warm.

If he thought he was going to divert me with big words, it was a forlorn hope. "You mean it's something like a potion—some sort of prescription, some sort of drug, some sort of medicine?"

"Yes and no," the physician mumbled. "It's—it's simply a by-product."

"A by-product. A by-product of what?"

"A side effect might be more precise. A benign side effect."

"Having any woman in the world you want screaming for your body is a *side effect?* Side effect of what, man? Side effect of what?" Were it any other man in Egypt save Yuti, I wouldn't credit what I was hearing. This pathetic, twitching little rabbit held in his sole possession a secret for which kings would give up their crowns, and to him it was but some sort of side effect, almost an embarrassment.

"Well, if you must know," he muttered, eyes downcast, almost in a whisper, "a side effect of a potion I've discovered that cures the dropsy."

"You're afflicted with dropsy?"

He flushed once more and nodded. "A mild case. But dropsy nonetheless."

"And you prescribe this potion for yourself?"

"Someone has to test it." He raised his head and his voice held the first tiny edge of defiance. "I'm a scientist, you know, and *somebody* has to test it."

"If you're looking for volunteers, seek no further. I'll do tests for you, and give you concise, scientific reports on the results."

I'm an incurable lecher. But then, few men, if they are honest, would say differently of themselves. Where was this potion thirty years ago, when I *really* could have used it?

Yuti made no response, so I pressed. "Is it a powder?"

He nodded again.

"How does it work?"

"I don't know yet," he mumbled, looking wildly around the room as though seeking a bolt-hole. "I haven't finished my research. Normally, powders of this type work on the female. She imbibes it, and it triggers a powerful response in her system. My discovery was truly accidental. Truly it was. Somehow, if the male takes the potion, it's the female that becomes electrified. And this particular powder requires no special incantations for efficacy. My best guess is that it somehow works through the female sense of smell. Right now, all that I know is that it works. And cures dropsy, too."

"I would like a sample."

"Do you have dropsy?"

I could have lied, but I didn't. "Not of a certainty."

"Then you can't have the medicine."

"I must have it."

With astonishing firmness, Yuti shook his head vigorously. "I'm a doctor, not a charlatan. Not a whoremonger either, for that matter." I was stunned at his vehemence. "I can't give you a prescription. I've sworn a medical oath. I wish I could help you, but I simply can't."

I had apparently entered the one area where his courage would not fail him. I had touched upon his professional ethics. I admired the man for it. I certainly wasn't going to give up on this project, but for now reluctantly decided to let it rest. I was truly taken aback by this unexpected display of resistance on his part, and didn't want it to carry over into what, for now, had to be the more important part of my inquiries. This other could wait till later.

"You know of the mission Tut's set for me?" I asked abruptly, swiftly changing the subject. Yuti looked enormously relieved.

"Indeed I do. Indeed I do. I was at the palace that night."

"Of course. That's why I'm here talking to you. As the finest physician in Egypt"—here I felt flattery might get me somewhere, not to mention that it was the truth—"I thought you were the one man that might give me some particularly valuable insights."

"I'll do all I can to be of service, Grand Vizier."

"Most patriotic of you. Tell me, Yuti, what is your experience of magical spells and incantations? Can they kill a man? Most especially, can they kill a man at a great distance from the one who casts the spell? And," I added, "who in your knowledge, if anyone, would have sufficient power to raise up a desert storm at his sole command?"

Yuti paused gravely, giving full consideration to his reply. "It's puzzling to me," he said at length, "but in my experience—in my observations—it seems that indeed these spells, this magic, if you will, can be quite effective provided the victim knows the spell is being laid against him. When this is true, distance seems no barrier. When the victim is unaware, somehow he seems shielded. The success rate falls drastically."

"And typically, how long does it take a magic incantation to work? Assuming the victim knows it's being used against him?"

"Seven days. Ten days. Sometimes even longer."

"How about two days?"

"Two days?" Yuti wrinkled that smooth brow of his in deep, professional thought. "Perhaps. Not likely. I've never heard of two days. The least I've ever heard of is four. Doesn't mean it's impossible, though. If the spell is laid by a supreme master."

"What about a single day. One single day? To raise a khamsin?"

"That I've definitely never heard of. Even Aanen himself couldn't raise a khamsin in a single day."

So much for that. Another blind alley. The khamsin must have been pure coincidence.

Yuti must have seen the look of disappointment on my face. "I'm sorry I'm not of greater help. It's a pity the pharaoh won't let you use torture. I'm sure it would make your job so much easi ˉruly, it seems most unreasonable to me."

That makes two of us. "I thank you for your concern, Yuti. I'm glad you understand the difficulty of my predicament. It's left me at a total loss regarding what on earth to do. But anyway, just a few more questions, if you don't mind. You were present when Akhenaten died, were you not?"

"Absolutely. And I will neither lie nor dissemble. I was delighted to see it happen."

I raised an eyebrow.

"The man killed my son, my only son. He killed my Paheri, my boy, my only boy." His eyes began watering, and I averted my face. "You've probably heard the story. Everyone in Thebes has heard it. Everyone in Egypt. I begged him to exempt Paheri from military service. Our family isn't warlike. None of us are. We serve our country better with our brains, with our family medical lore that has passed down from father to son since the beginning of time. Of what use did pharaoh have for another spear? But he wouldn't listen, and Paheri died. Worse than that, died in disgrace. The man ruined this family—extinguished our line. I felt no sorrow for his end."

"Yes, Yuti," I said quietly, "indeed I have heard something of this."

"There's more," he went on, as though he were talking to himself. "More that's less well known. It wasn't just Paheri. It was Chamartea too. My sister Chamartea. Pharaoh could have any woman in Egypt he wanted. Any woman he wanted. But he took Chamartea. Not as a wife, not as a concubine, not even as a mistress. He just *took* her. He didn't even want her. She wasn't pretty— quite the opposite, though she had the nature of an angel. He took her just because he was pharaoh. A lark. A whim. To show his power. She conceived." Yuti's face was suffused with a great sorrow. "She couldn't live with the disgrace. She killed herself." He paused, collecting himself, then continued, "No, I bore no affection for Akhenaten. If he was murdered, praise be the murderer. I say that openly. Now as for his son Tut, that's a different matter altogether. Tut is a fine young man and Egypt is lucky to have him on the throne."

This was my grandson he was talking about. And I doubt Yuti even made the connection concerning my relationship. He didn't seem the sort that would even perceive the niceties of social connections.

"You truly admire Tut?" I inquired, with an effort keeping the astonishment from my voice.

"Of course. He's always treated me and my family with utmost respect. He promotes my medical researches and encourages me to train new physicians in the healing arts. He genuinely reveres our ancient gods. He's restored prosperity to our land, and civil order. May he live forever."

I breathed a heavy sigh. So this was how people thought. Didn't Yuti realize *I* was the one who had restored prosperity and civil order to Egypt? Didn't he know *I* was the one who had taken over an empty treasury and a strife-torn land and restored it to some semblance of its former greatness? Well, Horemheb too, but for the most part, I. Still and all, I was surprised that Tut apparently had treated Yuti kindly. Maybe there was a side to my grandson I had never seen. But that wasn't important now. I had other things to do.

"Did you kill Akhenaten?" I asked directly, in my most prosecutorial manner, looking Yuti as fiercely in the eye as I could. It was a look that had made many a criminal grovel in despair. I hoped that the sudden, direct assault might disconcert Yuti, throw him into confusion. I was wrong.

Yuti smiled his benign, rabbit smile back. "If you can't torture me, even a Yuti would never be fool enough to answer that question 'yes.' But truly, I wish you well in your endeavors."

So much for Yuti, and my hopes for being able to browbeat something of value from him. I saw no point in pursuing matters further. He'd told me all I was going to learn, which was far, far less than I had hoped.

As I was about to leave, he brought me to an abrupt halt with a totally unexpected remark. "And I hope Queen Ankhesenamun is better."

Incongruously, the first thought that hit my mind was that indeed he was aware of my family relationships, and had said what he had said about Tut anyway. Remarkable. But I immediately realized this wasn't the case. I instantly set all that aside. Absolutely the next thought was about my granddaughter. "What are you talking about?" I barked sharply. "What's wrong with Queen Ankhesenamun?"

He looked at me with his watery eyes, all apologetic. "Oh. I'm sorry. I thought you knew. She's ill."

"Seriously ill?"

"I think not. At least not anymore. I'm sorry I'm not with her, but Tut insisted that I come here with him, so I had to leave her in the hands of my apprentice. He's a very fine lad," Yuti hastily assured me, "and has the touch. He'll be a better doctor than I am one day. I only had time to give her the most cursory inspection before Tut made me leave. I had no time for any diagnosis."

"What troubles her?"

"A fever. A high fever. It came upon her that night, the night of the audience, and by morning she was quite ill. I ordered Wenamun—my apprentice—to stay with her day and night, to let no one save him and her most trusted servants into her room. And by that I meant absolutely no one. Not even her mother. I would have ordered that the king himself be forbidden her room, but he was with me here in Karnak, so that wasn't necessary."

"She's better now?"

"Yes. Recovering nicely. So I'm informed. I get daily reports from Wenamun, and her fever's almost normal."

"Why did you order her isolated?"

"Just a precaution. I've learned a lot, serving the royal family."

"You suspect poison?"

"Not anymore. Not deliberate poisoning. Food poisoning, more likely."

"Did anyone else get sick?"

"No, but it happens that way sometimes with food poisoning. Just a small portion of the food might have been tainted. In any event, she seems to be almost back to normal."

I shook my head in disgust. My little Ankhy sick, really sick, and I so wrapped up in this absurd quest I hadn't even had the time to know about it.

I glanced at the sundial in the courtyard. Time to leave. Hours were getting increasingly precious. I bade farewell to Yuti, but not before managing to extract from him one last thing of great value.

I stopped on the way back to my palace to look in on the most expensive jeweler in Thebes. I really didn't have the time, but I wanted to order something for Tey before it slipped my mind. She'd more than earned it—and not just because of Yennah. Forty years of marriage do, in the end, count for something. It took the better part of an hour to find precisely the bracelet I thought would do. I have an excellent eye for style. The jeweler assured me that the design I selected was finer by far than anything owned by the pharaoh himself. For once I decided to hell with the pharaoh's petty jealousies, and I ordered it for immediate delivery. My holdings of gold would be somewhat reduced when the bauble was ready, but as Tey kept telling me, I already had more than enough.

My terrible mission continued to thrust all other thoughts from my mind. The irony—the supreme irony—of the whole thing was that after my investigations, after all my work, I rather admired each of those on my list more than I had before all this began. Horemheb. Nefertiti. Aanen. Yuti. I of course hadn't had a chance to talk with my dear little Ankhy yet, but how could I possibly think less of her? The whole situation was a supreme mockery. Whoever killed Akhenaten did Egypt a mighty favor, and certainly Tut as well. It was hard to imagine that the murderer really intended doing Tut a favor, but that was the inevitable by-product. If I succeed, I must expose this murderer. What happens then is a certainty, and the one who did the deed, the one who should have risen to immortality, shall suffer such a death as only Tut can imagine. On the other hand, if I fail, or if I learn the identity of the killer but withhold it from Tut, my own life will probably be forfeit. My fortune and my stature, absolutely. I was increasingly beginning to realize that as this was playing out, the end was getting far more complex than I'd originally envisioned, and that the consequences of Tut's rather childish little scheme were apt to be far more extreme, far more unanticipated, than either he or I had realized.

Still and all, there were now but two days left to me. Could I, by even a remote chance, find a way to spare Akhenaten's killer and at the same time be spared myself? A peculiar question, I know. Spare a killer. Yet by all accounts, including mine, the victim deserved to die far more than the culprit. Odd. Why couldn't Tut have just left the whole thing alone? Or was I again making the error of underestimating him? Perhaps I was letting my dislike for him get in the way of my judgment. His game might be far more devious, more clever than I'd even begun to suspect. If that was true, Tut might turn out to be an excellent pharaoh after all, once he matured.

Once I reached my palace I made it a point to go to my room as quickly as possible. I needed rest, and time for uninterrupted thought. You might think I'd have had enough of rest and thought by now. Not so. I'm an old man. I need the rest. And as for the thought, when someone is trying to kill you for solving a problem, and someone is almost certainly going to kill you for not solving it, the entire matter becomes something of an obsession.

I was on my bed but a few minutes when, without knocking, Yennah quietly slipped inside. I was annoyed. I wasn't annoyed. By Seti, she was magnificent for a girl not yet fifteen. She was magnificent by any standards. Now that she once more was here in person, in the flesh, so to speak, she was even more entrancing than my overheated mental visions. Still and all, how had she been able to get in so easily? There were, after all, two guards at my door. This was serious. If Yennah could get past them so easily, who else might do the same?

She came over to me, and her self-confidence and poise were absolutely astonishing in one so young. "I'm so glad you're back," she cooed throatily, and that husky voice sent shivers up my spine. "I've missed you, Eye. Really missed you." She reached out a hand, a soft, rose-petal-smooth hand, and gently stroked my face. I really wasn't in the mood for this. But you know how men are. In another instant I was.

I was going to ask her how she'd managed to get in, but knew I already had the answer. This is how palaces are. No doubt everyone knew of my—what might the word for it be?—*involvement* with this girl. I could think of no better one. It's truly amazing about females. Once they're perceived as being in some sort of relationship, they immediately start taking things for granted, and everyone else in the palace does the same thing.

"Aren't you happy to see me too?" she inquired kittenishly, trying to give an appearance of artlessness that almost, but not quite, succeeded. "I told the guards you wanted to see me the moment you got back, so here I am." She giggled.

There you have it. Here I am, grand vizier of all Egypt, and here she is, nothing but a slave girl, yet she assumes on the strength of nothing but sheer physical passion she's able to move back and forth between her station and mine at will. At her will, not mine. And the guards, knowing the palace gossip, simply let her in without question. What if she'd had a knife in the folds of her gown?

Those guards were going to hear from me. No matter how tight you try to maintain security, in the end your safety depends on men who wouldn't be guards if they had the brains to rise to a higher station.

"You had no right to say that to my guards," I answered in stern rebuke. "You've caused those men to be in really serious trouble."

It was scarce worth the effort. She ignored me. She fixed me with those incredible, almost violet eyes, all heavily made up and accented, and she moved even nearer, her right breast rubbing against my arm, and the gentle stroking of my face never stopped. Her perfume permeated my room, and her natron-sweetened breath touched my nostrils as she lightly placed a kiss, soft as papyrus in spring, upon my cheek, a kiss so soft it was impossible to know if it had really brushed my face.

"Have you found out anything?" she continued, and her smile grew ever more languid. "Anything at all?"

"About what?"

"You know about what. Don't be a tease. You know exactly about what." She pouted prettily, her lower lip thrust forward in mock dismay. I could feel the rise and fall of her breast against my arm, and I could see the spins and swirls of that incredible golden hair as it fell about her shoulders. Yennah was amazing. I knew exactly what she was doing, yet it made no difference. How do females learn all this so young?

"I have rather disappointing news for you, my dear," I said unhurriedly, and in a certain way rather enjoyed giving her her comeuppance. "I've visited with the High Priest of Amun at great length, and no one, not even a pharaoh, can set aside a principal wife without just cause. The typical just cause is adultery, but there's no hint of that in Tey's case, so I'm afraid the thing just can't be done. So there's an end of it."

Why was I even discussing this with Yennah? Why was I humoring her? Disposing of Tey had been all her idea. Yet here I was, pretending to give the whole thing consideration. And then there was that odd episode in the Temple of Karnak. What was going on here? Was I going to be led inexorably down a path I really didn't want to follow, by a determined, clever girl who knew her sexual power over me and knew how to use it? Seeing is one thing, resisting quite another. I guess that's why it's called temptation. Yennah pouted at this unwelcome news, and this time it wasn't in mock dismay. She thought about the matter for a while, a very short while. For just the briefest instant I caught a glimpse of the real Yennah, a look of granite on that lovely face, before she recomposed her features into a soft and honeyed facade.

"Well," she pronounced, with remarkable calm, "if you can't, you can't. That's that. I'm sure you looked into the matter thoroughly." She seemed to have taken the news quite well, had I not caught that one unguarded expression on her face.

"Most thoroughly," I assured her soothingly. "Searched back centuries for precedents. There aren't any. It simply isn't done."

She very lightly, with an almost feline grace, slipped out of her gown. Her body glistened, and I could feel my eyes widen as I once more gazed upon its glories. She again insinuated herself against me, and her fingers began making new explorations. "If there's not one way, then perhaps there's another," she whispered into my ear, stretching ever so sinuously full-length against me.

"What way?" I asked, trying my best not to get distracted, and succeeding none too well.

"There's always a way." Her husky voice was heavy-laden, pregnant with meaning. "If you want something badly enough, there's always a way. Particularly for a grand vizier. If you want it badly enough, you'll do it."

I didn't want to give credence to what I'd just heard. I sat bolt upright and pushed her sharply away. My hand left an imprint on her flesh, and the touch flashed through me like a lightning bolt. "You're suggesting," I bellowed, hoping to break my own mood, hoping to terrify her, "you're actually suggesting that I kill Tey? The woman I've been married to for forty years? This is unbelievable!"

"I didn't say that!"

"You didn't have to. That's exactly what you meant."

"I DIDN'T SAY THAT."

"It doesn't matter. It's never going to happen. I ought to whip your rump and toss you out to the guards for their amusement!"

My indignation was genuine. This girl was unbelievable. I thought the royal court of Egypt was corrupt. What must the royal court of Corinth be like, if this not quite fifteen-year-old princess could so calmly and dispassionately propose the murder of my principal wife?

Yennah went on as though my dismissing her proposal for murdering my wife was nothing more than a minor setback, perhaps just a whim on my part, to be reconsidered at a later date. She had the face and form of a goddess, but a will of polished bronze. Nothing fazed her. So here she was in my room, a truly flawless beauty, kittenish, but with the heart and compassion of a tigress.

"Let's not quarrel," she continued, purring. "We mustn't quarrel. Just think about things. That's all I'm asking. Just think about things." She stood up full-length before me, her shoulders back entrancingly. I looked. "I'd make ever so much better a principal wife for you than Tey. Tey's old. She's worn out. She has no ambition for you anymore. She's content to live out her days, and yours, locked up in this palace, doing nothing, and dragging you into isolation until, by the time you die, no one will even remember you ever lived. I'm not like that, Eye. I have ambition enough for both of us. You needn't be the number-two man in Egypt. Truly you needn't. You can just as easily be number one. In fact, you've no choice. I've told you this before, and you know I'm right. Either you'll be pharaoh or you'll be dead. You've not much time."

Carrying on a political conversation with a stark-naked beauty is an unsettling proposition. Every word she uttered was an outrage, yet I could feel my brain disengaging, slipping away. Will anyone argue that this was a most bizarre situation for the Grand Vizier of Egypt to find himself in? I suspect not. Would anyone, if he could see the naked Yennah, opt to be elsewhere—would he order her from the room? I suspect not also.

This bi-level situation was an intense strain. It would have been laughable had anyone else but I been right in the center of it. I wanted Yennah. Yennah wanted me. Not true. Yennah wanted power, and to get the power, she had to get me. She was giving it a most remarkable try, all things considered. And I'll give her this: she was proposing action, concrete, specific action. Her keen mind was cutting straight through to the heart of things. For that I give her credit.

She returned to her theme, with the barest flicker of annoyance. "It boils down to one simple fact. Like it or not, either you kill Tut, or Tut kills you. I'm right. You know I'm right. You just need somebody like me to make it all come clear."

"I'm not a regicide, Yennah."

"Then you're a suicide!" She pressed herself full against me, and began removing my robes. I made no move to stop her, and soon I was as bare as she. Of the two of us, she was by far the more attractive.

I reached for her, all thought of palace intrigue beginning to slip irreversibly from my mind. "Not yet, master," she whispered. "Not just yet. Think this through with me. I'm more than a silly girl, you know. Much more. Hearken to me. Tey has taken away your drive. I can bring it back. Together we can rule this land, rule it gloriously. But we must act, and swiftly. Tey has robbed you of your will to act. She's made you an old man before your time. I can make you young again. All you have to do is act, and act swiftly."

With a mighty effort of will I forced myself to address this peculiar situation. Her entire mind was set on power. My entire mind had abdicated, and I was obsessively, compulsively pursuing something else. Clearly, the two of us were at serious cross-purposes here.

In an agony of impatience I forced myself to keep the conversation alive for just a few minutes more. "Yennah," I said, not wanting to anger her but very much wanting her to understand the stark truth of the matter, "you're incredibly lovely, but still and all, you're not even fifteen yet. I know more about these matters than you do." I put both arms around her waist and pulled her firmly against me. What a sensation! She didn't even try to resist. But her honeyed voice could now whisper directly into my ear.

"I know more than you can imagine about affairs of state. I may be not quite fifteen, but all my life has been spent in a royal palace. I told you that before. I told you my name wasn't Yennah—that's as close as those oafs of yours could come to my real name. My real name is Helen. I'm a true princess, a princess royal. My destiny is to rule. I want to rule here, in Egypt, the most powerful, the most advanced, the most cultured, the most civilized nation in the world. I want you to rule with me. What a fantastic team we'll make! With your experience and skill and brains, and my drive and ambition and—I don't hesitate to say it—beauty, we can between us make Egypt master of all the lands surrounding the Great Green. It's in our grasp. You have to seize your moment. Tut leaves you no choice. You know that. I know that." She continued to undulate her glorious body against mine, and my response was increasingly evident to see. The girl was most persuasive.

"Tut's done you an enormous favor," she went on determinedly. "The chance has always been there. He's just forcing you to take it. Think about it, Eye. Think about it carefully. Strike! Make yourself pharaoh! Live forever! Be the god yourself, not just his vizier. Be a god after you die. What real man would do otherwise if he had the chance?"

I don't think I could have talked if I'd wanted to. It didn't matter. She was doing it quite nicely all by herself. And much of it made sense. "I want to be your queen," she continued fervently, and those incredible violet eyes of hers glistened. I wasn't born to be a slave girl. I was *born* to be queen. And had I not been captured by that pirate ship, at this very moment my father would be marrying me off to Minlos, and I'd be a true queen as we speak. But the very gods willed it that I be brought here, to a destiny far greater than the rule of a primitive rock pile in a fragment of Greece. *This* is my destiny, and yours. Between us we can make of Egypt an empire such as the world has never seen before. This is our moment. We must seize it, Eye, we must seize it. Together. The gods give mortals but a single chance like this."

[*Translator's note: I was so caught up in the, shall we say, imagery of this passage that I almost made the most egregious error of my entire academic career. My eye nearly skipped over the passage about "Minlos," king of a small state in Greece. But the word, several sentences later, must have struck some subconscious chord with me, for I suddenly and excitedly went back to it. I studied the hieroglyphic with intense closeness and excitement, but could extract from it nothing more than "Minlos." But this ravishingly beautiful girl had revealed her name to be* Helen. *Could that of the king waiting to marry her be* Menelaus? *For one whose entire life has been spent in the study of the ancient world, one even as burned out as I, the possibility that I had unearthed a manuscript proving the historical existence of Helen of Troy excited me, thrilled me, moved me more deeply than anything I had previously experienced in my entire life. And if indeed "Yennah" were to prove to be Helen of Troy, one can at once understand how Eye must have been overwhelmed by her presence. One can both sympathize with the man, and envy him.*]

"It's not all that simple," I managed to croak out, "plotting a coup. It takes time, and resources, and coordination. I have but two days left, and Horemheb stands in the scales against me, with an infantry force that outnumbers my horse by a staggering proportion. There's more to this than the mere death of a king. And mind you," I hastened to add, "I've agreed with nothing. The king is, after all, my grandson."

Yennah—Helen—pulled me ever closer to her, and her lips played about mine, and her tongue teased mine too. For one so young, her skills were truly impressive. "Last time I gave you a sample," she murmured. "This time you may have more. Not all. But more."

# 17

## DAY

## FIVE

## —

## EVENING

**G**et rid of that Greek slut! I won't have her under the same roof with me another minute! Not another minute!"

I've been married to Tey for forty years and never, ever have I seen her more angry. "What slut?" I countered warily.

"You know what slut!"

"Oh, *that* slut."

This is exactly what I need. I have important matters to discuss with Tey—she's the one person I can always count on. Before I was able to step a foot halfway into her bedchamber, however, this was the greeting I got. Good thing the jewelry I'd ordered for her wasn't ready yet. I sensed this wouldn't be a propitious moment to give it to her.

"I know everything. Everything! I want that Greek whore out of my palace this instant!" Tey wasn't kidding. I've seen that look on her face before.

"You're being redundant. You already said that." This did nothing to improve her frame of mind. She was quite literally hopping up and down, and since she had gout in her right toe I knew how painful this must be for her. Her face was contorted, and she sputtered. Her hands were fists, and her uncombed hair flew in tangles all over her face as she stormed at me as though ready to hit. I'd rather face crocodile-headed Min than face Tey in one of these moods. Luckily, they're rare.

I knew the source of her rage before she had a chance to say it. Not that that would stop her, of course. I knew I'd just have to wait her out, like a sandstorm. I also knew none of this had anything to do with sex. Tey couldn't have cared less about that. In fact, as far as she was concerned, the more young girls I had, the better, as long as I didn't bother her. No, sex definitely wasn't the issue here.

"That Yennah tramp of yours is trying to take my place—*my place*—after forty years. Forty years!" As you'll note, Tey does have a tendency to repeat herself when she gets worked up. I closed my eyes wearily and waited for more. Not for a moment did I doubt there'd be more. And there was.

"She has you groveling at her feet! Groveling! Why, if she ordered it, you'd get down on all fours and let her put a leash around your neck. You'd bark like a dog if she ordered it. You, Grand Vizier of Egypt, a lapdog for that slave-slut! It's a disgrace. And don't think everyone in the palace doesn't know all about it!"

Tey's imagery was rather imaginative and, in fact, provocative. I thought about Helen, the leash, the groveling—maybe even a whip? I don't think that reaction was what Tey had in mind.

Fortunately for me Tey couldn't read my mind, at least not precisely. "It's bad enough you humiliate yourself. That's your business. But humiliating me! That's something altogether different. I know you've promised that bitch she'd be principal wife. Principal wife! Well, *I'm* principal wife, and if you've forgotten it, I haven't. And there's nothing you or that [*Translator's note: Here I leave Tey's torrent of abuse untranslated. It's truly shocking for a woman of her time. Where did she hear such words?*]——can do about it."

It would be charitable to attribute this entire tiresome episode to Helen's youth and indiscretion, but not so. It would have been the same if she were twice her age. Women, for all their virtues, are simply incapable of putting a lock on their tongues. The gods made them that way. Helen had simply been unable to let her ambitions stay sealed in her own head. She just *had* to confide them to someone. In absolute, total secrecy, of course. And within minutes, ear by ear and tongue by tongue, Helen's thoughts had become Tey's knowledge.

I never relished being with the normally docile Tey when she flew into one of these rages. Who would? Sometimes they were irrational, but not this time. This time she was entitled. But why take it out on me? I hadn't even slept with Helen. Not yet, anyway. Technically. And that wasn't the point anyway. All this was Helen's doing. Was it my fault Helen had these big ambitions? I'd done nothing to encourage them. Still, the bill of sale for Helen was made out to me, so I suppose I really was the only one Tey could yell at.

I knew placating Tey wouldn't be easy, that I'd have to wait and let her run down, but I still had to make an effort. "Look, Tey," I said as soothingly as possible, and right away I could see my soothing tone was only irritating her more, "nobody can replace you as principal wife. You know that. I couldn't if I wanted to. Which I don't. Yennah (Tey didn't know her real name was Helen, and I didn't want to go into that just now) is just a girl—immature, flighty. You know how young girls are. All full of wild ideas and crazy dreams, always fantasizing. Why are you taking it so seriously? She's just a slave girl, and all she'll ever be is a slave girl. There's nothing here to be blown out of proportion, and still you're blowing it out of proportion."

"What kind of a grandfather are you!" she shouted angrily, so worked up that the corner of her right eye began to twitch.

Where did this come from? The sudden switch brought my mind to a numbing halt.

"You know what I mean!" she railed. "You couldn't wait to come home and screw your little Greek. And all the while our little Ankhy dying there in the royal palace!"

"Ankhy dying?" I exploded, suddenly deeply and totally concerned. "Ankhy dying! I was told she was much improved!"

"Well," Tey responded, sullen, averting her face, "for all you knew she could have been. For all you care. All you wanted was to play dirty sex games with that Yennah of yours. You didn't even ask about Ankhy. What kind of grandfather are you?"

"I didn't ask because I knew she was nearly well. Tey, I'm really getting annoyed at this." I put on as stern a face as I could. I'm the man, after all. Wives don't talk to their husbands like this. Not in Egypt. I was willing to make a few concessions for the forty years, but enough was enough.

"Look, Tey, I've come here to ask your help about something. If you want to argue with me, we can do it later. If I let you. But I haven't time for the rest of this now. I only have time for one thing. I have just two days left. Two days exactly. Two days from this very moment. That's it. And I still don't know who killed Akhenaten. In fact, I don't know an awful lot more than I did at the beginning. A bit here, a piece there. That's all."

"You've talked to all of them and learned nothing?"

"Nothing much. I'll tell you all I've found out. Maybe you can help me get on the right track." I was pleased she'd accepted the change of subject. The prospect of my being deposed or dead in two days' time did after all have priority of consideration. I didn't even correct her by pointing out I hadn't had a chance to visit with Ankhesenamun yet. As you'll remember, Tey very firmly refused to allow that either Ankhesenamun or Nefertiti could be suspect in the matter. I saw no point in getting involved in another quarrel by insisting that I couldn't look at it that way.

"Tell me all you've learned," she said. I was delighted she seemed to have dropped the Yennah matter so quickly. "Tell me again, everything you've learned since the start, and everything you found out at the Temple of Karnak. Try not to leave out anything. You know how you are, Eye. You skip over the details. Sometimes it's the details that are the key."

I complied. Tey had an amazing mind. She had superb intuition. She had the knack of being able to pick things up out of the air—subtleties, nuances. I wouldn't want to try to make a living fooling Tey. Hardly anything ever escaped her, and she exposed liars as fast as a cobra strikes. *Never* mess around with Tey.

I reviewed everything with her. It took time. She questioned. She probed. She interrogated. She inquired. All this was fine with me. I needed all the help I could get.

I saved what I felt was the most vital bit of information for the last. "I had a dream last night," I said flatly. "A very peculiar dream. I haven't been able to figure it out. Other than the Hebarews, who are the best dream interpreters in Thebes?" I knew she'd know much more about such matters than I would.

"A dream? A dream? That could be significant. Tell me about it."

Tey had had luck with dreams before. I would have told her anyway, of course, but I suddenly realized that in all likelihood my very own principal wife might well be the best dream interpreter I could find. More than once she'd shown me she had the knack, and certainly nobody in Thebes was more highly motivated.

"It was incredibly real," I began. "You know how some dreams are. They're, well, *dreamy* even while you're having them. This one wasn't like that. In fact, I was amazed that it happened at all, since I would have sworn I hadn't even fallen asleep."

"So what happened?"

"Well, I was getting ready to go to bed—the lamps in the room were still lit—when I looked down and saw this kitten on the floor."

"A kitty-cat? You saw a kitty-cat?"

"Yes. A kitten. A kitty-cat."

"What color?"

"Black. Pure black. With a little white on the front paws."

Tey pondered this. "Color could be important. Sometimes yes, sometimes no. Go on."

"I looked at it, and suddenly I saw a baby crocodile wriggling across the room right next to the kitten."

"All right. I'm working on it already." She sighed, and gave me a very pointed look.

"Eye?"

"Yes?"

"Get rid of the slut."

# 18

## DAY SIX — MORNING

It was a perfect morning. The day dawned clear and cloudless. It was pleasant and cool, but in another hour, as the sun rose higher in the sky, it would become seriously hot. Every day in Thebes is like this.

I prepared to make my way to the royal palace, and my heart was heavy. Maybe I've outlived my time. I'm an old man. I've served Egypt well, and done well for myself in the process. In the end, all men find their way to their House of Truth. Would it not be better if I were already in mine, with my reputation intact and no fear that my name be excised from all my works by some vengeful pharaoh?

Maybe I'm just cranky. I can't remember the last time I've had an untroubled night's sleep. After all this is over, a vacation. That's what I need, a vacation, at my villa on the shores of the Great Green. The thought buoyed me, but only slightly.

I was buoyed more by the thought of seeing my little Ankhy, my firstborn grandchild, my sweet little Ankhy. Although the royal palace is close to my own, I rarely get to see her. Even when I am in the royal palace itself, I seldom see her. For the most part she is secluded in the harem section, and in the heavy press of business—I am embarrassed to confess—more often than not I let other matters take me away without taking the time to call upon her. In this my melancholy state of mind I felt genuine regret for those wasted opportunities. I've let time and opportunity slip by, a little each day, and suddenly I've reached the point where I finally recognize that time is more precious than gold, only to discover that my supply of time has almost all been spent.

Was it truly possible that Ankhy might have murdered her father? It was difficult to imagine, yet I had to take that contingency into consideration. She had the opportunity, as did all the others I've been pursuing. And she had a most powerful reason. Other than the generalized welfare of Egypt, which would be reason enough for anyone, Ankhesenamun would be Queen of Egypt upon the death of her father, and with Tut but a child of ten, would have the opportunity, should she make the most of it, of truly exerting her influence in affairs of state.

The only problem with this hypothesis was that Akhenaten indeed had died. Ankhesenamun had indeed become Queen of Egypt. She had remained passive, had quietly accepted her subordinate status as befitted her gender, and made no effort at all to interfere in the workings of the kingdom. Even with Horemheb and me as co-regents, I would think that if indeed that was what she had in mind, she would have done *something* to exert influence. I could remember no single time when she did. Perhaps she had reasons of which I knew not. Of all those who might have accomplished the king's death, I wished most fervently that it not prove to be little Ankhy.

Knowing my granddaughter, of all those who had the opportunity to kill the pharaoh, Ankhy would be the only one apt to commit such a horrible crime without reason for personal gain, but only for the general good of Egypt and its suffering people. Ankhy is kind, generous, and genuinely good—good in heart, good in nature, in a way rarely seen in human beings, at least in those I've encountered in this lifetime. It was almost impossible for me to conjure a picture of Ankhy either personally or through a surrogate under her instructions actually accomplishing the death of anyone. And yet, given how Akhenaten had disrupted every aspect of his country's life, had caused so much hardship and misery, had been so depraved in his Aten-obsession . . . If indeed Ankhy had caused his death, she alone would, I believe, upon being asked why, say, "I did it for Egypt."

I arrived at the royal palace at the earliest possible hour, making allowances for the time it would take Ankhy to prepare herself for the day. Contrary to Tey's rebuke, I was truly very concerned about my granddaughter. What had happened to her? Why had she become so ill, right after the audience? Nobody else had. Might someone be trying to poison her? Why? As you can see, these days poison was very much on my mind. After being offered a poisoned cup from an apparently innocent hand, the possibility of poison lingers strongly on the mind.

Ankhesenamun greeted me affectionately, throwing herself into my arms and hugging me tightly to her body, covering my cheeks with kisses. But unlike Nefertiti, this was but a spontaneous display of genuine familial love, nothing more. Her voice had a genuine ring of joy in it upon seeing me, a lilt that I hear from no other, not even Tey. My little Ankhy is quite pretty and, at twenty-five, a fully mature woman. Her hair is dark, shiny, and lustrous, and her dark eyes dance with life. Though she is now indeed a woman, she sparkles and bubbles with energy and animation as though still in her teens. When she is fully well, that is.

Although I have to admit that in terms of pure physical beauty Helen by far would win the competition, in terms of purity of nature Helen wouldn't even be at the starting line. My Ankhy is one of those blessed beings that has a genuine warmth of heart. Everyone loves her—male and female; officials, tradespeople, servants.

Nothing she ever says leaves her lips in calculation. Her heart is a happy one, a gift of the gods far more precious than gold.

I pushed her away from me and looked at her closely. She seemed fine—a trifle pale, but otherwise fine. Her eyes were quieter than usual, but I took that to be the lingering effect of her illness.

I then noticed a man in the room. He stood quietly in a corner, making no effort to be seen, nor any effort to join Ankhy and me. I assumed he was Yuti's assistant, but he made no attempt to introduce himself, which is only proper, given the lowliness of his station. For the moment I ignored him.

"Are you well, Ankhy?" I asked. A not very original question, but my worry was genuine.

"Quite well now, Grandfather." In her turn she scrutinized me most carefully. "You look tired," she said. "Please do sit down. Yes, you look tired. And your face is drawn. You really must start taking better care of yourself. You're the only grandfather I have left, you know."

The nice part about this is that I absolutely know that her care and concern are genuine. How often can a man say that?

She didn't wait for a response, knowing that her observations really didn't call for one. "Grandfather," she continued, "I know why you look so worn-out. I know it's all Tut's fault. This whole thing is stupid—that's the only word for it, stupid. I've begged him to tell you he was only joking about finding Father's murderer all these years later. If there even was a murderer, which, until Tut started all this, really never seriously entered my mind. It's monstrous of him, and I've told him so. He should know without my telling him that you're getting too old for this sort of game."

She had given me the opening and I seized it. I would have done so in some manner anyway, but this made it appear natural. "Ankhy," I said, and rather hated myself for saying it, since it almost might seem a betrayal of her husband, "has Tut confided in you what all this is really about? If you know anything that might be useful, it would be an enormous help. You're absolutely right— this has been an enormous strain on me and I don't know how much more stress like this I can handle. Anything you can tell me—any little thing at all—could really be useful to me."

She shook her head. Her dark eyes clouded. I hated to see her sad, even for my sake. "Tut tells me nothing. He rarely if ever sees me, which is just fine as far as I'm concerned. The less the better. Anytime I ask him anything, he always dismisses me as a mindless woman unfit to even begin to understand affairs of state. And it's not so much that he says it, but the *way* he says it. So much contempt in his voice. And each day it seems to get worse. I wish I could help you, Grandfather, truly I do. If I knew anything at all, you know I'd help you with it. But I just don't."

She bowed her head slightly, but even in sadness the corners of her lips had difficulty turning down. It simply was Ankhy's nature to be buoyant. I knew for certain that she and Tut couldn't possibly have the same father. The man who had sired this delightful girl could never have fathered Tut. Once more I found this an oddly comforting thought.

With an inclination of my head I indicated the man in the corner. "Wenamun?" I asked.

She nodded, her short, straight black hair shimmering back and forth, bouncing. Her eyes lit up when they rested upon him, and her lips broke into the smile that almost always resided there. I could see the profile of her pert pointed chin and tiny upturned nose, the slim, demure, petite body. The old familiar joy at the presence of this my favorite grandchild came welling freely into my heart.

"Wenamun," she said in soft invitation, "please step over here. I'd like you to meet my grandfather."

Wenamun, clad all in black, and in every respect a perfectly ordinary specimen of humanity, walked toward us hesitantly, and as he drew near me, started to grovel the ritual grovel. With a movement of my hand I stopped him. "No need for that, Wenamun. This isn't a formal occasion." I turned once more to Ankhy. "Are you pleased with his treatment of you?"

"Most pleased, Grandfather. I couldn't have asked for better care. He's been with me day and night ever since I grew ill. With my maidservants always here too," she added hastily. "Please tell

Yuti how professionally he served me. It does Yuti honor to have such a splendid apprentice. I shall tell him so myself next I have the chance."

I bowed to Wenamun, a brief bow from the waist. "Wenamun," I said sincerely, "you have my deepest thanks for the care you have given my granddaughter. Be certain that I'll also commend you personally to Yuti the very first opportunity I have. But tell me," I went on, "was Ankhy truly in any danger?"

Wenamun nodded gravely. "Indeed she was. She was stricken almost the moment the audience was over. Her fever ran quite high, and my most powerful potions could do little to check it. I'm but an apprentice, of course, and my experience is limited. Between you and me—and I hope I get myself in no trouble by saying this—Yuti himself should have been here, but Tut would have none of it. The gods are kind to one of so fine a nature as Queen Ankhesenamun, for I was able to find the right chants to cause her fever to break. I'm sure Yuti would have done it all much, much quicker."

"Do you suspect poison?"

Wenamun looked genuinely shocked. "Poison? Who would want to poison the queen?"

"Nevertheless, Wenamun, is poison a possibility?"

He gave the question his best professional consideration. "Possible? I suppose. When I see Yuti I can ask him—his experience in these matters is so much greater than mine. Some poisons do cause high fevers. But there are so many natural events that cause high fevers, I find it difficult to isolate poison as the cause. In my experience—and once more I emphasize how limited it is—the queen suffered from a condition quite compatible with various natural sicknesses. In my limited knowledge there is no poison comes to mind that would act in the precise manner of the queen's illness."

"I thank you for your thoughts, Wenamun. And let me ask you, did you indeed stay with the queen all the time until the sickness passed? All the time?"

The man was genuinely shocked. "Of course, sir," he replied instantly, deeply offended. "The lady is Queen of Egypt. Would I desert her, even for an instant, until she was fully recovered?"

"And what of her maidservants? Did they approach her? Speak to her? Touch her?"

"Never. Not until she was almost entirely well. Believe me, your worship, at the height of her illness the queen was not of a mind to speak to anyone, even me. I personally supervised the preparations of her meals, right here in this chamber, and selected only those items which would be most gentle on her stomach. Other than wiping her brow with damp cloths and bathing her body in cool water from time to time, the maidservants never touched her. And they neither spoke with her nor gave her food or drink of any kind. And," he added in a voice edged in bitterness, "the king never once called to see her, nor did he send inquiries. I suppose I am taking a risk to say these things, but, your worship, I truly cannot understand how any man could neglect this lady once he'd had the privilege of being in her company."

Wenamun was indeed a lucky man. Only a half minute later, without any preamble or notification, Tut himself came into the room. Had he arrived the least bit earlier, Wenamun's head would now be decorating a royal palace gate pole. We all audibly gasped at his entrance, apparently not loud enough for him to hear.

"And how are you this morning, Ankhy?" he growled, though it was obvious he really didn't care, since he turned to me without waiting for a reply. "And you, Grandfather, how are you? Well, I trust." Then he frowned a deep, foreboding frown. "I'm disappointed in you, though. Most disappointed." Those cunning eyes of his narrowed, and I could tell he was going to enjoy this session. His dress was completely informal—rare for Tut, even when lounging about his own palace—and without his ceremonial robes he looked even smaller. He had the beginning of a mustache and beard—apparently finally being able to grow them—but they did nothing to enhance his appearance. They were scrawny, thin, and droopy. Pitiful things, really. Lifeless. He'd be well advised to be rid of them. And his voice grated. Or maybe it wasn't his voice, just my attitude toward him.

"Grandfather," Tut continued, and the way he said "Grandfather" was a taunt. He was the sort of man who could say "good morning" and his tone of voice would make you want to punch him in the nose. "Grandfather," he said, "you've failed to keep me informed. I've received no reports from you. None whatsoever. I'd expected to hear from you daily with reports of your progress."

"I regret, Majesty (Life! Health! Strength!)"—how reluctantly those ritual words rose to my lips—"I regret having disappointed you, in even the slightest manner. Alas, time has been most pressing, as you may well imagine. Also, I have little of substance to report."

He looked at me with genuine sardonic glee. "Then you've failed me?" Clearly, he relished that failure. What was he up to? I was frantic to know.

"I have a day remaining," I responded somewhat brusquely. We weren't in court now, and in this informal setting I wasn't of a mind to crawl or abase myself, to offer him anything more than the absolute minimum respect due him in his capacity as king. "Somewhat more than a day," I pointed out. "And certain of my investigations have promise. Since my banquet is tomorrow evening, I would think your Most Powerful Personage (Life! Health! Strength!) would prefer that my report be something of a surprise. I have marvelous other entertainment, of course, but still and all, I'd rather hoped that my report on this entire affair could be the high point of the evening. I truly would hate to spoil it for you by giving away any of it now."

Tut considered this. I could read in those malicious eyes of his how much he was going to savor my public discomfiture. "Quite right, Eye. Since the banquet's tomorrow evening, might as well wait till then. I can wait another single day. But only one. Don't disappoint me, Eye. I'm counting on positive results. Positive, you understand." His voice was dry but heavy with threat. "Even though you're my grandfather, other men can be grand vizier. Never forget that for a moment."

He must really be ready for his reach for power. Never, ever had he spoken to me in that manner and tone of voice during all the years of the regency. I shouldn't have been surprised, but it came as a very unpleasant shock. I'd heard Tut's tone of voice with others, but never before had I been the target of it. Up till now he'd always known that with me as regent, anything he wanted needed my approval, so he'd never before used his tongue on me this way. I should have deposed the little toad years ago, when I had the chance, even if it had meant making Horemheb pharaoh. It would have been an unnatural act, deposing my own bloodline, but I should have done it. Well, it was too late now.

Tut turned to leave, but I restrained him for a moment. "Divine Ruler (Life! Health! Strength!), I have but one request for you. I'm returning to my palace shortly to supervise the final preparations for the banquet. May I take Narmer with me?"

Tut's eyes narrowed. They frequently narrowed. The man seemed to suspect everything and everyone, no matter what the request, what the inquiry. He waited a long time before replying. Then all he said was "Narmer? Why Narmer?"

"Because Narmer's the best there is. That's why he serves you. His palate is so sensitive it could search out a grain of salt in a ladle of pepper. I want this night to be perfect—for you, for my guests, for my own good name. Everything must be prepared to absolute perfection. Only Narmer can guarantee that. I shall require him only for the balance of this day and tomorrow. It would be a kindness for which I would be forever grateful."

Tut pondered the request. I knew his natural instinct would be to say no—what little joy he found in life he found in thwarting other people's hopes. But this time I was talking about the quality of the fare that he himself would be consuming.

"Very well, Eye," he conceded grudgingly. "But he returns to my palace the instant the meal is served."

"Of course."

Once more he turned and left the room. I was thrilled to have him gone. Did something of my own blood actually flow in that man's veins? It was an extremely disheartening thought. But I knew Tey had always been true to me. So there it was, and I'd have to live with it.

In fairness to Tut, I had to consider the possibility that my animosity perhaps was based on the fact that I've always known one day I'd give up power to him. Dispassionately considered, Tut had more reason to dislike me than I him, considering that I was thwarting his legitimate claims to the full power of his throne.

Maybe indeed I'd played the game too long, had stayed at the table too long, and now my wagers were being called in. If I were in Tut's position, would I have waited this long to act?

I turned my attentions back to Ankhy, preparing to follow the same line of questioning I had with the others. But as I looked at her, I simply couldn't do it. If she had done murder, I'd have to find out some other way.

"I'm sure Wenamun would prefer that you rest until you're fully recovered, so I'll be on my way. It's always such a pleasure seeing you, Ankhy, and a particular pleasure to see you so well along in your recovery. I do have a favor to ask. Would you please arrange for Narmer to be informed of my need for him, and instruct him that he is to present himself to me at my palace absolutely no later than the setting of the sun?"

"Of course, Grandfather. Consider it done." She skipped lightly toward me and placed a tender farewell kiss upon my cheek.

Ankhy. Little Ankhy. I knew not what the purpose was in my being placed upon this earth, but if it took my blood, to be mixed with that of others, to produce Ankhesenamun, then I have fulfilled my purpose.

I took my leave of Ankhy and departed from the royal palace. I had no idea how I was going to fulfill my boast to the pharaoh. On the other hand, there was not much harm in it either. If I failed, Tut would make whatever move he had in mind.

At that moment, I had no way of knowing how vital my request for Narmer's services would prove to be; how my very life hinged upon this man of the fastidious tongue, how my pride in providing impeccable viands for the gaggle of spoiled nobles and aristocrats who would gather at my palace tomorrow evening would be the event upon which the balance of my life would turn. The gods. Oh, the gods. How peculiarly they shape our lives.

# 19

## DAY SIX
## —
## AFTERNOON

I returned to my palace, thoughts spinning through my head. By now my head was so full of thoughts that, for each new one pushed in, another would have to be shoved out.

As soon as I came through the front door, I stiffened. I knew something was wrong, badly wrong. A person grows to sense this sort of thing about his own household, and I was certainly sensing it about mine.

Sentib, my majordomo, came up to me in a state of extreme agitation, wringing his hands, quite literally beside himself with nervous anxiety. "Master!" he shouted, which was a rarity in itself, since Sentib never, never shouted, no matter what the provocation. "What are we going to do? What are we going to do!"

I hated to find out what we had to do something about, but I had no choice. "About what, Sentib? About what?"

"About the banquet! About the madam. She went into her room early this afternoon, and she refuses to come out. There are a thousand decisions that still have to be made. Everything still has to be coordinated. I can't do it by myself. Madam always takes charge of these things. But she won't leave her room, and she won't talk to anyone. And we've so little time! What are we going to do!" The poor man was practically clawing at me in despair, and suddenly this became one too many things for my overtaxed brain to cope with.

Now I don't think it's being self-indulgent of me to point out that I've gone through quite a lot these last several days. Ever since that fateful audience with Tut, I've had to live with the specter of public humiliation, or removal from office, or mutilation of my body, or even death. You know, it's usually not the big things that get you. I've borne up rather well under all the stress and worry, if I do say so myself. But this was too much. Tey *always* fussed incessantly about every social event we put on, even the most trivial. And this was to be a state banquet, unquestionably the most important of my life, and Tey was just dropping out.

This I couldn't handle. It was simply one thing too many. With a bellow of rage, an explosion of anger totally unexpected, I struck Sentib a smashing blow across the mouth with the back of my hand, sending the poor man, reeling and stunned, to his knees, and then to the floor.

I'm not proud to relate this, but it happened. There it is. He looked up at me with an expression of hurt surprise that I shall take with me to my grave. I couldn't believe I'd done such a thing. I make it a rule never to apologize to servants, no matter how in the wrong I might be. But this was so out of character for me, so totally spontaneous, so grossly unfair, that I had to make an exception. I didn't actually think of it in those terms. I honestly just didn't know what had come over me. I couldn't recognize myself.

I almost immediately reached down to help Sentib back to his feet. I could barely look him in the face. "Sentib," I pleaded, "do forgive me. I didn't mean that. It's inexcusable of me. It's not your fault. I'll make it up to you as soon as the banquet's over, and I assure you this will never happen again."

Sentib looked at me dumbly, stricken. He was bleeding from the mouth, and I gave him my own handkerchief to staunch the flow. Luckily, at my stage of life, the force of my arm isn't what it was in my youth, or Sentib's head at that very moment would have been dangling halfway torn from his body.

"Sit down and rest awhile," I said. "I'll find the madam and set things right. Have some wine. The good stuff. The wine we're serving the king. I'm sorry, Sentib," I said again lamely, not knowing what else to say. Again I got that stricken look, like that of a faithful hound suddenly lashed by its master for no offense at all. I was truly stunned by what I had done.

I stormed into Tey's bedchamber. All the draperies were pulled tightly shut and no lamps were lit. This brought me to an immediate halt, since I literally had to grope—the unexpected darkness brought me to a total standstill. It was several moments before my eyes adjusted to the gloom and I saw Tey huddled in the corner, arms wrapped around her knees, rocking back and forth, emitting a low, keening wail. It sent chills down my spine. I'd only heard that keening, piercing wail once, at the death of our son some—what must it be?—thirty-five years ago. I could see she'd been crying, was all cried out, but even if the tears were all spent, the eyes were crying still, and the inconsolable sounds still poured from her trembling lips.

I didn't know what to say. All the anger I'd felt when I stormed into her room instantly vanished. I was at a total loss. Instead of screaming at her, as I was coiled to do but an instant before, I simply said, "Tey?"

She made no answer.

"Tey?"

"Go away."

Even more quietly now. "Tey, I can't go away. What is it?"

Somehow she found a new reservoir of tears, and I waited several minutes before attempting speech again. "Tey. Please let me know what's wrong. Whatever it is, you've got to pull yourself together. Our lives are at stake. We just don't have the luxury for all this. And remember this: our blood is royal now. We must act like the nobles we are. It's the price we pay."

In retrospect those words sound pretty inane, but for some reason they seemed to work. Tey looked up at me, and I felt infinite pity for her, for she was truly devastated. Whatever it was, and the sick sense of dread in the pit of my stomach told me it was something pretty awful, it had apparently almost killed her.

She continued looking at me, her eyes lifeless, burned out, as though the very soul within her had been extinguished.

"I know who did it," she said, in a whisper so low I could scarcely comprehend. "I know who murdered Akhenaten. It was Tut. I know who tried to poison you. It was Nefertiti."

She said the words tonelessly, and this time it was I who reeled. Tut and Nefertiti. My own blood! Even though I had always had to consider the possibility of Nefertiti's involvement, this flat declaration that my own daughter had deliberately tried to murder me sent all the blood draining from my head. I felt myself faint, reeling, and I reached down with one arm, then slumped into a chair and for a few moments actually blacked out.

My mind must have continued functioning on its own, for I found thoughts free-floating through my brain while I simply sat crushed, mourning. That Tut might try to murder me would not have come as a surprise. But, as much in a state of shock as I was, the idea that Tut, at age ten, could have killed his father seemed utterly preposterous. Still, somehow or other, I knew it was true. Tey would never be wrong about something like this. If she said it was Tut, it was Tut. And knowing that your own daughter actually tried to poison you is a thought too painful to be borne, though bear it I must.

I asked the inevitable question. "How do you know?"

"Your dream," she said in a monotone. "Your dream. I understand your dream."

I said nothing, knowing she'd go on. And she did. "I lay down for my nap this afternoon like I always do. Just for a few minutes—

there's so much to do, but I really have to have my nap these days. And then it all came to me."

"You dreamed you had the answer to my dream?"

"Of course not, you fool!" She said it with a low growl. Ordinarily I would have rebuked her sharply for speaking to me, her husband, in such a manner and such a tone of voice. But now I was just happy that she was showing a little sign of life.

"So?"

"So I lay down to rest. And as I relaxed, my mind seemed to come open. I caught a little piece of it, just a corner, and once I did, I pulled the rest of it into place. All of it. Everything came clear. Once I pulled on that first piece, the rest of it just followed."

Once more I waited in silence, and once more she proceeded, in a voice so low I could scarce catch the words. "It was the gods that first started the unraveling. Bastit and Min. I thought to myself, Why Bastit? Why Min? There are many pairs of gods that are mother and son. And then I started thinking. Bastit and Min. Mother and son. What mother and son are involved in all this? Only Nefertiti and Tut. They're the only ones."

I waited, and now that she was speaking, the words wouldn't stop. "Bastit and Min. Bastit and Min. The cat and the crocodile. There are so many god-pairs, but you dreamed of the cat and the crocodile. Cat is a perfect description for Nefertiti. And as for Tut . . ."

Even at this moment, emotionally drained as I was, I couldn't help saying, "Crocodile? Your Tuttikins? A crocodile?"

"Don't, Eye. Please don't. It's more pain than I can bear as it is. I'm a grandmother. In my heart I've always known there was something strange about Tut. Truly strange. Almost inhuman. Still and all, he's my flesh. He's your flesh. I made excuses. Made allowances. It was the way Nefertiti brought him up, I told myself. It's all the special privileges, I told myself. He'll change. He'll mature. Just give him time. But deep in my heart, I always feared something dark about him. I called him Tuttikins, but I never honestly felt that way about him." Another brief burst of tears, which she wiped away with a corner of her hand.

"Go on, Tey. I'm listening."

"I didn't want to think about it. I didn't want to let my mind take it any further. But once I started, my mind took over all by itself. And once I started, I had that sure, certain feeling that I was right, and right away everything just dropped into place without my even having to work on it. In a minute. In half a minute."

Maybe Tey saw it all, the whole picture, but I still didn't. "Each element made the next one so much easier," she went on. "Re-Horakhty. How obvious! The sun-god! The Aten! Akhenaten! And the crocodile-god devoured him. Tut devoured him. Tut killed him. What else could it be?"

Somehow I knew she was absolutely right.

"And the water clock? And the sundial?"

"The most important proofs of all! Think about it, Eye! Think about it! You went to see Nefertiti to let her know your suspicions, hoping she'd spread the gossip and perhaps unnerve whoever killed Akhenaten enough so that somehow he'd reveal himself. And it worked. Nefertiti revealed herself. It had to be her. Time! It was time! And it was Bastit that held the water clock. It was her time that was draining out!"

I was genuinely puzzled. "I don't quite see."

"You have to see. You *have* to see! There was no time! Nothing speeds faster than gossip, but even gossip had no time. Not enough, anyway. How long was it between the time you talked to Nefertiti and the time Oudah tried to kill you? Four hours? At the most?"

I thought about that. It was true.

"So!" she exclaimed triumphantly, starting to get a little life back in her voice. "It couldn't have been Horemheb. He was in the desert with his troops. There was no way he could have heard a thing. Tut and Yuti and Aanen were all in the Temple at Karnak. Even if she would have sent a horse galloping after them, there was no time. The only one that had time to terrorize Oudah and force her to try to poison you was Nefertiti herself!"

All of a sudden I remembered Oudah's death. The poor girl, unable to speak, had tried to tell me something. She'd clawed at her breasts. She's tried to tell me her poisoner was a woman. She's placed her hands to her head in an odd manner—probably trying to indicate a crown. Then she'd slipped into a pose of prayer—to a crowned goddess. Nefertiti. It was all so clear when you knew the answer.

Tey hadn't mentioned Ankhesenamun. She still obviously clung to the idea there was no way it could have been her. But Tey was right. Ankhy had been desperately ill in bed, and no one had been in communication with her. For whatever reason, Nefertiti had panicked, had tried to kill me. But why? Had she been involved with Tut in plotting Akhenaten's murder?

"What about 'Unfair! Unfair! Unfair!' "

Tey pondered the question. "I don't know. Not yet. All will still come clear. There will be more to come, of that I'm certain. Your investigations put all those pieces in your mind, and the gods sent you the dream to put them all together. Whatever 'Unfair!' means scarce matters at all. At least to me. My daughter, my grandson . . . murderers! I don't want to live anymore."

"You have no choice, Tey. You have to. We both have to. There's Egypt to think about. There's Ankhy to think about. We have to rouse ourselves. We have no choice. It's a terrible thing to be relatives of a god. We must behave nobly. It's the price we pay. Nothing in this world comes without cost, and we're paying full measure this day."

Tey's interpretation of my dream was flawless. Once explained, it all made perfect sense. I still had a hard time accepting that the ten-year-old Tut could actually have done such a thing. But there it was. Or was it? The dream interpretation was absolutely, precisely correct. I somehow intuitively knew this. There was that quality about Tey. In matters of this type she was always right. But a dream interpretation is far, far from proof, and what I desperately needed was cold, hard proof, and that I totally lacked. But I was a giant leap ahead of where I had been moments ago.

I said what I was thinking. "Proof, Tey. I need solid proof. I don't know for sure what I'll do with it when I get it. But I must have it. And quickly."

"Then send for Yuti and Narmer."

Of course! I don't know what I'd do without Tey.

"Akhenaten was poisoned. Obviously. Yuti knows about poisons. He's a physician. Maybe he was even involved in all this somehow. And Narmer was involved in the preparation and tasting of all Akhenaten's food. And ever since Akhenaten's death, Tut's treated him like a member of the family. Tut doesn't even treat members of the family like members of the family. You have to get the truth from Narmer."

"How?"

"Torture him."

"But—" And then we both shouted it simultaneously. "Unfair! Unfair! Unfair!" And then, for once, I was way ahead of Tey. I'd get the information I needed from Narmer, and I wouldn't torture him either. But what I planned was indeed "Unfair! Unfair! Unfair!"

Narmer was already in my palace, so I had no need to seek him out. But Yuti was either still at Karnak or back at the royal palace with Tut. One of the perks of being grand vizier is that you get to summon people anytime you want. I sent my two swiftest chariots for Yuti, one to each possible destination, and within a few hours he was in the room standing before me. I'd imagined he'd be with Tut and I was right, which pleased me, since the time to and from Karnak would have been far greater.

Yuti clearly was in a highly nervous state when the guard dragged him into my presence. He groveled miserably before me, and I let him. Normally I found the sight of that enormous bottom pointing straight up into the air highly amusing, but not now. The sun had not yet set, and although the distance traveled was relatively short, his albino skin was already turning red and blotchy. He looked miserable.

I let him stay down in the grovel position. "I need answers from you, Yuti, and I need them quickly."

"I'm anxious to help," he muttered.

"I can't hear you!"

"I'M ANXIOUS TO HELP!"

"Much better. Tell me about poisons."

"Poisons?"

"Yes. The various kinds."

I suppose he was pondering the question, since I couldn't really see his face. "Fundamentally," he said, "there are two kinds of poisons. There are the earth-based poisons. The ones that come from substances dug from the ground. Like arsenic. These, in general—and there are exceptions—are the swift-acting poisons. The plant-based poisons tend to work more slowly."

Suddenly it struck me. My conversation with Nefertiti. It seemed like a year since I'd talked to her, but it was only a few days ago. And now that I knew Tut had killed his father, her words suddenly jumped out at me. "Yuti," I asked eagerly, "is there any sort of poison that's a mushroom?"

"None that grows in Egypt," he answered. "But there's a strange plant that grows across the Great Green. It's called deadly cort. Or, by other physicians, deadly galerina. For obvious reasons."

"It's a mushroom?"

"A most delicious one. Or so I'm told. For obvious reasons I've never eaten one."

"And how long does it take to act?"

"That would depend upon the dosage. Normally, a day. Sometimes two. And there's no antidote. When someone suffers deadly cort poisoning, it attacks everything. Autopsies show heavy damage to almost all the organs—intestines, heart, liver—even the genitals. I've never actually seen one case of deadly cort poisoning in all my career, but you only have to hear about the effects of one for it to make a lasting impression."

"And these things look like ordinary mushrooms?"

"Experts can tell them apart. They can tell them apart better in the lands across the Great Green than here. In those countries they're aware of the danger. Here in Egypt we have no native poisonous mushrooms, so we think all we have to worry about are toadstools."

"So you were the one who told Narmer what to search for when Tut sent him across the Great Green to find special treats for his father!" I stormed, relentless, giving him a firm kick square in the middle of that oversized bottom.

"No, master, no!" he wailed piteously. "I don't know what.

you're talking about! I never talk to Narmer! Why would I? He's nothing but a court servant. I would never be called on to treat him. Never! How could I ever have anything to do with him?"

I had heard all I had to hear. Call it intuition, but somehow I knew Yuti was telling the truth, that he had had nothing to do with Akhenaten's poisoning. Still, I ordered him confined to a locked room until I had full confidence I'd discovered all the facts. Just in case.

Once more I reflected on the providential ways of the gods. Narmer was already here, in my own palace. How lucky for me. How unlucky for him.

I was truly in a grim mood when they brought the man in to me. I'd made a few preparations before my guards dragged him in. I didn't have the time or the inclination to fool around with him. I needed the truth, and I needed it now. I now knew the who and the how of it, but I had to have confirmation, and I wasn't too fastidious about how I got it.

I disliked Narmer. I'd never thought much about him before. He was, after all, Tut's servant—and had been Akhenaten's before him, for that matter—but servants tend to be invisible. This time I looked more closely. My dislike doubtless was colored by the circumstances, since this was the very first time I'd ever had reason actually to notice the man. I'd had him roughly pulled and hauled into my presence, but he still had a certain arrogance about him, the reflected arrogance of a little man who has spent his entire life serving royalty and has come to think of himself as somehow having absorbed their aura. This was probably why I conceived the instant dislike.

He failed to grovel. Technically he didn't have to in this informal setting, but I slammed his head to the ground anyway. I wanted to get this over with fast.

"All right, Narmer," I snarled without any preamble whatsoever. "Tell me how you and Tut did it. Everything. Tell me how the two of you killed his father."

"Highness, I have no idea what you mean!" The man was a cool one, I'll give him credit. "I'm but a servant," he continued, and his voice was rock-steady. "I have no knowledge of such things. I've killed no one. I've helped to kill no one. And the former great pharaoh died naturally, as far as I know."

"I haven't the time for this, Narmer. I'll make it totally clear to you, right now. Right this minute. Tell me what you know, or I'll make you tell me."

I swear I heard a suppressed chuckle. I'll again give the man his due. He had spunk. "You can't do that!" he answered calmly, lifting his head slightly from the floor. "You can't use torture. Every man in Thebes knows that. Even the peasants in the fields know that. If the pharaoh hears about it—and he will—I wouldn't be in your sandals for all the palaces and all the titles in Egypt."

I pulled Narmer up from the floor by his hair. He gave a yelp, half of genuine pain, and half of genuine surprise. He'd never before seen the violent side of my nature. I took a wickedly curved, wickedly sharpened bronze razor and waved it under his nose. "You recognize this, don't you, Narmer? You know what it's for?" By the way his eyes widened I knew he did. It was a razor specifically designed to geld horses.

I took the razor and slowly and carefully slit his robe from top to toe, so that it fell inelegantly at his feet. I did the same to his loincloth with a brief, sharp flick, and Narmer was completely naked before me. In my experience, there is nothing more humiliating than for one man to stand naked in the presence of another, and I wanted all the mental advantage over him I could muster.

The terror in his eyes was palpable. "This is insane!" he shouted. "I was there when pharaoh gave his command. He'll destroy you when he learns of this! It's pharaoh's command! You can't do this. It's—"

"Unfair!" I exclaimed gleefully. I think at that moment I had indeed gone a little mad. "Unfair! Unfair! Unfair!"

Narmer broke into a sudden, profuse sweat. A cold sweat, I presume, though since it was his body I have no way of knowing. "Narmer, I have no time to explain, and in any case I never waste explanations on a servant. Rest assured, however, that you are going to tell me everything you know. Everything. And now. This very minute."

I lifted the razor toward his mouth, and pulled out his tongue. I held the razor but a few inches away. Then I lowered it. "No, I think not," I said, as though musing. "No. Your tongue is a national treasure. I could no more destroy that superb instrument than could I deface the statues of the gods."

I gazed downward. Naked, the man was an amusing sight. I moved the razor downward. "This," I said, indicating the portion of his anatomy for which my razor was designed, "is another matter altogether. I see nothing special there. In fact, a certain deficiency, if you don't mind my saying so." I again pulled his head up by the hair, so we were eyeball-to-eyeball. "Let me make it totally clear. You tell me right now, right this second, everything I want to know. The full and complete truth. All of it. You have two choices. You can talk. Or, if you have any decent kind of singing voice at all, I'll have you sent straight from here to Aanen the High Priest at the Temple of Karnak. I'm sure his choir can always use another soprano."

Narmer didn't have to give the proposition an instant's thought. "Very well," he gasped, his eyes bulging with fear. He knew I meant every word I was saying. And I absolutely did. "I'll tell it all to you. Every bit. Just put that damned thing away!"

"Fine. Talk."

"It was all Tut's idea. He'd heard about the mushrooms, and he asked me to cross the Great Green and find them for him. I was Akhenaten's servant, but Tut managed to prevail upon Nefertiti to devise the subterfuge so that I could be away for the time it took. How he persuaded her I have no idea. I'm just a servant. I do what I'm told."

This was totally unexpected. "Queen Nefertiti had no part in this?"

He shook his head.

"You're certain?"

"Of course. Well, I have no way of being *absolutely* certain. But no, as far as I could tell, Queen Nefertiti had no knowledge of the matter whatsoever." She knew of course that Akhenaten loved mushrooms and was thrilled that Tut wanted to go to such lengths to surprise his father. She had no way of knowing just how big a surprise for Akhenaten it was going to be.

Then why did she try to poison me? Another mystery. But a subsidiary one. I'd have time to deal with it later.

"Go on."

"When I brought back the special mushrooms, Tut had me carefully arrange them on pharaoh's plate. Akhenaten was a gourmet, you know that. But these mushrooms, when cut and diced, look scarcely different from any others. Akhenaten couldn't be everywhere in the kitchen at once. It was simple, really. I knew which portion of the mushrooms to taste. I ate of the good part. He ate all the rest. And Tut kept all his promises to me. I'm the wealthiest servant in Egypt, and more than that, I share his confidences."

Indeed, I thought. Two of a kind.

So now I had my answer and my proof. But how to use it? How does one bring a pharaoh to justice? More important, proof or no proof, how does one prevent a pharaoh from simply doing one in? A vexing problem. And all mine.

"Narmer," I said, allowing the man to pull the cut fragments of his robe about his body (and I certainly didn't particularly want to see it anymore), "as I see it, you now have a terrible problem. The banquet goes on tomorrow night. I will be there and the pharaoh will be there. I need your living witness to what you've just told me. It's perfectly clear now that tomorrow night there will be a confrontation between the pharaoh and me from which only one of us can emerge alive. You seem to be an intelligent man. I suspect you're already trying to figure out where your interests lie. Let me assure you they lie with me. Let me give you some further assurances lest you have any doubts in your mind whatsoever. I am a desperate man in a desperate situation, and I have absolutely nothing to lose by doing exactly what I am telling you. For one thing, from this moment on there will always be at least two armed men within an instant's reach of you. For another, at the banquet, there will be many armed men dressed as guests, seated all throughout the great hall. Should you make the slightest effort to communicate with the pharaoh, at a nod from me they'll be all over you. Your throat will be slit like a pigeon. And you won't know who they are, so you won't be able to run or dash or scream to avoid them. You're in this now up to your neck. Tut may be pharaoh, but where you're concerned, right now *I'm* your pharaoh. I have power over you, not Tut. And I give you a solemn promise. If I survive, you survive. I will do you no harm. Think well on what I tell you."

I had him taken away, with the severest instructions that he never for an instant be left unguarded and never allowed to have any sharp instrument in his hand. "Unfair! Unfair! Unfair!" I fairly sang to myself. For some reason I took enormous pride in the fact that I'd found out everything (save for the nagging puzzle about Nefertiti) without violating my promise to the king. I had promised Tut I would use no torture. I never promised that I wouldn't *threaten* torture.

[*Translator's note: If you find it incredible that the ten-year-old Tut could actually have plotted and killed his father, roughly thirteen centuries later, Caligula would plot and kill his father Germanicus. Caligula was seven. On further reflection, perhaps it's not all that incredible after all. In England, yes, it's difficult to imagine. In America, children seem to be killing people all the time, although rarely do they* plot *the killing, they just seem to do it.*]

I had much to do this night, and while I now had in my grasp the answer to much, much remained unknown. If Nefertiti hadn't been involved in the death of Akhenaten, I still didn't know why she'd tried to kill me. And since Tut *had* killed Akhenaten, why had he sent me on this quest? Most important of all, what should I do now? For whatever Tut had had in mind when he started down this road, if it was a game, it was a game no longer. I couldn't pretend I'd learned nothing—eventually I'd have to free Narmer, since Tut would be clamoring to have him back at his palace. Having Narmer die while in my custody would raise more awkward questions than I would want to cope with. And feigning failure would still leave me open to whatever outcome Tut had had in mind in the first place.

If I couldn't tell Tut I hadn't found his father's killer, the only remaining option was to tell him that I had. This was fraught with even more peril. If Tut hadn't blanched at killing a father, he certainly wouldn't hesitate at killing a grandfather. This was now a duel to the death between Tut and me. He had every advantage but one. I knew it. As yet, Tut didn't. I had one additional advantage. I have a will of steel, and courage. For the most part, Tut has only seen me as a courtier, appearing to accede to his every whim. He doesn't know the risks I've taken to negate the most outrageous and damaging of his offhand impulses. He hadn't seen the wounds on my body from enemy swords and spears. Whatever his game is, he thinks he's invulnerable. He underestimates me.

On the other hand, it is vital that I not underestimate Tut. Much as I dislike him, I cannot fault him for lack of intelligence—or shrewdness, which, for a pharaoh, is probably an even more important attribute. Tut is cunning. No better evidence of that is needed than this grotesque game he is playing with me, a game designed to lure me to my own destruction. Now that I know the name of my adversary, I'll need to get inside his mind and anticipate his next moves. If I can. As a first step I sent a messenger to summon Houy. Quite obviously I needed to beef up my cavalry guards here in my own palace.

I had many tasks to accomplish this night, but I resolved to tackle the most disagreeable first. I owed it to Tey. Much as I hated it, I would have to banish Helen from my palace. Tey deserved that much from me. Were it not for her, I'd know nothing. She'd solved the riddle. The bulk of it, anyway. And as I thought about it, thought back forty years, I remembered the Tey I knew then, a girl but slightly older than Helen is now. And as beautiful. Well, that's not true. I had to be honest about that. Tey in her youth had been most attractive, but at her best no match for Helen.

But one day Helen would be as Tey is now. The difference is that Tey's heart had remained golden. Whatever passion, whatever lust, whatever desire I had for Helen, I still saw her as she was.

The child-woman was intelligent, she knew what she wanted and she knew how to get it, and though she might play the kitten, there was nothing kittenish about her. Helen was not a nice person. Given the choice between Helen and Tey for principal wife, I simply had to pick loyalty and time-tested love over pure physical passion. Particularly considering that, as Helen had demanded, though not precisely in so many words, if I wanted her, there was only one way to get her.

I do admit that the rather bizarre partial consummation of my lust for Helen left me totally salivating for more. Still, I had to resolve this issue, so it might as well be now. If I knew anything at all about women, it was that Tey and Helen could no longer sleep under the same roof, no matter how large my palace was. Not to mention that for me ever again to get any sleep, one of them had to go.

I had Helen summoned to my chamber. As soon as I saw her I knew this was going to be even more difficult than I had thought. She entered, and her entire body had that sinuous, hip-swiveling motion that immediately began distracting all rational thought processes. By every god in Egypt, wasn't she fantastic! She was wearing a sheer, billowing gown that covered her from throat to foot but revealed every bit of her at the same time. It was rose in color. I think rose—it was so filmy it was almost invisible. Around her neck she wore a magnificent pure-gold necklace, exquisitely crafted from the workshop of the very best artisan in Thebes. You may wonder where a slave girl could acquire a wardrobe like this. I probably have forgotten—or, to be more honest, I've been too embarrassed to mention—that I've been rather generous to her. It's a vulnerability of older men in their relationships with women young enough to be their daughters. Or granddaughters. And to avoid rebellion among the other slaves, I had to be generous with them too, since by doing so I counted on their treating Helen well in return. The more generous I was to Helen, the more generous would I be to them, and thus it would be to their interest to treat Helen with deference lest she mention any ill-treatment, thus not only bringing down my wrath but cutting off my largesse. I hated to calculate what my lust for this Greek girl had already cost me, and I *still* hadn't truly possessed her. Well, from time immemorial they've always said there's no fool like an old fool, and if I'm not living proof, I don't know where you'll find it.

"I'm so glad you summoned me, Eye," Helen cooed in that husky, sultry voice of hers. She positioned herself to display her fabulous body to best advantage, and swayed her hips provocatively. "I've missed you so! Why are you neglecting me?" She moved toward me, and with her tongue out-thrust, slowly and with great deliberation moistened her lips. Once. Twice. Thrice. In the corner of my chamber there is a stone statue of the male god Seth and I glanced nervously over my shoulder to see if it had stirred.

I simply couldn't help reaching out a hand to stroke her face. That flawless, perfect face. Yes, perfection is the only way to describe it. And lest you think I exaggerate, I have known more than my share of women in my time.

Helen took my fingers and began kissing the back of my hand passionately, and her tongue flicked over it like the wings of a hummingbird. She looked into my eyes with such fire that I felt my robes would ignite. As I thought about it further, I began to think that Tey hadn't done all that much after all. True, she had interpreted my dream. But I would have arrived at the same conclusion all by myself, and soon. Had I not been so busy and so exhausted, I would have solved it long before her. And after all, I was the one who'd assembled all the pieces, wasn't I? I was the one who had searched out all the facts. And it was the gods who put the dream in my head so that understanding could come of it. Anyone could have done what Tey had done.

Helen took my other hand and pressed it lightly to her breast. "Eye," she murmured gently, "you've thought about it, haven't you? What we talked about? Surely by now you've found a way. Wouldn't you rather have this every night than—than what you've got?"

I have to say this for Helen, she knows what she wants and she knows what she has to offer. I shook my head, and removed my hand. "As a matter of fact, Helen, let me ask the same of you. Look at me. Look at me closely. Look at me and tell me if this isn't exactly what you want." I removed my robes and stood before her stark-naked, posing, not too ridiculously, I hoped, like some irresistible satyr. "Say it. You want me. No conditions. Just me. Say it. I want to hear it."

She looked at me with a startled, puzzled look on her face, and suddenly she was all over me. There was no stopping her, nor did I try. I shall not describe all the minute details of this encounter, other than to say, with a certain amount of pride, that within but a few minutes the consummation of my lust for Helen was no longer a partial one.

We lay on the bed together, and her fervent kisses cascaded over my cheeks, my lips, my chest—well, you know how it goes. I'd had a difficult day, and I deserved this little relaxation.

I'd like you to believe that Helen had, after having so much chance to know me, suddenly found me completely irresistible, more than her feminine nature could withstand. I'd like you to believe that, though it would cost her any chance at being principal wife, that she simply couldn't play her teasing game with me any longer, that I'd lit fires in her that her own reciprocal lusts simply no longer could hold in check.

I'd like you to believe that, but the truth of it is that Yuti's dropsy prescription had a certain amount to do with it. As you will recall, he had been most adamant about not issuing a prescription for use other than for its intended purpose. Yuti, so mild-mannered, so meek, so submissive, was as of stone when anything touched upon the practice of his profession.

"Yuti," I'd asked, following my interview with him at Karnak, "I truly would like to have some of that powder. For medicinal purposes, of course."

He looked at me with what, for Yuti, he must have thought was withering scorn, although in truth he looked more like a rabbit twitching its nose and ears. "I told you just a few minutes ago that that is not possible, much as I regret it," he said, inevitably falling back into his passive mode even as he refused me. "I must be true to my oath. I must prescribe this medicine only for its intended use."

"How do you know I don't have dropsy?"

He looked me over carefully, as though he were about to give me a complete medical examination. "You just told me you didn't. Besides, I know all about dropsy," he stated flatly. "I have dropsy myself, which is why I take this medicine."

Of course, I thought, remembering the temple girls fighting for the privilege of giving him his bath. Perhaps that's an unfair thought. Knowing Yuti, maybe the man really *does* have dropsy.

"What if the disease is merely in the incipient stage with me?"

He again looked at me doubtfully. He considered the matter. I pressed my advantage. "You are a physician, Yuti, a healer. You have a sworn duty to your fellowman. If this prescription can treat and cure my symptoms before they become disabling, is not that the highest calling of the physician's art? Would you force me to wait until I'm all bloated and disabled before dispensing this boon?"

He considered the matter most carefully. He approached me, pried my eyelids wide, poked at my body, squeezed my limbs. "Dropsy?" he said suspiciously. "You have symptoms of dropsy?"

"Now that I think about it, I'm certain of it."

"Do you feel sluggish and uncomfortable in the morning?" he inquired.

"Absolutely," I lied.

"Do you get up many times during the night to relieve yourself?"

"I certainly do." This was not a lie.

"Shortness of breath?"

"All the time."

"Unusually heavy sweating?"

"Like a pig."

"How long have you had these symptoms?"

"Well, like I said, I seem to be in the incipient stage. But I'm sure without treatment I'm going to get much worse, and soon."

"Very well," he sighed, and turned over a packet of his magical potion to me. "Try this for a week and see me at my office."

"Thank you, Yuti," I responded fervently and effusively, "you are a noble man and a credit to your profession."

I could hardly wait to leave, this promise of paradise clutched tightly in my hand. He called me back briefly. "Vizier," he continued, "stay out of the sun for at least two hours after you take it. Otherwise your skin gets all prickly and blotchy."

Thus did I come into possession of enough of the witching powder to have the divine Helen practically drooling for my body. Yuti's prescription also had the side effect he'd warned me about, and which I forgot. I did go out in the sun, and my whole body was itching miserably. Luckily it was temporary.

In any event, the intervention of Yuti's medicine certainly had a bearing on the outcome of my relationship with Helen, although I'm certain that, given time, I could have accomplished the same thing without it. I am an experienced man in these matters, so it came as no surprise to me that, having had her, she no longer obsessed me. Don't misunderstand. I certainly would find further episodes of this sort most pleasant. But that mindless, unbound, all-encompassing, all-consuming passion simply wasn't there anymore. No doubt for the best, too, since keeping ahead of this woman was more of a challenge than any man needed to be up to if there was any way to avoid it. And, to be perfectly honest, now that my obsessive lust for her had been slaked, her calm willingness to have Tey murdered in order to get her way didn't sit all that well with me either.

I pushed her away from me and got up, securing my robes around me. What I had to say was best spoken at a distance, and besides, saying what I was about to say, I needed as much dignity as the situation could muster. It's virtually impossible to be manly, forceful, and dominating while lying shriveled and naked on a bed.

"Helen," I said, trying to make my voice both stern and tender at the same time, "Egypt is no place for you. You have royal blood in your veins, but it is the blood of Greece. It is far better that you return to your own land, to return to find the destiny that awaits you there. Go back to Corinth, where your family will explode with joy at your safe return, where you will be in the company of your relatives and all who love you. Marry your Minlos and become Queen of Lacedaemon, and pass your blood to future generations of fine Greek warriors, as the gods intend for you."

Fortunately, I know little Greek, for I fear I would not have been pleased at the torrent of words that poured from her lips. Helen knew that those fine words simply meant that I was kicking her out of my bed.

[*Translator's note: Lacedaemon! Lacedaemon! Eye specifically mentions Lacedaemon! The proof! Helen, wife of "Minlos"—Menelaus—Queen of Lacedaemon, the lady whose face launched a thousand ships, lived! She is no myth after all. My reputation is made! My colleagues will be insane with jealousy. I love it! Oh, they'll carp and tear every shred of evidence apart they can. Good luck. What are they going to say? That the* Iliad *states that Helen was the daughter of Zeus, not the daughter of Jason, King of Corinth? Of course, the* Iliad *also states that Leda was her mother and that Leda's husband was Tindareus, King of Sparta. It would have been nice to have received confirmation of this too, but one rarely gets everything. Helen's flat statement of her own parentage simply further clinches her historical existence. And the time is exactly right—historians agree that the Trojan War took place just about the time that Tut ruled Egypt. Life never ceases to be strange. I went digging for a pharaoh and I found Helen of Troy! I had been skeptical of Eye's extravagant descriptions of Helen's beauty, but now I have to conclude that, if anything, he probably was a master of understatement. The man's been dead 3,400 years, but how I envy him!*]

# 21

# THE

# FINAL

# DAY

I awoke in the morning feeling truly rotten. I'd had barely two hours sleep. This time it wasn't from tossing and turning. I had had much to do, and I'd been up most of the night doing it. I looked at myself in my mirror. There were huge dark circles under my eyes. My skin was pasty and the jaw muscles slightly slack. I shook my head wearily. Maybe I shouldn't worry about Tut. At this rate, stress, sex, and lack of sleep would finish me off if Tut didn't.

My palace was already clattering with activity. My normal household staff was far from adequate to handle all the details of a state banquet, and new temporary servants were being carefully screened and instructed. I tried to keep out of Tey's way—this was her department—and besides, I felt sick just looking at her. She was back in the swing of things, everywhere at once, checking every detail, screaming, scolding, commanding, but I could see her heart wasn't in it. Her eyes were dead. Ordinarily, Tey lived for these banquets. Not today. But she knew her duty, and Tey never shirked, no matter what.

Time. Again, my enemy was time. That's true for all men, but I wasn't just philosophizing. Originally, I'd thought that I needed the time to locate a murderer. Now I needed time to figure out how to kill that murderer before he killed me. I had very little left. My head felt as if it were filled with sheep's wool. I was having a hard time thinking straight. Despite the absolute, vital importance of this day, I was even having trouble staying awake. Everything was finally catching up with me, one day too soon.

My plans were those of desperation, and if any single thing failed, I might as well say farewell to my head. I was under no illusion. If only I'd had time to contact Horemheb! With his troops and mine, we could depose Tut. That is, of course, if we trusted each other. Which we didn't. And if only I could persuade Horemheb to help me get rid of Tut, rather than have Tut order him to get rid of me! My mind kept trying to squeeze these thoughts through my fuzzy brain. Most of them were old ideas— they just kept going around and around in my head to no useful purpose, but no new ones showed up of any value either. I don't know why I was still thinking about all this. I'd already made my plans, such as they were, and put them into motion. I was irretrievably committed.

An invitation from the grand vizier to a state banquet amounts to a command. None invited would dare not appear, unless they were on their way to their House of Truth. Quite often men arrived quite horribly ill, and had I known I would have insisted they stay home, for they dampened the appetites of those who looked at them, and quite often others quickly came down with the same complaint.

I kept gazing nervously at the water clock. The water dripped out at what seemed a torrential rate. Not only that, but I was constantly checking to be certain it functioned properly. All my plans, my very life, depended on the accuracy of that clock.

Details. There were so many details. Irrationally, there were details about the banquet itself and I allowed them to divert my attention. These banquets were my pride too, and I demanded of my staff that every most minute item be checked and rechecked for absolute perfection. The public rooms of my palace gleamed, with platoons of servants on their knees scrubbing, washing, polishing. Row upon row of new lamps stood arrayed in artistic, graceful placings, many of them elaborately tall candelabra, so that when the proper time came, the great banquet hall would blaze with such brightness it would seem the sun had failed to set this day.

My own preparations took hours, and though I bitterly resented the wasted time, it was mandatory. I chafed at the ministrations of my barber as he painstakingly applied the hot iron to each and every curl of my beard, creating curlicues that were then trimmed to spade-shaped perfection. Tey had often suggested that I darken my hair and beard. No doubt it would make me look younger, but it seemed too effeminate an affectation. My chiropodist worked manfully on my feet, which was a blessing, since I'd walked blisters on them just running back and forth through the palace. My masseur was a godsend—my neck muscles were so taut, a pebble bounced off them would fly a hundred feet into the air. It goes without saying that I was bathed and scrubbed until my skin was nearly raw. My entire body was perfumed and oiled from top to toe, and whether by men's hands or women's was a matter of perfect indifference to me. My eyes were carefully painted in the traditional almond shape, though, as dark as the bags were under them, they really needed no highlighting. What little hair I had was carefully combed and pomaded. I sweetened my breath perhaps overmuch with natron. I was ready to dress.

Even with all my worries I could not help taking pains with my appearance. I am Eye, Grand Vizier of Egypt, and if this was my last night, I wanted to be remembered for the magnificent figure I cut. My slave brought me my boots, and I fondled them lovingly. The crimson leather was of an astonishing suppleness. Buckles of gold drew the leather together, and an intricate stripe of gold ran unbroken up each side, from toe to top. A cloth of gold tunic, everywhere sewn with precious gems, was overlaid with a black cloak, from which dangling heavy sleeves fell in graceful folds. I placed a white linen scarf at my throat. It set off my dark complexion rather well. I placed a white turban on my head into which I affixed a huge, perfectly cut ruby. A slave placed my favorite massive gold-and-ruby necklace around my neck, and from a huge and glittering tray I selected a jeweled ring for every finger.

I looked at myself in the mirror. Was it possible I was overdressed?

I also looked at the water clock. It was approaching the time for my guests to arrive. As was the custom, I waited at the door to greet each one personally. Punctuality was absolutely demanded, save, of course, for pharaoh. Even pharaoh wouldn't abuse the privilege of arriving late by more than the narrowest of margins since he knew that the food was prepared with exquisite timing, and if it was served even a few minutes too late, he would miss the peak of its perfection. Perfectly prepared food waits for no man, not even pharaoh.

I felt more than a little uneasy as I awaited my guests. My household guards, though somewhat augmented, still were minimal in number. This troubled me deeply, since these men weren't trained soldiers, just household staff being used for security purposes. For certain I couldn't call on any of my household cavalry guarding the royal palace. Tut would be immediately suspicious if I drew down from his guards for the protection of my own palace. In fact, any meaningful increase in the size of my household guards, from any source whatsoever, would immediately catch his eye. Pharaohs very quickly learn to become suspicious of everything.

The first sedan chairs began to arrive, each more elaborate and gorgeous than the next. Long, gilded poles extended from the bodies of the coaches, and each wooden carriage, elaborately lacquered and polished, intricately carved, bore the gilded hieroglyph proclaiming the name and rank of its owner.

The bearer-slaves numbered eight to a sedan chair; in some instances twelve, all perfectly caparisoned and matched for height and appearance. Each guest's retinue tried to outdo the next. There were huge Negro slaves, bodies oiled, naked to the waist, loins wrapped in cloths of gold, headdresses of the same material dotted with a profusion of amethysts; Egyptians from the lower Nile, dazzling in white tunics all washed and chalked, striped in silver and black, with silver headbands from which gilt arrows protruded in all directions; Numidians, all in black from throat to foot, cross-belted with rhinoceros skin studded with gold medallions; swarthy slaves from Cyprus, resplendent in mock uniforms of the temple's sacred guards, breastplates gilded, helmets gilded, stiff, all capped with bristling horsehair crests. Each retinue bespoke the wealth and social status of its owner. It was a magnificent sight. What a pity I was in no mood to appreciate it.

My guests were men of power. The elite of all Thebes, the great capital of Egypt, were swarming into my palace tonight. These were men to whom luxury, fame, power, slaves, women, culture, a life of ease, a life of refinement were but their expected due. These were the high aristocracy, and they carried themselves with an air that cannot be learned, only bred from the cradle.

I stood at the door busily greeting each of them, not knowing what I was saying. The usual meaningless gibber that passes for social conversation. Occasionally one of them gave me a strange look. I probably had made an inappropriate reply to something he'd said or asked, for in truth I wasn't paying any attention.

Finally the last of my guests made their entrance, entering the Great Hall and heading for the tables laden with exotic viands I had scoured the entire continent of Africa to provide. These tidbits would keep them amused until the arrival of the king.

This was always an awkward time when the king himself was a guest at a state banquet. I knew all my guests would be well provided for with nibbles and drink, but nonetheless, for me, being kept waiting outside, not knowing exactly when to expect the royal appearance, the time passed excruciating slowly.

I went over all my plans in my mind, although there was no point to it. What was done was done. I could change nothing. I could only await the outcome.

How much time had passed? Fifteen minutes? Twenty? I have no way of knowing for sure. What I do know is that when I finally did hear the approach of pharaoh, I heard the approach of doom.

In the distance I heard a sound, muffled at first, then louder, louder. I'm an old military man—I knew that sound at once. It was the sound of marching feet. Step—CRASH—step—CRASH—step—CRASH! It was the sound of the Egyptian military parade march. The sound is distinctive and peculiar to our armed forces. The soldier lifts his left leg stiffly, into a locked position. As he then slams it earthward and takes a step with his right foot, he smashes his unsheathed bronze sword in unison against the metal rim of his shield. Step—CRASH—step—CRASH—step—CRASH! I could feel my heart sink deep into the very bottom of my gorgeous crimson boots.

To my trained ear, I knew this wasn't the sound of the ordinary royal guard. The normal guard would be perhaps a company of men, no more. This was no company approaching. This was a full regiment, at least.

It took but a few minutes for my fears to be confirmed as the head of the marching column swung into view, illuminated by outriders on horseback carrying lighted torches. At the van rode Horemheb, mounted on a pure black stallion, a beast as black as King Tut's heart. He wore a parade dress uniform of purest white, and upon the tunic and around his neck were the emblems of the military decorations he had earned during his distinguished career. Normally Horemheb was totally indifferent to pomp—he rarely even bothered to don officer's dress but most often wore the dirty and shapeless uniform of his field troops. Not tonight. Tonight was obviously different. Had I had any doubt of the fate Tut had in mind for me, the inexorable approach of Horemheb's superbly drilled guard regiment dispelled it at once.

Tut himself was in the center of the regiment, borne on a palanquin of indescribable magnificence by sixteen slave-bearers. Naturally, his equipage had to be far finer than that of any of his subjects.

My mind ceased functioning. My palace was about to be surrounded by a full regiment of the king's own elite guard. I was to be taken prisoner.

Horemheb galloped toward me, sword raised in his right hand, a broad grin of triumph spread joyfully across his face. He'd struck first. He'd preempted me. He reined in his mount and brought it to a halt almost directly in front of me.

I composed my features. There was no way I was going to give him the satisfaction of seeing me surprised or chagrined. I looked up at him and gave him a salute, soldier-to-soldier. He deserved it. Even though he was my adversary, my enemy, by the gods, the man was magnificent. Horemheb was everything a soldier should be.

He looked down at me from horseback, and his eyes were alive with victory. He waved an answering salute and slipped lightly from his mount. "Welcome, General," I said courteously, making a supreme effort of will to appear nonchalant, as if this were nothing at all unusual. "Welcome to my home. As always, it's my deepest honor to have you as my guest."

"Thank you, Eye, for your invitation. I always look forward to sharing an evening with you." He smiled broadly. "I would deeply appreciate it if you could accommodate these men of mine in your palace. I wouldn't expect you to furnish them with food or drink, of course. Still, at the request of the king, I would like them quartered inside."

I tried to keep my head from slumping, but it was difficult. A regiment of guards inside my palace and all was over for certain. All seemed over anyway, but this there would be no way of overcoming.

"I will of course be delighted to do as my pharaoh commands," I replied formally. "But of course I had no way of knowing I would be honored by the appearance of so many of his splendid guards. With over six hundred for dinner this evening, my palace, I fear, is simply not large enough to accommodate so many unexpected guests. Would perhaps one hundred inside be sufficient?" I looked significantly at my own household security guards, who in their entirety numbered perhaps forty. Rather poor odds.

Horemheb looked them over, considering. It was quite obvious that one hundred picked guardsmen would be more than a match, particularly with an entire regiment immediately on call outside. "I'm a reasonable man, Eye. The king didn't specifically state that

*all* the regiment had to come inside. I'll leave the rest out here."
With a sweeping gesture he indicated that indeed my palace would
be tightly surrounded.

I inclined my head in acceptance. So be it. It was the will of the
gods.

Tut had by now also reached where I stood, and descended re-
gally from his palanquin, followed by Nefertiti and Ankhesenamun. [*Translator's note: They were appareled in full royal regalia as
befitted the occasion. Eye describes each item of clothing and each piece of
jewelry in exquisite detail. The description covers many pages. Suffice it to
say they looked great.*]

I immediately dropped to my knees in groveling obeisance, and
in that absurd posture poured out the ritual effusive pleasure I felt
in having him honor one so low by appearing at my inadequate
and humble home. Tut said nothing in reply, and with my forehead pressed down to the marble entranceway I could see nothing of the expression on his face. He allowed me to remain in this
position for an unconscionably long time, giving me one more in-
dication, had I needed it, that the only question was how deeply
I was in trouble, not whether I was in trouble.

At last he bade me rise. Unfortunately, on this occasion I did not
carry my cudgel of office. Having been on my knees so long, it was
extremely difficult for me to stand. He merely laughed mirthlessly
as he watched me struggle to my feet. "You aren't all that spritely
anymore, are you, Grandfather?" There was oily menace in his
voice. "Oh well," he continued grimly. "It will be of little matter."

He wasn't subtle, and I got the message.

I escorted Tut and Horemheb into the Great Hall, where the roll
of drums and the blare of trumpets brought all the guests immediately to their knees. Nefertiti and Ankhesenamun walked demurely behind, as was their station. With a nonchalant wave of
the wrist Tut signaled all to rise, and all gratefully complied. The
hundred guardsmen, in double file, entered the Great Hall with
us and stationed themselves along the perimeter of the room,
swords unsheathed, standing with feet spread, and eyes alert. The
guests looked at each other nervously—this was novel in their experience too—and I'm sure each wondered if somehow he should

personally be worried by this unusual display of heavy security.

Tey is a woman who knows how to structure a state banquet, and she had outdone herself this night. Potted lotus trees in huge brass planters lined the room, their bright-orange blossoms exuding a heavy fragrance that filled the evening air with sensuous perfume. Two long, shallow, narrow, specially constructed mirror-pools ran down the center of the Great Hall, reflecting the intricate paintings on the ceiling and serving to give proper balance and separation to the myriad tables set and ready for the main banquet. The floor swam and swirled with elaborate polished terrazzo mosaics—hunting scenes, battle scenes, mythological scenes, god-scenes—and Tey had had the walls hung with huge paintings and tapestries, some woven with strands of pure gold. The artists had had to work almost without sleep for the full six days since the banquet had been announced, and all these wall hangings were new and depicted recent events in the life of the pharaoh. Tut looked at them and was clearly pleased. I could not hold this against him—they had been commissioned to flatter him, so how could I be resentful if flattered he was?

The chittering gossip of the guests made it virtually impossible for conversation to be carried on other than at the top of the voice. The wives had outdone themselves in the splendor of their dress, considering that they too had had but six days to prepare. [*Translator's note: Again Eye goes into elaborate detail, including the cones of ointment on the women's heads which, as the evening progressed, melted and released continuing sweet aromas.*]

Female slaves, gowned in spotless saffron robes, circulated trays of goblets—pure gold, of course—brim-filled with the finest vintages imported from across the Great Green. The females were of every nation—some brown as ripe almonds, some sallow as balm, some black as petroleum pools, some light tan, some few from Circassia fair as reflected mirror-light.

Some had been sold by parents too poor to keep them, some acquired by sailors who had won them at dice, some had come as captives from fallen cities, some were former prostitutes worn out by lovemaking, some had simply been stolen by slave traders and sold at auction.

The youngest, the best-formed, had their breasts brazenly exposed. These carried trays heaped with cheeses; small stuffed sausages, smoke-cured and tender; flat circles of unleavened bread, heavily seasoned and heaped with fish eggs; broiled swallow's legs in garlic butter; cucumbers carved into scalloped circles; celery filled with ground chestnuts and honey; raw oysters on shells, seasoned with paprika; eggs of every sort and description—hen eggs (a rarity), duck eggs, pheasant eggs, peacock eggs, gull eggs, swan eggs—boiled in the shell, each shell painted in an intricate pattern. Carved and seasoned tidbits of meat were offered in profusion: deer meat, ostrich meat, giraffe meat, owl meat, lion meat, oryx meat. I felt it was certainly enough to tide them over till the main meal.

Magicians, resplendently robed, circulated through the crowd, making doves appear from nothingness and gilded canes disappear in puffs of smoke. An orchestra, specially and personally selected by me, played songs of love and loss, though if many of the guests paused to listen I would be greatly surprised.

The sound level rose incessantly, each guest raising his voice louder and louder to make himself heard above the general din.

My majordomo signaled the guests to take their places at table; he was a man of peremptory and haughty mien and somehow was able to command the attention of the entire room by a mere gesture of his hand. The orchestra struck up the royal anthem, and as all assembled once more dropped to their knees, Tut, Nefertiti and Ankhesenamun took their places of honor.

The guests returned to their feet, and my majordomo's assistant entered the room, carrying in his hands an upright skeleton whose bones dangled loosely from the pole to which it was affixed. "As you are now," he intoned, acting the voice of the skeleton, "so once was I. As I am now, so shall you be. So eat, drink, and be merry, for tomorrow we die." This he repeated many times, making a complete circuit of the hall before exiting with his grim relic.

I am of two minds regarding this particular custom of ours. It certainly drives home the point, but whether it truly puts one in a happier frame of mind I'm not at all sure.

My menservants, resplendent in jet-black belted tunics, began attending to my guests. Dancing flames from burning torches reflected off their silver breastplates. My dishes sparkled and flashed from the encrustation of precious stones surrounding the rims of each one. Drinking bowls, similarly bejeweled, contained the finest vintages the world offered: potations from grapes both red and white, from berries, from grains, from fruits, exotic and pleasing to the palate. For the ladies, of course, the libations were heavily diluted, not out of parsimony but for the sake of their virtue and decorum.

The profusion of fare was, if I may say so myself, more than adequate. The presentation upon each plate was a work of art, so perfectly arranged one hated to disturb it. The guests, by a nod, could indicate their choice. Great slices of elephant steak, broiled and seasoned to perfection; roasts of ibex, aromatic and succulent, their powdered horns sprinkled lightly into the sauce in which they simmered; venison strips, chewy and seasoned in savory blends of herbs and onions; roast birds in greatest profusion: swans, geese, ducks, hens, pheasants, peacocks, albatross, all stuffed with various succulent breadings; salads in eye-catching array: cucumbers, radishes, wild cabbage; cauliflower, leeks, celery, all intermixed with olive oil seasoned lightly with garlic.

Female servants strolled unobtrusively among the diners, strumming lyres and singing ballads of love, occasionally bringing tears when a particularly poignant verse struck a resonance. I do know how to give a banquet.

One of the crucial moments of the evening arrived. Only I knew it, and I quite literally held my breath. As was customary, Tut had not participated in any of the food or drink prior to sitting at his honored place. But now he was prepared to dine, but of course would taste nothing until it was first tested by his trusted Narmer. When I borrowed Narmer (was it only yesterday?), I had no idea how pivotal his role would be. All I thought I was getting was a superbly trained tongue.

What would Narmer do? There was no way I could keep him from serving as the king's taster. I had, once more, just prior to the banquet, met with the man. I did everything in my power to convince him that I was a desperate man with nothing to lose. I had even, though it galled me bitterly to have to do so, revealed nearly all my plans to him, so that he would have as much reason as possible to side with me till the evening was over. All he had to do was keep his mouth shut, nothing more.

But would he? He knew that I truly did have armed men stationed throughout the room who would cut his jugular at the merest nod from me. But all that had occurred before the room had been lined with the king's own guards. What would Narmer do now? Would he blurt everything to the king and run for sanctuary behind the back of the nearest soldier? If that happened, what would I do next? I could but watch and wait.

Narmer approached the king. My brow broke out in sweat, and I took a handkerchief from my robes to wipe it dry. Narmer took the plate from my servant's hand and inspected it closely with his eyes. Satisfied, he used his personal silver spoon to take a portion into his mouth. The palate of a trained taster is incredible. Obviously, he does far more than simply taste the food and, if he doesn't drop dead, certify that it's all right to eat. Most poisons don't work that quickly. But all poisons distort the natural taste of the food or drink, and if the taster detects anything even slightly off about the flavor, he rejects it immediately. Considering the consequences, tasters are the most highly motivated of men.

I don't know if eternity itself will seem as long as it seemed for me before he finally, with a nod, signaled his approval. He said or did nothing, and the king, satisfied, ate. Narmer left the king's side, and my heart returned to its normal rhythm.

The desserts were soon finished, and with an almost imperceptible nod of the head I motioned to my servers to begin removing the plates. I kept glancing nervously at the water clock. The next few minutes would determine my fate.

Tut rose from his seat, and the room immediately fell into a total hush. I could see from the look on his face that he was enjoying this moment immensely. I had announced this banquet, in a burst of bravado, at that audience which now seemed a thousand years ago. Tut was clearly delighted—the task he had given me was impossible, and he obviously relished the prospect of my utter humiliation before the aristocracy of Thebes—men I had personally selected to attend. This was Tut's idea of a good time.

Tut carried his symbols of authority with him—the crook and the flail, and he crossed them over his chest in the classic position. "We thank you, Vizier," he intoned, striving for a sepulchral voice, "for your hospitality, which as always is unsurpassed in Egypt."

I nodded my head in acknowledgment of his compliment.

"But now, this is the end of the seven days allotted to you to discover the murderer of my father. This was my command. My vizier must accomplish my commands to retain my confidence. Have you retained my confidence, Eye?"

I glanced briefly at Horemheb, who clearly was savoring the moment too. He was a splendid man of war, but no match for Tut's devious mind. Once I fell, his turn would come with startling swiftness. I knew that, but regrettably Horemheb didn't.

I brought myself before the king's table but made no obeisance. "Indeed I have, Pharaoh. I know the man."

"Mazel tov," the pharaoh replied sarcastically. Another dig. A reference to my unsatisfactory dealings with the Hebarews. But I could see I'd unsettled him.

I stared him straight in the eye, and had the satisfaction of seeing an answering flicker of surprise and fear. Suddenly he took his flail and struck me a savage blow across the face.

"How dare you!" he screamed. "How dare you fail to kneel before me? How dare you mention the name "pharaoh" without offering life, health, strength! How dare you?"

"Because, Tuttikins (and I drew out that 'Tuttikins' to make it as demeaning as possible), you shall nevermore know either life, nor health, nor strength."

My guests audibly gasped in shock at my unbelievable insolence. Horemheb drew sword and started for me, then abruptly stopped, stunned. My manservants had swung the massive doors to the Great Hall open, and with measured tread, in double file, row after row of my dismounted cavalrymen marched resolutely into the room, their swords unsheathed and at the ready.

This was the absolute moment. Anything could happen. I had not wasted my night. After patting Helen on her rump and sending her back to her room, the rest of the night had been spent in frantic and urgent business. There was no way I could summon my royal horse guards from the king's palace without arousing immediate suspicion, but unlike Horemheb, I had kept the bulk of my regular forces barracked in Thebes, not out in the desert, training. These, my regulars, I had summoned. Houy, totally faithful to me, had done a superb job in following my instructions to the letter. A palace, by definition, is a very large building, and mine well merited that description. It has many rooms, and Houy had been able to sneak half a regiment in during the darkest hour of the night.

This caused a few problems, but it couldn't be helped. Any servant who saw any of the guards had to be immediately put in detention. Secrecy was everything. Since quite often my cavalrymen had to be packed into the servants' rooms, many servants saw them, and this made Tey frantic since consequently many of her most experienced help simply disappeared.

Another problem was sanitary facilities. The palace wasn't equipped to handle the needs of so many men, and in any event they were strictly forbidden to leave the rooms to which they were assigned. The palace would suffer for this, but it was a trifling price to pay.

My half-regiment of troopers outnumbered Horemheb's hundred guards by roughly five to one. In addition, we had the element of surprise. But surprise or not, Horemheb was a fighter. What would he do?

I again looked agitatedly at the water clock. Everything depended on it. I'd taken an identical one and given it to the colonel, Macramun. As both sides in the Great Hall faced each other, indecisive, weapons drawn and ready, I breathed a great sigh as I heard the sound I had to hear if all had any chance of coming out right. I heard hoofbeats, and bells. The water clocks had been perfectly coordinated. Amun be praised.

The sound of mounted men is unmistakable, and the thunder of hoofbeats reverberated throughout the Great Hall. In addition, to gain mental ascendancy over my enemies, I had ordered Macramun to round up as many bells as he could find and place them around the necks of his horses. The clatter of hoofbeats, the clanging of bells—the surprise served to overwhelm and demoralize Horemheb's regiment completely. More than that, they were hugely outnumbered. *All* my regular cavalry now surrounded my palace—regiment upon regiment. Horemheb's hundred guardsmen were outnumbered inside, and his single guard regiment was outnumbered outside. I commanded the situation. For the moment.

My guests were starting to panic, but I had the doors closed and compelled them to return to their tables, with repeated apologies for the inconvenience.

I returned to Tut, whose face was ashen. I walked over to Horemheb, and with a look of both triumph and sorrow, for Horemheb had been my friend, I put out my hand, into which he relinquished his sword. He gave me a sardonic salute, which I acknowledged with a nod of my head. Nefertiti and Ankhesenamun remained seated, eyes wide, faces drawn, speechless.

I motioned to the room for silence, and all instantly complied. "This man," I shouted, "commanded me to find the murderer of his father. I have succeeded. This," I said, pointing dramatically at Tut's chest, "this is the man!"

I'll give Tut credit. He may be a weasel, and a slime, and a serpent, but he's no coward. He stared fully back at me, standing tall and straight, every inch a pharaoh.

"Congratulations, Grandfather," he said evenly. "I truly never thought it was possible. I should have listened to Nefertiti. She warned me not to do it, but once the idea came to my mind to rid Egypt of my father, who in Egypt isn't the better for it? I was only ten years old, but I could see what he was doing to the country, and I was the only one in Egypt willing to do something about it, even though I was just a boy. Of course," he added with what was one of the most genuine, likable grins I'd ever seen on his face, "I also got to be pharaoh. But I don't notice any of you complaining. The country's prospering again, the priests of Amun have their revenues back. The ancient gods are being honored with their ancient rites. Where's the harm?"

I looked at Nefertiti. She looked back at me, cold, without expression. "One thing I fail to understand," I said to her, and I couldn't have meant it more, "if you had nothing to do with

Akhenaten's death, why on earth did you try to have me killed?"

She stood, and indeed looked absolutely a queen in her long, flowing, jet-black gown. "I warned Tut not to underestimate you," she answered evenly. "I knew his plan was ridiculous and unnecessary, but you know Tut. He wouldn't listen. He's my son, but he's well past the age where he listens to his mother. He really was looking forward to tonight. But, Eye, I know you too well. I was deathly afraid this would be the outcome. I didn't know how you'd manage, but somehow or other I knew that you would. I told Tut just to kill you then and there, if he wanted to be rid of you. But no, he wouldn't listen. And if something like this happened, where would I be? In exile again, like when Akhenaten set me aside. Tut at least let me be at the center of things, let me have a share of real power. What do I do now . . . if you don't execute me? What is there left in life for me? Once a person has known royal power, what's left when it's taken away?"

I was truly aghast. Truly, truly a knife had just been stuck into my heart. "Nefertiti," I cried, and by this I mean I really cried, "you're my daughter. I'm your father. You'd have me killed for the sake of some secondhand power?"

She drew herself up, proud, regal, Queen Mother of Egypt. "Yes. I tried to kill you. And Tutankhamen killed his father. Did anyone," she said icily, "ever say that we were a close family?"

I looked at my Nefertiti, the daughter who used to play at my knee and jump into my lap when she was frightened or tired. Suddenly I too was tired, terribly weary, and rather than hear what I had just heard, I felt it would have been better if I had drunk from Oudah's cup.

I turned my attention back to Tut. "Did you enjoy your meal, Pharaoh?"

Whatever Tut is, he's no fool. "What do you mean, Grandfather?" he asked warily.

"The mushrooms, Tut. In particular, did you like the mushrooms?"

His eyes widened.

"You know, if a certain species of mushrooms is kept in a cool and totally dark place, they keep almost indefinitely. You might ask Narmer about it. He brought more than enough back from beyond the Great Green, and at your very own instructions has kept them preserved all this time. In fact, they become more potent with the passage of time. Were they tasty?"

Tut gave me a look of pure malevolence, then slid slowly down into his chair. "Life! Health! Strength!" he shouted sardonically. His face paled, and he collapsed.

I did not execute Nefertiti, but, as she had feared, I did send her into exile. I also extracted a small price from her. I made her reveal which of my servants she'd subverted to get the information about my whereabouts. All right, so I'm a softy. I didn't even execute the servants. They suffered, of course, but I didn't kill them. I didn't execute Horemheb either. I had him in my absolute power at this one moment, but it just wasn't my style. He was my enemy, but in truth only because my ambition was every bit the equal of his. Though I knew I would have to face him as an adversary at least once more, I could see no crime he had committed that would warrant his death. He had obeyed his pharaoh's command. I would expect the same of any general of mine.

How, once having permitted Horemheb to return to his troops, I once more had to face him as an adversary, how I resolved another mystery to became pharaoh of Egypt myself is another story, and another scroll.

THE END OF SCROLL ONE.

[*Translator's note: I could not resist opening the next scroll before completing the translation of this one. It too is a an amazing document, and our understanding of the Exodus will be significantly expanded once my translation is fully polished and complete. Eye lived in truly remarkable times.*]